I0675021

The Gem Testament

Joseph P. Stringer

Vivere Press

ISBN: 978-0-9903301-0-3
e book ISBN: 978-0-9903301-1-0

Printed in Charleston, South Carolina, USA

Vivere Press

www.chosen4life.org

www.ingramcontent.com/pod-product-compliance
Lightning Source LLC
Chambersburg PA
CBHW020636260626
47157CB00008B/2764

DEDICATION

To my wife, Kathleen, whose strength and character are the inspiration for Gem. She has been my muse, my best fan and my love for over forty five years.

ACKNOWLEDGMENTS

Although this book is a work of fiction, it has several real settings.

Back in the 80's, Time Traxx was a real business in Cleveland, a recording studio on the east side.

Also, "Roxford" and its "University College" will be recognized by many who attended a similar school in Southwestern Ohio. I chose not to use its exact name though many street names and building descriptions remain. No academic monitoring programs exist in the real college, nor would I wish to disparage your beautiful school's reputation.

Unfortunately, some of the economic, social and political environments which affect our friends in The Gem Testament are swiftly coming to pass in this nation. I can only pray that we do not bring into reality the dystopian futures which are part of my books and those of other writers'. I hope that what we write will awaken us, help us to reflect and to pray for God's grace.

I could not have finished Gem without the help of many friends who read, critiqued and commented on it. Among them are my friends, Larry and Nancy, who helped with the final edit for both content and for context. Finally, the support and urging of my loving wife is the reason I completed this book.

The Gem Testament

Prologue

Wurttemburg, Tubingia Province, (now part of Germany.)
August. 474 A.D.

"For evil will whisper lies into your hearts."

The demon whispered from the cave. His words invaded, cold and malevolent, feeding on the darkness within. He yearned to extinguish the light and the life. He sought the girl...and the man...and the sword. In the future, the demon found them all.

The sorcerer knelt in his own cave and watched in horror. The angel had been wrong; wrong to trust him with the sword. He moaned, keening at the pain and loss, "...by my fault, by my fault, by my own most grievous fault..."

*　　*　　*

Cleveland, Ohio. The near future.

"The Spirit blows where it wills."

The breeze wandered off the lake past burnt out hulks of towering office buildings, storefronts, apartments and condos. Occasionally, it would brush past someone working at the cleanup and lift the terrible toll of the last two days; ease the despair, and the exhaustion. A fleeting sense of hope filled them, freshened them and made them smile.

The breeze continued until it reached down to

gently rock a sign on one particular building which stood untouched amidst the destruction. The sign was written in an Old English script, dark green on a white background.

$$TIME\ TRAXX$$

$$AMERLINZ\ ENTERPRISES$$

The words resonated with ancient power, whispered secrets. Roger Noguchi looked up at the sign. He now knew the secrets and the power the sign heralded. A vibrant aura of violet roiled about him, the color of the sky moments before a promised sunrise.

People brushed past him in their haste to clean up the city. Many of these same people had been part of the army which, two days ago, destroyed what they now were rebuilding.

Others passed him by and did not notice the color, the man or the sign. No one noticed other signs: the Artificial Intelligence computer; the presence of the sword; the evil of the demon; the war waged on American soil, here within their sight. Roger wondered how they could not notice. Then again, he knew how. *"They have eyes but do not see."*

One: Gem

Three years earlier. University College

Three in the morning. Gem Matthews sat up in her bed, gasping for a breath she knew would not come. She reached out for her purse and pulled out her asthma medication. She held the inhaler, and looked at it like the enemy. She hated having to take it. *"Why now?"* she thought. *"That was over long ago."*

Gem shrugged, then inhaled the vapors which relaxed the muscles and let her breathe. Only then, with the first breath out, did her mind snapped fully awake. She knew why she had awakened. Why the asthma had returned. She was frigid. The room temperature had dropped at least twenty degrees. Gem Matthews knew what that meant too.

She switched on the light and stumbled over to the mirror. Gem knew what she'd see. Her eyes were wide with fear and loathing, black, the irises gone. From those eyes poured a cold malevolence which threatened to engulf her.

She stared at those eyes. *"No! This is where I was meant to be. This is where I belong! I will not let this happen now."*

Gem was beginning a promising course of study

at one of the country's most prestigious universities. She was completely in charge of her life. *"At least that's what I've told myself. I know I can beat this. This is my own mind working. I can stop the dreams."*

But she couldn't. For the first time since Gem was six, the dream had returned to haunt her. She shook her head hard. Then she went to the windows and threw them open to let in the hot night air.

How long would it last? Why did it come back now? Anxiety? No, that wasn't it. She belonged in this place. She sat on the window sill to look out at the dark night and it comforted her.

As she sat there, a man walk across the green. He was tall and lanky. He looked like he was walking in a dream. He stopped and turned as if listening. Then he continued on. Right in front of her dorm the man stopped again. This time he turned around in a circle and paused. He shrugged and walked on.

She wished that she could have a dream like this charming scene. Such dreams were not for her. She sat, breathing in the warm breath of the night, and waited for it to warm the room behind her.

A memory rose from her past. She leaned over a smelter, her thin arms black with soot and sweat as the blast of heat from the furnace washed over her. Her father hovered close, guiding her as she poured the liquid fire into the molds to reshape and recast it. *"Vulcan, the god of fire. That's who I am."* she had thought. She was seven at the time. Now, looking back, she wished she really *were* a god. One who could control the metals...and her own mind.

Two: Broddin

2:30 a.m. James Broddin stood in the classroom in Roberts Hall. He was alone. He was thankful that Roger Noguchi wasn't sitting in the back. Roger was the autistic son of Kerian Noguchi, a mathematics professor at the college. When Broddin first came to University College, Roger saw him in a hallway, turned and began following him. Since then, Broddin had never stepped on campus without Roger right behind him.

This summer had been a welcome respite, since Mrs. Noguchi visited her family in Japan and insisted that Roger go with her. Broddin supposed that was about to end since a new semester was starting.

He stared at the VID virtual interactive display board where he had written a complex equation. He had been wrestling for years with this particular problem in creating Artificial Intelligence and he could not break through a certain wall.

He had been at it for hours: changing, writing, wiping, rewriting. His fingers ached from the charge the virtual display left on the skin. His eyes burned from concentration.

He knew this equation was too complex, not "elegant," as Einstein would have said. He couldn't find the element which would simplify those bits of data and make them resonate with each other in between levels like brainwaves.

He swiped the equation off the display, irritated. "What am I missing?" He closed the display and left the classroom to walk home.

As Broddin crossed the center of the campus, three drunken frat boys were coming the other way. The larger one, a football lineman, saw Broddin. "Hey genius, where's your shadow, gay Roger? We've never seen you without..." The lineman stopped abruptly, a raw pulse of fear in his chest. He was close enough to look into Broddin's face.

"You were saying?" Broddin's eyes held him.

The lineman backed away, crowding his two buddies. "Hey, I was jus' kiddin.' Didn't mean nothin'." The three walked around.

Broddin turned, and watched them stumble away. As he turned back to continue he saw Frank Riley, one of the campus police. Riley walked over to him. "Hey, Broddin. Those guys giving you any problem?"

"No. They're all talk. Harmless."

"I'd watch them. They've been around two years. They're trouble.

"Thanks, but I don't think they'll bother me."

"Take it easy, young man."

"You too, Lieutenant." Broddin continued on toward his home on Bishop Street but some sound in the dark night drew his attention. It sounded like a distant, pure tone; someone singing, though he could not catch the words. The sound called him.

He stood listening to the distant beauty of it on the

breeze. He turned, trying to track its source. Then he reversed his course and headed back through the Hub past the Lieutenant.

"You forget somethin'? You're not going back to take on the frat boys."

"No. It's just too nice a night to take the direct route home. Hey did you hear anything, like someone singing?"

Riley stopped for a moment. "Nope but if somebody's singing at this hour I'm going to hear about it real soon."

Broddin chuckled and waved, then walked back past Roberts Hall and across the road.

Now the strange song came more clearly from the South Quad residence halls. It almost sounded as if the wind came to life to voice some crucial thought. He walked slowly and stopped at intervals trying to track it's source.

Broddin followed further down the path but lost the sound again. He stopped to listen. He turned in a circle trying to hear it's call again, but the night was silent.

He shrugged, then walked on down the path headed to his home.

Three: University College

Saturday.

James Broddin walked across the green campus toward Roberts Hall. This was Saturday morning and he had a special class he looked forward to leading.

As he stepped onto the campus, he saw Roger Noguchi angle toward him with his hunched over sideways gait. "*Some things do not change. First day of classes...and there he is.*" He shrugged. "Hello, Roger." No response. There never was.

Roger fell in several steps behind Broddin and shuffled along quickly to keep up with Broddin's stride.

Broddin retraced his steps from the night before hoping that he could figure out what that sound on the breeze had been. Also, he hoped that he could fool Roger by coming another way. He failed at both.

Broddin puzzled over how Roger knew things. How could he possibly know when Broddin would show up and where he'd be on campus? Yet, he did.

Gem still sat in the window watching the coming dawn. She saw the same man walk back on campus. A boy was waiting for the man and angled over with a shuffling gait to walk behind. As they passed by, the boy stopped, then turned to look directly at her as if he knew she was there. He stared for a moment then turned, put his head down and shuffled on.

"Strange." She turned back to her room and dressed for the day.

University College is located in the town of Roxford, Ohio. UC is the jewel of the Ohio University system, an old line college with a history dating back to the early nineteenth Century. In the last two decades the vast wealth and ardent loyalty of its alumni funded an aggressive campaign to recruit scholars in fields as varied as Ancient Middle Eastern Studies and advanced research programs in the applied sciences--like the one Broddin was in.

The wealthy alumni sent their children to the school because of tradition, or ease, or because their contributions earned their kids a place there.

The primary reason the wealthy sent their children to Roxford was for protection from the violence in the coastal cities and to avoid the draft. The draft had been re-instituted by Washington out of necessity.

The terror wars had come home to America again. In the last decades America's enemies waged a constant war of bombs, murder and assaults in the coastal population centers. The nation took the war back to the enemy in the Middle East and on the North African continent.

Social wars also plagued cities, a result of the rising shortages of food, fuel and health care. The constant tension between the young and the elderly over scarce resources broke out in violence. Youth gangs attacked the elderly on city streets. Nursing homes were bombed and destroyed.

The government, running out of options, instituted a program of voluntary euthanasia called "Relief" in order to create a "fair" means of sharing resources. No one protested. The constant death around them exhausted their ability to care.

Yet, in the center of the nation, especially in fairly rural areas like Roxford, the wars, the terror and anarchy seemed distant and unreal. So the parents sent their children to UC of Ohio. Most times, these children of privilege attended for the football, the fun and the booze; another strong UC tradition.

Another quiet scholarship program was in place at UC which brought young people from all over the country. Those children were, for the most part, from underprivileged families. They were all exceptionally gifted. They came to learn from the scholars.

No one really followed the college tracks of the first group. As to the second group, their sponsor closely monitored their performance, activities, writing and research. They were not made aware of that monitoring or of the sponsor.

James Broddin was one of the second group. At eighteen years old he was a graduate student researching Artificial Intelligence and was a teaching assistant for the best professor in the field. He had written software programs which became the core of a new academic file sharing network, Intellisearch. The school funded a startup company.

Broddin opened up the classroom and began to write equations on the Virtual Display while students started to sign on. Few students ever came to these classrooms anymore since the VID's made it seem like they were right in the room. The lack of adequate air conditioning in the ancient buildings made the rooms hot even in the early morning.

The only other person in the room was Roger Noguchi, who sat in the same chair he always used. Broddin ignored him. Roger was wrapped within his own world. He sat hunched over, oblivious to all, continuously writing nonsense: letters, symbols, words, numbers; page after page, book after book, with no discernible meaning.

One of the new students looked through the virtual display. "Who's that with you?"

Weng, who had been around awhile, said "That's Broddin's pet, 'It.' 'It' follows him everywhere. They're inseparable. Maybe they're...."

"Knock it, Weng. And don't call him 'It.'" To the new student. "This is Roger. He's autistic. His father allows him the run of the school...and he's latched onto me."

Roger did not acknowledge his name, did not look up or respond at all. As he wrote, he mumbled unintelligible words to himself.

Broddin continued. "Let's get back to the problem I've outlined here." Watch how I expand this equation." He began to write a complex formula onto the display.

As Broddin wrote, a bright shaft of sunlight reflected off a car windshield into his peripheral vision. He turned toward the source and a lance of light drove into his eyes...

Four: Angel

...and he could clearly see an angel, bathed in a brilliant white light, holding a sword. Runes of an ancient language ran down the blade, broiling with every color of the rainbow.

The angel looked right into Broddin's eyes. Then its focus shifted as a massive dark tide of creatures descended upon it. Once in a while a face or form appeared from the dark, the horror shapes of every child's nightmare. They looked like the opposite form of the angel, black where white should be. They attacked the angel with a fierce vengeance born of absolute hate; of envy, lust and greed.

Broddin thought that the angel would be annihilated in an instant but the flame of the sword pulsed out in every direction. Its might crushed thousands into grey powder which blew away with the force of a hurricane. Yet thousands more came.

Occasionally, a suicidal slash from one of the creatures drew fresh blood from the lone angel. With each slash, Broddin flinched as if he could feel the pain. The pain took the form of a thought, accompanying a constant flow of tears: *"My brothers!"*

Five: Scientist

The pain of the Angel focused straight into Broddin's mind and he turned away from the sight, closing his eyes. As he did, he heard someone singing behind him and turned. Roger Noguchi sat upright in his chair, staring beyond Broddin to his left. He was singing in some strange language. "Roger?"

"Hey, I thought 'It' never said a word...and what kind of equation is that?"

Broddin turned, irritated at Weng, but stopped, stunned. To his left a series of symbols were written vertically on the display. They looked vaguely familiar. "Weng, did you write this?"

"Your color on the board, my man. Blue on the display. That's you. Mine's red, Tobe's is green. Way the system works. I can't write blue on your board. You wrote that."

"What are you talking about?"

Now Weng looked serious. "Broddin, you just stopped mid-equation, and stood staring off into space for about three minutes..."

"Three minutes?"

"...then you wrote that equation with your left hand. Wanna tell us what it represents? I've never seen those quantum elements."

Broddin was getting a massive headache and he

was annoyed. He reached out and palmed the symbols off the display. "Drop it. Let's continue. How does this formula affect wave certainty equations?"

Roger's singing had drifted off to silence again. Broddin looked back at him, puzzled, then shrugged. He had work to do.

He continued with the discussion but a separate part of his mind kept coming back to the "daymare" as he would come to call it. It would be years before he'd accept these "daymares" as visions. Visions were for mystics and prophets. Broddin was a scientist and a realist. Oh he believed in God, went to church faithfully. God had Broddin's faith. But science was his passion. The two were separate, entirely different areas of concern.

Broddin shrugged to himself *"Must have been a minor heat stroke or something."* He needed to cool down. At least, he'd be able to do that when he got to his business this evening.

Intellisearch was housed in a new building and, thank God, the air conditioning was efficient. It had to be since a room full of the most advanced servers had to stay cool to function properly.

He finished the class, closed up and walked out to his car. Roger followed.

The car was a furnace. He reached in and turned it on to let the AC cool it before getting in. As he stepped back and closed the door, he heard a noise behind him and turned...

Six: The Meadow

...to see a quiet green meadow dripping in the heat of a summer afternoon. A few horses cropped grass within a hastily constructed pen. Soldiers lay everywhere, collapsed in exhaustion from the heat and the day's march. They followed their king and waited for the campaign to be finished.

Two men stood in the midst of the soldiers, watching a large tent being erected with poles and ropes. Servants laid rich bolts of cloth under the tent to make a floor. One man was close to six feet tall. He wore a gold crown woven through his flowing white hair and rich blue robes of silk for he was a king.

The other man looked much younger, was considerably smaller, and wore only a plain white tunic. Power radiated out from him in waves of green color. He looked up at his companion.

"My lord Uther, you have driven your troops mercilessly on this campaign for the last seven months. They need rest. You need rest!"

"Do not tell me what I need, Sorcerer." He spat the title out as a challenge. "I must conquer the petty Dukes and Barons of the middle plains. You know it is right! This is not for me. It is for my son, Jared."

"But, my lord..."

"Do not speak of it! I know what you told me, that

my quest is futile." His voice dropped to a whisper. "I will **not** see those Norman fops as Kings over this land! Jared *must* be King, even though he is slow! After all, he has the *best* of advisors...and I have the sword."

"It is not enough, my King. I saw..."

"What have you seen?"

"I cannot tell you other than Jared will not be King."

"This is about that bastard son I sired. He is a threat to Jared's legitimate claim. I know that you aid in hiding him. If the bastard will rise against Jared, I will kill him, infant though he is."

"He will not rise against Jared, but he will someday unite all the Britons."

"Not while I live and still hold your sword, he won't!" The whole camp could hear Uther, but hardly anyone paid attention. They had heard all this countless times. Then Uther's voice dropped to a deadly whisper. "And you, counselor, plot against me! Shall you take the sword from me also?"

"I do not take back what I have given. Furthermore, you know that even I could not take it without your agreement."

"You'd best remember that, Sorcerer. "I will continue this campaign. Tomorrow, again, I will ride with this sword and conquer. *You* will come with me! Uther opened the flap of his tent to go in, then turned on his heel to yell **"And you will watch me find that bastard son of mine and kill him myself!"** Then the King threw himself into the tent.

The sorcerer waited. In a moment, the King came back out of the tent. "Why do you stand there?"

"Because I knew you were not finished with me."

"What is it about Jared? I command you to tell me." The old man's shoulders fell with worry.

"This is one command I cannot obey, my Liege. You are not ready to hear this news."

The King sighed. "I have asked you for advice in peace and in war. You never refused your counsel, nor have you ever been wrong. My entire Kingdom rests on your advice and on Ex...this sword." He touched the hilt unconsciously. "Though my queen tells me I should not trust you, I have never seen even a shadow of deceit in you."

"And you will not my King. The only one above you I serve is our Lord God. I trust my Savior before I yield to your need, Sire."

The two men stood staring into each others eyes for a long moment. Finally, Uther threw up his hands. "You try my patience, wizard! I do not trust this Servant Lord of yours who delivers so much power into the hands of one such as you. I do not trust you." "*And,*" he thought, "*I do not trust myself, for I cannot but like you in spite of your plotting.*"

The King turned to walk back into his tent and said, without looking back, "Stay, sorcerer. Gather my men around you and tell them a story. One you have not told before. Speak!"

"Mr. Broddin." Someone was calling his name. He turned around to see...

Seven: Kendo

...his kendo instructor, Yamato, walking toward him across the parking lot. "I am glad you are here. Why do you stand out in this heat?"

Broddin tried to shift his mind away from what he had just seen. This was no dream. He had *been* there. But that was impossible! His head started to ache again. He bowed to his instructor. "Forgive me, sensei. Did you need me? I'm waiting for my car to cool off."

"Ah. Come to the studio tonight."

"I was hoping to get some practice in, but..."

"This is not a request."

"Yes, sensei. I need to stop at the office. Then, I'll drop off Roger..."

"Bring the boy."

"But..."

"Bring the boy. He's of Japanese descent."

"He's not going to watch anyway."

"Bring..."

"...the boy. Yes, sensei."

Yamato turned and walked away. Broddin grimaced. For the longest time, his Kendo dojo was his only refuge. Now even that was infringed on. "If only! Ah what's the use! Roger, get in the car!"

Kendo, the sport of Japanese sword fighting, is

unique in many ways. The training techniques, the forms and the culture all descend from hundreds of years of tradition which originated in the Samurai warriors of the ancient Japanese dynasties. Broddin fell in love with the sport the moment he entered Yamato's dojo.

Seven years ago, he discovered the dojo two blocks from his home and stopped in to watch. He never had any desire for physical activity, was always too busy with his studies. But the precision of the movements and the discipline moved him.

Three nights a week he drove to Dayton. His Shidachi, the master of the school was the only person other than his father who referred to him by his first name. Seven years later his master still called him "Mikey."

Now, Broddin went through his forms. The master took the floor and beat him around for a time before Broddin could better him. "You improve every day. I will soon not be able to challenge you myself."

Bowing, Broddin said, "You humble me, Sensei. I am flattered, but I think you're holding back."

Yamato did not answer him. "The boy. He has benefited from being here, seeing you spar."

"He didn't even notice."

"His mother called me when they returned. The boy's uncle is a grand master of Kendo. The boy was taken to their dojo. He did not watch, but every day afterward, he went there. Kendo calls him."

"Forgive me sensei, but I know Roger. Nothing in this world touches him. Nothing but his notebooks

— and they're just scribble."

"'Nothing in this world.' I am glad of your certainty. Meanwhile, bring the boy."

Broddin looked quizzical.

Yamato turned to walk away, then as if reconsidering, turned back. "Roger is descended from Samurai. He *is* Samurai. Do not forget that. Whatever he is now he deserves respect for what he is within."

What he said struck a chord. Broddin's face colored. "I apologize, sensei. I do not see him as you but you're right. No matter what his limitation, he deserves respect."

It was almost ten by the time that Broddin dropped Roger off at his house. Dr. Noguchi looked at Broddin. "It is good that Yamato called to say Roger went with you to the dojo. We're used to seeing him home at 7:15."

"Sorry, sir. I should have called, but the Sensei caught me off guard — twice, today."

"That is not a problem." Noguchi looked at Broddin. "Again, I thank you James that you have shown patience and gentleness in allowing Roger to...to *be* with you."

Broddin started to brush this off, then remembered the incident from earlier in the day. "Sir, may I come in a moment? I have a question." They walked into the hallway. "Has Roger ever sung?"

"What?"

"Does Roger sing? Earlier today..."

Noguchi looked back toward the kitchen. "Come into my study, please." He guided Broddin in and closed the door. "What are you talking about?"

"Earlier today, I was at the VID in Roberts hall for one of my classes. I had a...a momentary lapse. I was out of it for about three minutes, or so the others say. When I came to, Roger was singing."

"You had a daydream?"

"Well, I was somewhere else in my mind. I wrote some symbols on the board which made no sense. An angel fought..."

Noguchi looked concerned. "Are you saying you had a hallucination?"

"I wouldn't call it that. It was like some daydream, but none I would've ever thought about."

"And you say that you heard Roger singing?" Noguchi's tone was doubtful.

"Yes, when I came back to myself."

Noguchi shook his head. "You must be mistaken. Roger has never uttered an intelligible sound. He simply mumbles nonsense, just like he writes in the notebooks."

"But I heard him....and I saw him looking at something, too. First time I ever saw that."

Noguchi thought for a moment. "It must have been a part of this cerebral event you had. I cannot believe that Roger truly verbalized."

"Perhaps you're right. Maybe it was all part of this daydream." Broddin had forgotten that one of the others mentioned Roger singing.

"Please do not mention this to my wife. She has prayed for a 'miracle' for our son ever since we first learned of his autism. I would not want her to latch onto some...false hope." Noguchi now looked more closely at Broddin. "Young man, you look worn. How many hours of sleep have you had this week?"

Broddin thought back. "About six."

"This week?"

He winced. "Yes. I've been preparing for my teaching assistant duties, working at the new business. I don't have time for sleep. The room in Roberts Hall was hot and maybe I had a minor heat stroke."

Noguchi did not look convinced. "You will report to me immediately if you have any more 'daydreams.' Do you understand me?"

"Yes, sir."

Broddin left. Noguchi waited for a few moments then unlocked a drawer in his desk, pulled out a secure phone and dialed. "I want to see the reports for today, the work done on the Virtual Display in Classroom 4, Roberts Hall, and video if you have it. We may have an incident, a cerebral event of one of our charges."

Eight: Gem

Three nights in a row she sat bolt upright, gasping for breath, the darkness invading. She felt the violation, her breath being choked out of her...again!

She picked up the phone and hit send. "Mom."

"Gem, are you all right?"

The tears were close. "Mom, it's back."

"Oh, no. Is it...the cave?"

Now the tears spilled over. "Yeah, the cave." She wished her mother were close enough to come to her, to comfort her, to rock her like she used to.

Estelle Matthews gripped the phone. She knew all about the cave. "Tell me about it. C'mon, honey. I'm here. Talk to me."

Estelle felt that familiar coldness again. The hairs on her scalp bristled. "Is he there?"

"No, Mom. He hasn't gotten the better of me..." She hesitated. "...yet."

"Fight it!"

"I am!"

"You know what I mean. Pray."

"I'm doing what I can! Mom, I just need you to listen for a while."

"Okay, honey. Tell me. I hate it but I know it helps you to talk it out."

Gem closed her eyes, steeling herself against the darkness of the vision. "The cave sits alone..."

Nine: The Cave

Near Wurrtenburg, Tubingia. August, 474 A.D.

The cave sat alone...dark...in the deepest part of the forest. It was formed from a shattered hillside which once had seen light. Now, ancient trees lifted their foliage far above this place and blocked the sun. No light filtered through. No path led to the cave. No animal used its careful secrets as a lair. Killing had been done here and not their kind of kill.

T'an crouched, waiting. He had followed some wolves stalking a wounded elk. He smiled. They hadn't smelled or heard him, but he didn't expect that they would. He was the best stalker in the clan. This brought him no recognition though, for he was small and the size of his kills usually small.

Three hundred years before when the paths remained clear and the owner of the cave was present, no creature would have ventured within a mile of this place, not even T'an's ancestors. They were such good trackers and hunters that any person who came near their village never came out again. They killed for food and for sport and for spite...and for no reason. T'an's ancestors still were close enough to the land that they remembered the smell of evil in the cave. They stayed far away from that smell.

In desperation, the elk began to crash through a

deadfall of timber. Ahead it could smell the growing stench of death. Behind were the wolves. The sun was setting. Darkness falling. T'an crept closer.

As the sun set in the heat of this August night, a pile of dead leaves on the cave floor came to life, swirled and danced. The darkness of the cave coalesced, then opened into a void. From the center of the darkness he reformed himself.

Slowly the thickness of the void took the form of a being which looked much like a man. He was over eight feet tall and wrapped in a black cloak closely resembling wings. An ice cold wind blew from the cave sweeping out the leaves which heralded his arrival. The Ishar Crull had returned.

The elk pulled itself to a stop. A frigid breeze blew into the elk's face. It turned to face the wolves. Three of the wolves leaped upon it for the kill.

T'an could smell death on the elk as the wolves brought it down. The elk would be theirs.

Yet suddenly the wolves halted, their hackles raised. They backed away from the elk, growling. T'an rose from his crouch. The hair on his neck stood on end. The wolves kept backing right past him, though he knew they saw him now. Then they turned tail and ran. He felt a strange buzz in his head but he ignored it. What a stroke of luck!

For a time Crull stood rigid, lost in thought. He felt a human intelligence outside the cave and turned to concentrate on it.

T'an smiled. The elk lay dead, awaiting only his effort to drag it back to the village. He raced forward...and crashed straight into a wall of pain which ripped at his entire being. Images entered his mind, grew stronger, demanding. He welcomed the darkness which overtook him.

The Ishar Crull looked at T'an's writhing form. "A puny excuse for a man. But then, aren't they all?" His voice was cold and painful to hear. Yet, less painful than the feeling of that mind probing.

A deep rumble, a cruel parody of laughter, erupted from the being above him. "I know you, T'an. I know what lusts drive you in the darkness. I see you stalk the young women and children while they bathe at the river. And you sneak in to stand over them at night. No one would ever suspect!"

"From now on you won't need to worry about being caught, or ignored. They will fear you, all of them. You can satisfy your lusts to your heart's content and no one will dare touch you. You will have my mark upon you...and my power."

That evening, the wolves slunk back to their lair, hungry, growling, their tails pulled down. Before the night was out, they would turn on one of their own, kill and eat it — an act unknown to their kind.

Miles away a young girl turned in her sleep, moaned and shivered as the cold blew in through the holes in the hut her father had built. Her mother lay awake, eyes wide, wondering at the fear which made her heart pound at nothing.

Later, the mother dozed only to awaken to the sound of her daughter choking and gasping for breath...

Ten: Warrior

"...and that was me, choking. I awoke to a full blown asthma attack." Gem fell silent. Her mother could feel the coldness radiate across the phone line.

"Why don't you come home?"

"I can't Mom. My place is here now. I just started my courses and research. I'm not giving into this."

"Gem, you're so young. You should be closer...and I miss you already."

"I know. I miss you too, Mom. I just needed to talk it out. Sorta makes 'em just that, dreams."

"Yeah. Sure. Dreams." Gem's mother fought her own trembling to reassure Gem. "I want you to call me if you have any more dreams. I love you. You know I'm always here, and you are in my prayers."

"Okay, Mom. I love you, too. Goodnight."

"Goodnight, honey." Gem's mother hung up the phone She would have little sleep, maybe not for many nights. She went to make some hot tea and turn up the heat. While Gem told the dream the temperature in the room had dropped twenty degrees. Her hand ached from holding the phone, from the cold radiating out from Gem's voice.

Estelle Matthews was afraid. She had no one to call. She could only do what she knew she needed to do — pray.

Eleven: Sorcerer

Broddin left Noguchi's house and drove out toward IntelliSearch. He had work to do to make sure the accounts were on line and functioning.

He pulled into his parking space and turned off the car. He thought back to Yamato's comment about Roger. *"He is Samurai. He deserves respect..."* Movement caught his eye to the right and he turned...

...to see King Uther walking towards the tent. "Tell them a story. One you have not told before. Speak!"

Emrys Ambrosius — counselor and advisor to the King, wizard, sorcerer — looked askance at Uther and chuckled. "Indeed, Sire, I would be delighted. Today I want to tell you about the first naming of your sword, Excalibur." (He heard the ting of a response from within the King's scabbard.) "It was not always named as it is today. That sword was first named by the Lord our God himself."

Uther paused at the entrance to his tent and now looked at his counselor with obvious disbelief. "Really? Tell us."

Emrys gathered the men around him, then settled back in a camp chair he had fashioned from tree limbs and woven grasses. This would be a long one. "The story begins, really, with Seth."

Twelve: Genesis

"You all know the Genesis story of how God made Heaven and Earth and Man and Woman. How eventually the evil one tempted our mother Eve. The father of lies gave us the opportunity to sin. Yet we cannot blame him. The sin was our own choice."

Uther walked back out from his tent, looking vexed. "Will you preach to us, wizard, like some wandering priest? Or will you tell us what we have not heard before?"

"I am coming to it, Sire. What you do not realize, what is left unclear in that account are the days, the eras, the millennia which followed those first times when God saw that 'it was very good.' His 'very good' included all of creation. It included Adam and Eve...and all of those sons and daughters they brought forth in obeying the Lord's command to 'Be fruitful and multiply.'"

"If you remember, the third son of Adam was named Seth. Here follows his story."

Thirteen: Seth

Seth, the third son of Adam, was very different from his two brothers: they chose to live near the Garden and their parents. Seth grew up running. He ran, simply for the joy of it and his running carried the multitudes of mankind out to far lands along the Gihon and the Tigris rivers, out to the South and the East and the West.

He would run out upon the green grasses which matched the color of his aura. Often sons and daughters, each shining with their own colors, came with him. Their different auras seemed to form a rainbow which flew through the grasses and forests just for the joy of the run.

In those days, time was not measured. Death was simply...not. Only the joy of each day and night need be reckoned for the Lord provided. Many generations of children and grandchildren and so on grew up, until Seth could no longer number them and could barely remember his children's names.

The Earth was a place of immeasurable beauty and joy untouched by any taint...except one: the Nephalim, the sons of God who lived among men.

These Nephalim were the only check to the unlimited joy Seth felt in his runs. They stood in the shadows, their wings folded close. As he passed them in his run, their eyes tracked his every step, their faces expressionless grey shapes. Their mouths moved constantly with their whispers.

He knew that they found the daughters of man fair, and had taken to wife a number as they chose. He found a vague disquiet in that fact but did not have the knowledge to name its root. It was part of the Lord's creation that men shared this world with such. With greater knowledge, Seth might understand that disquiet, but he did not seek such knowledge. Such things were for the Lord alone.

At times, when his running brought him close to a group of the Nephalim, Seth could hear their constant whispers. Their tongue was not man's. Seth could only thank God for that fact because the constant *whisper* of their voices also stirred that disquiet. He had no word to even describe the feeling he held.

What further disturbed him was the look in their eyes. When they were not watching men, they turned as one toward the garden in an unconscious act of yearning. As Seth watched them their eyes reminded him of his mother's eyes when she gazed upon *that* tree.

Here was the crux of Seth's disquiet as he ran. It lay not in the Nephalim, but in the brightness of his mother's eyes; a special brightness when she gazed upon that one tree. The same burning gaze he had observed in the Nephalim! He did not want to know its origin or meaning. Perhaps if he ran *from* anything, it was that look in his mother's eyes.

Fourteen: Visions

The security guard's knock on the window jolted Broddin back to the present. "You okay, kid? Saw you pull up fifteen minutes ago and you just sat there."

Broddin felt fuzzy but said, "Yes, I'm fine. I was thinking about a problem." The transition from the reality of listening to Emrys tell a story to being awakened in the parking lot made his head ache.

He was really worried now. He'd had a vision while in the car. What if he'd been driving? He didn't want to risk getting someone killed. He thanked the guard, got out of the car and stretched. "Probably need to get into the AC. The heat is draining."

The guard looked at him. "You do look beat. Take care of yourself kid."

Broddin went on into the building. The guard remained at his post, waited a few moments, then took out a secure phone. "I thought I should report this to you sir...."

Several hours later, Broddin sat in his office. Only two personal ornaments were in the office. The side wall of the office was polished black marble. Engraved within that wall was a crucifix only Broddin could see when he sat in the chair at his desk. It reminded him that he had purpose beyond simply business.

The other ornament sat on the desk: a plaque which read "Man — the Irrational Animal." Once, one of his investors picked it up. "What's this mean?

"That plaque is my general assessment of men. Just as we have the capacity for goodness but we always sin; we also are capable of rationality...yet so few people are rational and even they aren't fully so.

I do not tolerate irrationality in my business or my work. Most people are hopelessly irrational, especially in their personal lives. That plaque is a reminder to all those who work with me: I won't tolerate that."

Now as he sat there, he picked up the plaque. "Man--The Irrational Animal." He looked at the image on the wall and then at the plaque. The contradictions were too great: the difference between what God designed men to be...and the hopeless disaster they made of themselves.

He felt frustrated. Kendo practices usually invigorated and relaxed him, but this workout left him empty. Where were the rational people? What were men thinking? Or did they think at all? *"How could this be? Where did it all go wrong?"* If only he could *make* men think, *make* them rational!

He heard a noise behind him and turned...

...to see that Emrys was still telling his story. Many in the camp had settled around him to listen. The King sat in the shadows of his tent, did not look at his counselor and pretended not to listen. Emrys knew he heard every word. As did any person who needed to hear.

Fifteen: Transformation

Seth was many leagues from the garden when he felt the first ripple of wrongness enter the world, a cold feeling which suddenly seized his heart...and Seth stopped running.

He turned to look back and disquiet grew in his chest. He stared out across the hundreds of leagues he had run, toward the garden. It felt like he could see across that distance into the perfection which reigned from Eden. A shadow fell upon that perfection.

"Mother!"

Then a second pulse.

"Father!" And Seth knew.

A tidal wave of wrongness pulsed out from the garden, a ripple of change. Seth wheeled and ran faster than he had ever run. But the tidal wave caught him, lifted him, carried him downward, smashed his body against a hard rock surface and knocked the wind from him. He fell into blackness.

Pain wracked the man who awoke from that darkness. As he stared at his hands he watched his green aura fade away. Grief, loss and loneliness bombarded his mind. Knowledge he did not *want* to know. Emotions he did not *want* to feel! Anger flared. **"NO!"** His head pounded with knowledge and a flood of images he could not stop. He looked down upon his naked body and was ashamed. "Help me, Lord." But, the Lord had left him. The Lord was in the garden.

Seth turned back to race toward the garden, sure only of its loss and of a danger he could not begin to understand. As he ran, he could see the Earth change before his eyes. He knew now what the change was: death began all around him. It pained him to look upon the places he had loved.

On the sixteenth day, Seth came to a place of dry ruin. Nothing was left alive here. As he raced on, the grey sand burned his feet. Gaining the last rise, he saw to his relief that Eden still stood, pure and pristine.

Yet Seth stood in horror. A vast tide of the Nephalim waged war to gain entrance. He had heard the whispers of the Nephalim and now knew their fury and lust. *"They seek the Tree of Life to destroy all of creation with their hate."* A single angel stood against that army, wielding a weapon: a *(sword)* — the word came directly into his mind. Its light flamed outward, killed the Nephalim in every direction and swept away the grey ashes as dust before a hurricane.

Renewed fear for the angel propelled Seth forward. He could not let the angel down! He leapt across the remaining fields. He saw the last stroke as the flame of the blade fell quiet...and to Seth's horror, the angel fell.

Sixteen: The Gift

Seth raced up to the Angel, seeing only its need, feeling only the will to aid it. He stopped in fear and wonder. At his feet lay a creature of fearsome beauty, over eight feet tall, a winged creature (like the Nephalim). Such a pure white radiated from it that Seth's eyes hurt to look upon it. A wing was broken and bled. Terrible gashes cut across its chest.

Seth thought for a moment that he was too late and he fell to his knees. As he did so the creature opened its eyes. Pain radiated from those eyes, so intense that Seth could feel it directly. His body trembled. Then the angel smiled. "Seth, do not fear. I am Michael, Archangel of the Lord. Welcome, true man of God."

Seth looked away in shame and fear. "Do not welcome any man that way now. We all have fallen."

"Yes, I know." It chuckled. A sound of deep and painful knowledge. "Thus the Lord sent me to guard this gate. The Nephalim would have entered and eaten of the tree of life...and then the purpose of the Lord would have been dismayed."

"What?"

"Never mind. Some thoughts are beyond..." The angel sighed. "...beyond even Seraphim to know. Now help me to gain my feet. I must go."

Seth was horrified. "But what if they return?"

"They will not." The statement brought an image directly into Seth's mind: a view of the total of what this particular devastation encompassed. Then Seth knew. No Nephalim would come...because none were left. "I killed them all save one who fled." The angel looked at him. "They were my brothers." The flashing pain of that simple statement summarized an ancient knowledge of rebellion, of envy and coveting, of lust and hate that ended in eternal death. Seth did not know how much more pain he could endure.

"So much more, you will not conceive it, nor would you want to know now or you would surely despair." The angel had answered Seth's innermost question, one he had not even spoken. "My Lord knows your heart, Seth. Thus he has commanded me to give you this gift."

For the first time Seth looked at the object in the angel's hand. It was long, sharp on two edges. The Lord's hand formed this...sword and wrote its name down upon the blade: "Lehat Chereb," "Flaming Sword." The sword shone the brilliant color of a thousand suns so that Seth could barely look upon it.

The angel regarded him, now more seriously. "Seth, Seth, son of Adam." He recognized the voice which rose from the angel. It now had power, immense and timeless, boundless in its love. "Give me your hand to lift me up."

Seth reached out. He felt a slight resistance when his hand neared the angel, but his concern overwhelmed that resistance. He pulled the angel to his feet.

Suddenly, the angel was filled with power, his wounds healed. He towered over Seth, the sword grasped in his hand. He looked down upon this man with deep love. "Seth, the Lord has chosen you, to give you what you did not seek. In the end, you will find the Lord's choosing a burden as much as a blessing. Yet, you are faithful."

"Seth, man has chosen. You, too, have fallen. You now have choice with the knowledge of good and evil. This instrument will do either good or evil, for any creation now within man's grasp can be warped unto his own purposes. I do the purpose of the Lord."

"The Lord commands me to give you this gift." He lifted up the sword and his whole demeanor shouted reverence. Now the angel smiled. "Seth, son of Adam, I give you Lehat Chereb."

A weight of immense power fell upon Seth's mind. It almost drained him before filling him with a new power and strength. Set felt the strength of his pure green aura grow once again. The angel handed him the sword.

Seth reached out and grasped the *(hilt)*. Now he knew what brightness lived in his mother's eyes for this object commanded a power so immense that it was desired for itself. Seth looked upon its blade. "Lehat Chereb." A prayer, a dedication. In reply the sword sang out a tone of pure sound, and turned green! Seth was so startled that he almost dropped it. He turned back to the angel and saw that both the angel and the garden were fading.

"I don't understand! How am I to guard Eden? I am no angel!"

"An angel is one who does the bidding of the Lord. Seth, you are now that angel. Watch and Ward, for the remaining Nephalim will seek to trick the sword from your hand. Yet beware. You alone cannot face the absolute hate of the Nephalim. You lost the total love it requires. If you are to defeat him, you must gather six true men to join you; six — whose auras form the colors of the rainbow — join to complete the purest white. Only then can you hope to stand against him."

Seth looked back down upon the sword. Now he spoke to the Lord across the divide his father and mother had begun. "This is wonderful, Lord. I will honor not the gift, but the giver." As he turned back, Seth saw that the angel and the garden had passed from sight.

He turned his gaze upon this tool which had now become the center of his life. All of his life he had been whole, complete--until the fall had broken him and brought emptiness. Now, holding the sword, he felt complete again. He gazed upon its green radiance, looked at the words written down its blade. "Lehat Chereb." It responded in a pure, heavenly tone.

Seventeen: Camp

By now evening had fallen and the fires were lit. Emrys looked across the fire at the King. "The runes over which you puzzle, written upon the blade you carry, are the ancient language of the Lord Himself. They are the first name of your sword."

Uther guffawed. He unsheathed Excalibur. As he did so, a faint color of sky blue roiled around him. He waved the sword around so that the runes on its blade reflected a myriad of colors in the firelight. "You mean to say that *this* sword, wonderful as it may be, is *the* sword? Who, then, guards the gate to Eden now? Me?"

"Yes, you my liege." Emrys answered, then under his breath muttered, "but, I am afraid not too well."

"Humph! Lake at Cherub my foot! A great story, wizard! This sword has given me and my army exceptional service. And I credit its effectiveness to your magic. After all, *you* are the glowing fool who gave it to me. But no creation of God's would be in *your* hands and..." he turned to look behind his back, "...I see no wings on me!" He and his men laughed until they fell over.

Emrys smiled. He had accomplished the goal he was given. He knew and accepted that Uther did not understand the gift he had been given. Uther had not used it wisely. That would come later. Emrys bowed and took his leave, his page following.

During the long campaign, Uther granted only one deference to Emrys: that was to place his camp some distance from the others. Uther did so partly because of the enmity between the two, and partly because the men feared the sorcerer and avoided him. The most obvious reason for the distance of his camp, though, was Emrys' page Revyn, who happened to be a strikingly beautiful young woman.

As they walked toward their tent, Revyn was obviously irritated. "They falsely accuse you of sorcery, of serving the gods of this earth. How can they not see you are a man of God?"

Emrys mused. "Do not be angry, Revyn. They do not understand the power which rests in us is a power given by God, one possible to any man who would seek the knowledge of the sword. Uther has it but it lies so feint on him that he no longer notices. They fear what they do not understand, so they believe we obtained our knowledge through bargaining with the evil one. We cannot counter their superstition with reason. Why argue the point?"

"Because they say you are evil! They should know better."

Emrys sighed. "What men say is of no consequence. What matters is that which the Lord commands of me. That is all."

She thought about the story for a while, then made the observation Uther and all his men had missed seeing. She was quiet for a while, then said, "I felt the pulse of white power reach out from within Uther's sheath when you stated the name 'Lehat...'"

"Shh, child. Do not say it. Names have power. That name is so sacred, so filled with the Lord's purpose we do not want to use it in vain. That is one of the Lord's reasons for renaming the sword."

"Why did you say it?"

"The Lord told me to tell that story. I am not sure yet why he brought that to my mind after so many years. I guess, for anyone who listens. To listen is the greatest of gifts. 'He who has ears to hear, let him hear.' That was the Lord's word."

Revyn was quiet, then said, "I could see the pulse of white, feel its purifying force. Yet none of those men even noticed. Why are we different from others?" Her aura shone crimson red with her concentration. "Uther called Excalibur by...by its other name, yet it had no response. And the colors surrounding the others are pale. Ours are vibrant."

"You answered your own question. Their faith is pale and weak, as is their thinking. Uther is a good man, else I would not have even given him the sword. Yet he lives only on the most basic level, as do most men. The strength of Excalibur's response reflects the wielder's depth. What you and I share is much more powerful than they could ever conceive."

She smiled at that. "Mmm. What we share." They sat in silence. As they stared into the fire, its flames rose to reflect power and dedication and intensified until they gave off a brilliant light...

Eighteen: Night's Whisper

...which blinded Broddin so that he closed his eyes and turned away. He opened them to find himself sitting in the dark of his office. The visions of Emrys's story, the brilliant white power of the sword, the smoke of the campfire burned in his eyes. He had a headache. He could not understand what was going on. He closed down his terminal, took a couple of aspirin and headed home.

It was close to three in the morning. For a change the night was cool. Broddin decided that he would walk back to town. He could use the air, and he was a little afraid of driving.

He had passed Elm Street headed home. Again, a sound whispered to him on the night breeze. He could hear more clearly now. The pure, clear resonance of a bell sounded across the night. The sound pulled at him. He had to find its source. *"Now, auditory illusions?"* he thought, but shook his head.

The sound came again from the South Quad and drew him to stand in the same place he had stood a few nights before. It had sounded *right here!* Yet he stood in this spot and listened to silence so deep that he might have been deaf. As he stood there, a light came on in an upstairs room. He saw a shadow cross past the light. *"Hmm. What do they hear in the night?"* Broddin continued on home.

Nineteen: Battle

She could feel the clamor of alarm bells ringing in her chest. She was frigid underneath the covers. Her windows were thrown open to the night. Hot air beat at the sill. But cold air conquered from within to dominate and subdue; to take her away from here to a hillside, naked and freezing. An army of monstrous men covered the hill, leered at her, barked and growled and lunged. What held them back was far worse than the army itself. The Ishar Crull held her up by her neck, shaking her senseless, and probed at her mind with a force against walls her mind could barely hold. The coldness of death radiated outward from her. Her will was imprisoned by Crull's grip and by her unbelief that he could possibly exist.

The bells tolled their alarm once more, then a brilliant light flashed across the hill from below. It pierced the army, dividing it. The cold clamped down on her...

...and she woke, gasping. Again. "No.... No!"

She turned on her light to make sure the room was still here, still real. She got up, walked across to her closet and threw on a top and sweatpants for warmth. "Will someone help me?"

The room was frigid. "I've got to get out of here, get warm." She slipped quietly out into the night.

Twenty: The Sacred

Atlanta, Georgia

Gem's mother sat drinking a cup of tea. It was three in the morning and she had work the next day. Yet, she knew she wouldn't sleep. Her heart was focused on her daughter. The attacks had been gone for so long that she had forgotten the pain and cold, and the physical aspects of these spiritual attacks. She thought back to the time when the attacks first came, when Gem was six.

On a hot night in August the air conditioner in Gem's room blew a frigid breeze across her. She turned in her sleep, moaning, and shivered at the cold.

Estelle lay, eyes wide, wondering at the fear which made her heart pound at nothing. Later, she awoke to the sound of Gem gasping and choking for breath. She raced in to find her daughter doubled over and blue from lack of oxygen, her eyes wide and pupils dilated. Estelle gathered Gem in her arms and screamed to her husband **"Call 911!"**

The paramedics arrived within ten minutes. The girl fought for each breath. She was soaked with sweat and ice cold. The paramedics administered inhalants and oxygen which brought relief to her lungs. Within minutes she lay back down to sleep, exhausted from the ordeal.

The doctors who examined Gem the next day could only diagnose an onset of juvenile asthma, and prescribe the usual inhalers.

The attacks continued night after night for months of endless exhaustion. Many nights Gem lay trembling in her mother's arms, describing the dream that always came with the attacks: the dark man who choked her, who hurt her. The detail of it filled Estelle with horror, for this young girl described details no child should endure.

Worse were the nights when Gem couldn't defeat the dream. She would lay in bed, her eyes wide, pupils dilated so much that the green of her irises disappeared. Then, the hairs on Estelle's neck stood straight in horror, for from those eyes poured cold, malignant blackness.

Estelle tried every specialist within the Atlanta area, seeking to find some answer to the horror of the dreams Gem described. Finally, a psychiatrist from Emery University suggested she speak to a local Catholic priest who specialized in occult possession.

Estelle scoffed at the idea. She was a research scientist in applied physics. Joe, her husband, was a metallurgist and sculptor. He had a forge in their back yard where he fashioned sculptures of soaring beauty with compounds he created himself. They both were steeped in reality. *"Witchcraft, demons, holy water, crosses: that stuff was fiction for feeble minds."*

She was at her wit's end and she decided that it couldn't hurt. Nothing else had worked so far. She broached the topic with Joe, but he was incredulous that she even entertained the idea. Many days of arguing ensued while Gem kept getting weaker.

Finally, Estelle decided she needed to act on her own. She went to Father Perry of Immaculate Conception Catholic Church and talked to him.

After listening to her, Father Perry closed his eyes in thought, or prayer. Then he looked at her. "This child is not baptized, is she?"

"No."

"And you?"

"Oh long ago when I was a child, but we don't believe in that stuff now. No offense, Father."

Father Perry looked at her. No expression revealed his thoughts. He turned to a shelf behind him and picked out a book which looked to be hundreds of years old. "Let me read you a passage. 'The demon of cruelty has certain specific characteristics which accompany his attempts at possession. They are: restriction of breath, darkness, full dilation of the iris, coldness to touch, general coldness of the area in which it operates...'" He went on to read an exact medical diagnosis of Gem's condition.

"Let me see that!" She was trembling. "It can't be! It can't be real!"

"Because you can't see it? But you *are* seeing it. I am afraid that it's *very* real. Your daughter is in grave danger, Mrs. Matthews.

"What can I do? I don't believe in God."

Father Perry looked at her and smiled gently. "Estelle, do you remember the Apostle Thomas? Doubting Thomas. For some of us, belief comes only after we have seen with our own eyes and placed our fingers in the holes of Jesus' wounds. Even for those who knew him best in Galilee."

"At this time, it's not *your* belief that is important. That will come later. For now, I ask you to act on what you *know*, what you saw today with your own eyes and on *my* faith. Will you do that?"

She thought of Gem growing weaker. "Yes."

"Good. First, I'm going to give you is some specific prayers to repeat as constantly as you can, to shield Gem against this demon. It doesn't matter if you believe or not at this point. I want you to pray these prayers. Then, understand, prayer is just talking to God. Talk to him like you would anyone else. You used to do a lot of that when you were a young child."

She looked up, startled. "How did you..."

He laughed. "Don't look so shocked. We all did. Some of us simply forgot how to listen when He answers us.?"

"But he never answered my prayers!" Her voice was teary now. "That's why I don't believe!"

"Estelle, He answers us all the time! We've just closed our ears. Often because we don't like the answers. Sometimes we're too busy running our own lives. Trust me. Start talking to God, and listen. You *will* hear Him answer. I believe that Jesus especially hears the prayers of a mother for her child.

Estelle began her regimen of prayer that night and every night and day afterward. Her constant prayer, her call to God's protective embrace was the only help in easing Gem's breathing.

The attacks lasted for several months, then ceased as abruptly as they had come. Whatever the battle, Gem had won it. She was more direct, more at peace. During this time, Gem began reading voraciously. To her mother's curious questions on why she read their college texts on physics and metallurgy, she answered simply, "I'll need to know this stuff someday."

Gem began working with her father in the back yard forge, learning the craft, watching, helping. She loved being with him and he loved her company. They forged a bond in that shop, one focused on metal and on this earth.

Joe Matthews had gone to church with Estelle and watched as her prayers eased Gem's breathing. But after the crisis passed, he went back to ignoring the church. Gem followed her father's inclinations.

Estelle understood how they felt, but she had seen a deeper reality. She never ceased praying, yet she didn't impose herself on either Joe or Gem. Faith was personal. Each of us has to find it in his own way.

Now, eight years later, Estelle thought back to that first attack. Like her father, Gem would not acknowledge that evil exists, or that evil had attacked her. She had scoffed at the idea. "C'mon, Mom! There's no such thing as demons."

So Estelle went to do the only thing she knew would help her daughter. She prepared for war; a war she had fought before. She kneeled next to the bed to offer prayers for Gem's protection.

"Lord Jesus, I beseech your protection over my daughter, Georgia..."

Twenty-one: The Profane

Dr. Kerian Noguchi stood in his study, the phone pressed to his ear. "No. He hasn't made any progress. He keeps reviewing and working on the same equation hours on end. The security guard at his office said that he may have had another event.

The voice on the other end spoke. "What were the symbols he wrote?"

"Not sure. They look like some type of Middle Eastern language. I asked one of the professors here who is versed in this type of study to take a look.

"Who is this? Is he one of us?"

"No, but I see no harm in..."

"Brief me *before* you approach anyone else, do you understand?"

"Yes, sir."

"Report to me when you hear back from this man. Isolate this so he doesn't know where the writing came from. Do you have any other successes to report?"

"One in the Agricultural Sciences Department. Our research student has been able to increase the growth rate of the GenArbor formula by a factor of five. And he has been able to atomize an aerosol delivery method to bypass the usual genetic modification requirements. We're going to apply this quite soon to the Fallow Lands.

"Good. We are hoping this program will aid in quicker regeneration of our native forests. The Mother needs more oxygen."

Noguchi's heart raced at this reference to such important work. "Save our Mother Earth!"

The voice on the line responded in a bored tone. "Yes, Save Her. Now report on the boy. I believe we have reached the limit of our patience and he should be sent for Relief."

Noguchi stiffened. He knew his son Roger would come up. "I don't think that's wise yet."

"You don't? Do you have an undesired loyalty to this boy because it's your offspring?"

"No, but...he fulfills another function. I am using him to gain Broddin's confidence."

"It's a waste of valuable assets when we are *all* limited by the diminishing resources plaguing our nation. We made an exception for this boy because of some possible future potential. Unless his usefulness can be demonstrated, we will no longer accept excuses. He will be sent for Relief."

Noguchi answered. "I understand."

"Follow what's going on with Broddin."

"Yes, sir." he said to an empty phone line. When the voice spoke of 'relief,' of putting the boy down, he felt only a slight twinge. He thought that he should feel something. They *were* talking about euthanizing his son. But it *was* for the greater good of Mother Earth.

Twenty-two: Roger

2:30 a.m. Roger got up quietly. As usual, his parents slept. He had awakened every night like this for many months, beginning in Japan. He would go out to the back yard in the shadowed dark. He practiced the kata he saw that day, repeating until he knew it perfectly. Then he would go back to bed.

Once he was startled to see his Sosobo, his great grandmother, as she sat quietly in the shadows, and watched him. She was the oldest of living family. When not at the Shinto Shrine saying Christian prayers for her ancestors, she went out to the rice fields of local farms and help the farmers to plant or harvest.

That night, she waited until she knew Roger saw her. She stood up and bowed very low. Roger immediately dropped the shinai he was practicing with and bowed back to her. No words were exchanged. She simply turned and went back into the house. Roger wondered if she would say anything to his parents, but she never acknowledged what she had seen.

This night in Roxford was different. He slipped down to the basement. A back room was locked with an old heavy key. Within the room stood an ancient armoire. Roger paused in front of it, then opened the double doors. A suit of leather armor hung, facing outward. Though probably hundreds of years old, the leather still felt supple, still smelled fresh. Battle marks scarred the arms and the headpiece.

He knew that his mother came down here to carefully clean and condition it twice a month. His father would not have approved. These were the old ways. The ways of war, of combat and of honor. They weren't...scientific.

Roger looked for a moment at the armor. The pattern woven into the leather on the chest was the image of a cross. Roger bowed low. He took the armor down and slipped the vest over his shoulders. He was surprised how comfortable it felt. He took the headpiece down and carefully placed it on his head. He knew he wouldn't really need it but there was a reason to wear it.

He looked at the sword which lay cradled above the armor. Would this be needed? He thought for a moment. Not tonight, not for this task. He closed the cabinet and went quietly upstairs. On his way out the door, he picked up the walking staff he had earned upon climbing Mount Fuji this summer. It would do.

Roger Noguchi — autistic child, writer of nonsense notes, named 'It' by his contemporaries — slipped out into the dark night and began to make his way across campus. He kept to shaded grassy areas. He walked in total silence. He was a ghost, moving among the sleeping.

He knew his destination.

Twenty-three: Samurai

Gem almost stumbled as she walked out of the dorm. She was freezing. Needed the heat of the night. She headed across campus. She tried to control her breathing was slightly dizzy from the cold and the exertion.

Three frat boys crossed the campus. They had been out boozing and "smoshing' salts all night long. As they headed back to the dorm they were complaining that they hadn't gotten lucky. Across the green they saw a girl come out from one of the dorms. Whispers invaded their thoughts, grew stronger, demanding. They welcomed the darkness which came into their minds. It brought to the front images they had watched online late at night. It refreshed those images, and reinforced the desires until their heads were clouded with its power.

"Hey, Bill, looka that. I think we jes got lucky. You know some of the vids we watched the other night?"

"Yeah. Three on one."

"We can make that happen...right now."

"Ummm. Delicious! Do it."

"You guys circle around and flush her this way. I'll be waiting."

Gem heard someone cough behind her and turned

to see two boys. She heard one say "Hmm, what do we have here? Check out this sweet little thang." They started to jog toward her and Gem turned, but ran into a third boy. He was big, built like one of the jocks in her high school. He picked her up off the ground and clamped a dirty hand on her mouth. "Hey guys, cmon. We got a cute one." The others jogged up and the three wrestled Gem toward a dark area.

Gem tried to scream, but the hand over her mouth felt like Crull's choking grasp and the cold, already invading her heart, paralyzed her. *"So this is what it's like for real."* She was close to blacking out.

The larger boy held her. "Pull her clothes off. Man, she feels cold!"

A voice from behind them, clear and deep, said, *"No!"* They turned to see a small man standing in the shadows. He wore some type of headpiece which prevented them from seeing his face. He held a long staff at his side.

"Who the hell are you? And what's that costume? Jim, get rid of him."

Before Jim could move, the figure came at him, slashing with the staff. He went down, his legs swept out from under him, his wrist broken and the air punched out of his lungs. The larger boy dropped Gem and stood up. "Nobody does that to my friend. Whadya think, you're some kinda ninja?" The two boys charged at the figure.

Doing the kata night after night was not the same as real combat but the muscle memory from the practice worked. Roger ducked a punch, jabbed into the solar plexus, then spun around to bring the stick down onto the large boy's knees. The boy went down, trying to grab for his opponent, but Roger skipped backward and dealt a blow to the side of his head. The angle and force was enough. All three boys would awaken with a knot and severe headaches.

Roger Noguchi, descendant of Samurai, paused to make sure the three were done. He went over to where Gem lay and knelt down. Her top was torn and she was shivering uncontrollably. Her eyes looked back into his with implacable hate. He looked into those black eyes. "You do not frighten me." He swung his staff and struck the ground beside her head. A blast of violet colored light rippled outward.

*   *   *

Gem sat up. A rasping breath tore at her throat as she took in oxygen. One deep, deep breath. As her head cleared she saw her attackers on the ground a few feet away from her, unconscious. She looked around. No one else was here. Then she remembered. Suddenly, fearing the worst, she touched herself, but her clothes were intact. They had not touched her. She had a vague recollection of a voice, deep and powerful, clear and strong. *"You do not frighten me."*

She shook her head. "What just happened?"

She was warm. Warm down to her bones. It felt good. She felt good. She stood up, walked away from the darkness of the bushes and back to her dorm. That night, she slept in peace for the first time in weeks.

Twenty-four: Sorcerer

The fifth vision came to Broddin a few days later, as he sat at his computer. He was staring at the equation he'd been working on when the screen saver timed out. A galaxy field flowed in its usual rainbow pattern. Then, to his wonder, the galaxy changed to a rainbow of swords streaming toward him on the screen and right off the screen past him. Broddin turned to watch the little swords fly by...

...and was at the camp, watching the sorcerer write. "The year of our Lord, Four Hundred Seventy-four. I fear for the King. The hard riding and the fighting drain Uther, until he lays near death."

"Still, he refuses to give up this hopeless quest. He is dying. I will miss him."

The sorcerer looked up from his writing, thinking. He knew that men feared him. Wished they wouldn't, but he understood why. Uther was young when Emrys first arrived, but now lay at his deathbed. The sorcerer looked hardly a day older.

Revyn sat next to him, her head on his shoulder. Her glistening black hair reflected the flames of the fire, her brilliant green eyes, the flame of his aura. She looked up at him and smiled.

"I love you, Emrys."

"I love you, too."

She sat for a while and looked into the firelight. "I listened to your story yesterday about Excalibur. Why did you change its name?"

"I didn't. The Lord God changed it."

"As He changed your name?"

Emrys smiled. "Yes."

"Why?"

"You are full of questions, as always. The Lord has purpose in all He does. My role has changed for Him many times. Names are important, because they define one's purpose. My purpose outlived the name."

Revyn smiled. "What of your first name?"

Emrys deflected her question. "Oh, that was such a long time ago."

"I wish to hear it! Anyway, I think I know it."

"Shhh, love. Do not say that name."

"Why?"

Emrys remained quiet for a long time. "Only one woman had the right to say that name as you would say it. That was my wife."

Revyn's face fell and she looked down. This was the crux of her secret pain. His wife had been dead long ages ago, and yet he chose to take no other. She thought that they shared a deeper emotion. Out of that crucible of pain came the question, asked only a few times in the last three years. "Why can you not love me like a wife?"

"I am not a man at liberty to be like others."

"Regardless! That does not answer me."

"You are not my wife."

"In every way but one, I am."

Emrys sighed. "You know, Revyn, that it is forbidden. Your commandments are mine too. Even having you as my companion is wrong, but..."

"But what?" Revyn's eyes brightened.

"Nevermind." He looked into her eyes for a long time before continuing. "This is very selfish on my part. You knew even before you came to me that we could never consummate our love. I was lonely. That still does not make it right. Besides, I could not bear seeing you and our child die..."

Her passion flared in the flash of crimson in her aura. "Our child! We will *never* have such a gift! I would not *care* if she died. I *want* you." Her voice became deeper, more intense. "Emrys, I don't want *anything* between us! A gulf separates us. I feel it. Only our lovemaking can mend it. You had it with...*her* and you will not give it to *me*." She turned away, hurt.

Emrys sat and stared into the fire for a long while. He turned to see silent tears streaming down her face. He reached out and touched her cheek. "Revyn, I *do* care! I love you. I will see you grow old and lose you too soon as it is, before..." His eyes now grew tears.

"Understand, child." He whispered. "I had but one wife. I cannot number my sons and my daughters to you, or their children and children's children. I live...while all of them...*all of them* died. An endless progression of grief..." He fell silent, his throat taught, thinking of the loss, seeing the faces over the ages. "Give me your hands." Emrys opened his memory to share with Revyn the images washing through his heart, the grief he had borne alone for so long. Now Revyn's tears flowed freely.

This, then, was the manner they became as close to one flesh as possible. They became of one mind. In prayer, they grieved together for his loss. Together they drew upon the strength and peace of the Holy Spirit to carry them across this chasm of grief. They shared in the joyful knowledge of a communion to come.

She lay in his arms, accepting that this was to be the way of their lives. The closeness brought expression. As she kissed him, she said, "I wish we could consummate our love as it should be."

"I know. We may do nothing about that." Then, he smiled broadly. "Besides, intercourse is forbidden, but we have other ways, so tonight we shall cuddle."

Much as she tried, she could not keep her frown. She laughed at the delight in his face. "All right," she whispered, "tonight, we cuddle!" She rose from his arms and hurried off toward their tent to prepare, but suddenly whirled to look east.

Emrys marveled at her sensitivity, for her reaction came an instant before he felt that cold, probing force reaching out. It felt weak as of yet, but it was there. "No!" Instantly, he dampened the brilliance of his aura, closed his power upon itself.

The look of horror on Revyn's face reflected what she felt coming from the east and what she saw in Emrys' actions. "What is it? What assails you?"

Emrys felt her fear and anguish. "Do not fear for me, Revyn. Come here. I need to hold you. I will need to present no face of power for a while, until I can plan." He looked directly into her eyes. He had warned her that this day might come. "The Ishar Crull has returned."

The color faded from her cheeks and she moved to speak, but he held her. "Hold quiet, child. I am in command, but I need time. Go to your bed."

She wanted to protest, but she straightened and looked at him. "I'll be awake waiting for you."

"You fill me with hope, Revyn." He kissed her warmly and held her close for a while.

While Emrys and Revyn spoke quietly, one of Uther's attendants came hurrying over to the fire. "Lord Emrys, you must come! The King calls for you. I think...I think he nears death."

"I will be there shortly. Go tell him."

"Yes, sire."

Emrys sighed. Of course this would happen tonight. The cold force of Crull's evil whispers alone would hasten death's hold on the weak. Emrys knew now he must truly plan. No matter what happened in the next few moments, some factions would blame him for Uther's death and try to harm him in any way they could. Worse, they would be even more zealous in their hunt for Uthur's child, the future King.

He sat back down by the fire, stared into the flame's whispered secrets. Broddin followed Emrys's gaze and looked deep into the flames. They crackled, and danced around the wood, took form as little swords, and suddenly a tiny swirling rainbow galaxy which raced out toward his eyes...

Twenty-five: Nightmare

...and James Broddin almost pitched backward off his chair. He was back at his computer. In the present. Something was very wrong. He was not in control and he did not like it. He would call Dr. Noguchi in the morning. He knew he could simply not continue having these visions.

Broddin called Dr. Noguchi to tell him about the visions. "One of them happened while I was driving. Then there might have been some auditory..."

Noguchi interrupted him. "Hang up. Stay at your home. I am sending an ambulance for you."

"What? Professor, I don't have time for this! I have classes and my own studies. I don't think..."

"Do you really seriously want to convince me that I should let you continue until you have a cerebral hemorrhage which destroys that valuable brain? Stay where you are. We have a great clinic here with all the newest technology. I am calling a friend, Dr. Lewison, who will check you over."

"But the time!"

"Forget it. Someone will cover your classes. We need to find out what's going on. Do you understand?"

"Yes, sir."

That was two days before, when Lewison had

admitted Broddin for tests. Now Broddin sat in Lewison's office. He looked across the desk. "Well, what'd you find?"

"Nothing. It's frustrating. Physically, you're fine. No chemical imbalance, negative scans on MRI, CT, quantum and every other scan I could think of. You're in fine shape."

"Then what's with these episodes?"

"The hallucinations?"

"I wouldn't call 'em that. How about 'Daymares'? Sort of nightmares during the day."

Lewison looked at him. "Whatever you call them, I think we'll need to pursue them from a psychological point of view. I want you to write the daymares down in as much detail as you can remember. And you are not to drive for a while."

"Do you really need to know this stuff?"

"Young man, you know I am primarily a psychiatric specialist. I have an MD/PHD in genetic pharmacology. Tell me about the dreams. Maybe if you do, we can understand this and get you out."

"Time! It's going to take time that I don't have."

"Do you have a choice? Want to be driving your car when the next one hits you?"

Broddin brooded a minute. "No. Let's get on with it." The delay irritated him, but he could see no other way. "One thing about these dreams is interesting. These dreams at least give me a clue to the identity of the girl in my other dreams."

"Other dreams?"

"Yeah. These daymares only bothered me for a

few days. One of the characters in my other dreams is this girl, Revyn, in the visions. Of course, it makes sense that I might populate these visions with other dream characters."

"How long have you had these other dreams?"

Broddin paused. "It's only one dream. The same one. Every night. For eight years."

Lewison looked up at Broddin. "Earth Mother! Eight years? Did you tell anyone about this? This could be crucial! Tell me about this other dream."

Broddin sat in the chair, thinking. He looked away, embarrassed. This one was harder to speak about. Too personal. Too close. He grimaced. "All right, Doc. This dream is much less detailed, and more abstract than the others. It's different. It didn't grab me out of a conscious state, but in a way it's more powerful than any of them. More powerful."

"It's about a woman. God, she is gorgeous! She looks like this Revyn in my other dreams. Long curly dark hair. Brilliant green eyes." He could feel himself blush, but he kept his eyes closed and concentrated.

"We're about to begin making love." As Broddin describes the scene, it captures him, compels him into the dream. "I'm holding this girl. We hold each other and begin to make love. I think, 'So this is what it's like to feel joy. Absolute joy!' I feel like I was never complete."

Broddin's brow darkens. "An ice cold darkness rips me away from her, throws me aside, knocks me down. I can't move and I watch helplessly as a dark man begins to assault and choke her."

"I'm filled with a killing rage. It boils up inside me, completely out of my control. I lunge out at him and I kill him...but it doesn't help! Each time I kill him, I feel like I become darker myself, like I take on his character by the act of killing him. I kill him for nothing, though! When I turn to my love, she's dead."

"I hold her body, but nothing, nothing will bring her back. I've lost her again and...and I can't stand it, can't stand it, **can't stand it!"**

Broddin's own shout woke him from the dream. He stood, shaking, tears in his eyes. Dr. Lewison stared at him, transfixed for several seconds before he could recover his professional demeanor. "Okay Mr. Broddin, sit back down. You're back and awake."

"Sorry. I didn't think it would affect me like this."

"No, it's okay. I needed to see that. But Mother! You have these every night?"

Broddin looked haunted. "Yeah."

Lewison sat for a long while, writing in his pad, thinking. "Young man, I've heard all about you from Dr. Noguchi. He tells me how hard you work. How much you cling to 'your schedule,' 'your work.' You are a classic case of an obsessive compulsive personality. Perfect for a genius. "

"Yet, this seems like a type of psychosis...now don't get bullheaded." He saw how Broddin's face hardened at his words. "Just listen. Psychosis has many causes, including some chemical imbalances, but we've ruled those out."

Broddin frowned. "I'm not nuts, Doc. I function fine except for these daymares."

"Really? Except now some other kinds of dreams have invaded your waking life."

"Apart from the dreams, I lead a pretty normal life."

"Really? Have you actually ever been involved in any activity on this campus other than study?"

"No."

"No relationships?"

"No. No time."

"No hookups, just to...release the juices?" Lewison smirked.

Broddin looked up and bristled. "Doctor, aside from the fact that it's none of your business, I don't believe in 'hookups.' I value my body as well as my mind. I'm not interested in casual sex or any kind of sex outside of marriage."

"Ahh. One of the Clingers! You're what, Catholic?" He waved his hand. "No need to be embarrassed. My parents still cling to their private beliefs."

"Yes if you must know, and it *is* my private life. It has nothing to do with my research. Leave it alone."

"You'll note I am not writing any of this part down. I wouldn't want any...marks on your record later. Dr. Noguchi says you have a very bright future. Let's not screw it up with any of this religious mythology. Then again, perhaps that *is* having some impact on these visions you're having. I suggest that you leave this church stuff behind and really concentrate on your science. You can't have both.

"Drop it. I've heard all the lectures."

Lewison responded, "I suggest you remember that beliefs like that could cause your dismissal from your academic program. They may be private, but they can affect the public interest. If they do, they will not be tolerated." He paused, then nodded.

"Back to your issue, I think I see one possibility. You've suppressed your libido so much that I think it's coming out, at least in this dream you're having. You've repressed the sexual urge unnaturally and I could see a dream like that plaguing you. Perhaps, because your quaint views of sex make it a dark lustful urge to you, you're dreaming of yourself as a dark man assaulting what you love. I think you're battling yourself." Dr. Lewison sat back with a satisfied smile on his face.

Broddin frowned. "Doctor, I am not going to debate church teaching on the Theology of the Body. I'll only say that the church does not teach that sex is evil or lustful in itself..."

"Really? You're kidding!"

"...our fallen nature seeks empty sex outside of marriage and that demeans sex...and demeans who we truly are."

Lewison was humming to himself during this last statement. "No, no, no; we aren't having this conversation. I'm not listening to silly nonsense."

Broddin stood up. "We're done."

"Not until I say..." Lewison stopped talking abruptly. He felt a raw pulse of fear in his chest. He had looked into Broddin's face.

"We. Are. Done." Broddin walked out.

Dr. Lewison was perspiring. "These Clingers. So serious! Talk about delusions!" He wrote in his notes. *"Religious delusions may be leading to repressed sexual urges. Violent tendencies readily displayed upon therapeutic confrontation. Recommend closer observation of the subject."*

Broddin was irritated. Lewison's nonsense wasn't any different from the drivel he heard every day on campus. As his temper cooled, though, he wondered about what the doctor had said. Was this 'dark man' really a manifestation of some dark self living within him? He knew what the church taught, but what was this *thing* he dreamed?

He called Dr. Noguchi. "I'm out. What kind of quack did you put me with?"

"He's an MD/PHD."

"Yeah, so he told me." Broddin told him some of what Lewison said.

"Perhaps he just used the challenge technique, to push you into confronting an emotion you don't want to admit. He's very good."

"Find someone else. I won't go back to him."

Noguchi didn't like it, but didn't want to push. "Let me work on it. Meanwhile, I think he had a good idea about you writing down the visions. If you want, you could show me the diary. I'd be glad to give you my thoughts on it. After all, you're almost like Roger's brother and therefore like a son to me."

Broddin hesitated, but thought of how the visions had taken over his life. "Maybe. At least, I'll start to write them down. Let's see where it goes."

Twenty-six: Sunday

James Broddin sat in St. Mary's Catholic Church on High Street. His father sat next to him. They had kept this ritual for years. William Broddin was a machinist at an aluminum foundry in Dayton. He'd never gotten beyond high school, but he'd made certain his son had the best schooling. He was thrilled that his son had a full-boat academic scholarship to University College.

He got up at five o'clock every Sunday morning to make the trip down from Dayton and sit in Church. He'd nod to his son. "Hey, Mikey. How ya doin?"

"Fine, Dad. Nothing to do today?"

"Nah, just thought I'd come down here to make sure you're keepin up with God."

Broddin laughed each time. "I am."

"Sayin' ya prayers?"

"Cmon, Dad. I'm not a kid anymore."

"Yeah, you're a smartass. When was the last time you made confession?" Broddin shrugged. "Thought so. Have some breakfast after church?"

"Sure."

A scattering of others came in, most of them elderly, none of them students other than Broddin. St. Mary's was the only church which still held services within the town. Many of the smaller Evangelical churches still thrived in the outlying countryside. Out there, people could more openly practice their faith. Here, close to the academic center of town, your attendance was noted...and was not appreciated.

Broddin had never gone to the priest for confession, or for any real spiritual leadership. Now he sat in the pew and wondered if he should have confessed about the dreams.

He certainly couldn't discuss them with his father. They felt wrong in so many ways: a naked woman; making love to her. Then, the viciousness of the dark man and the assault. For eight years, he had put them out of his conscious mind. Now, they had broken through. Why? Was the quack right about them, that they represented repressed sexual desires? *"How can I confess them? I didn't **do** anything."*

People slowly filed in to take their accustomed seats. Always the same. The *structure* of it somehow reassured. He looked up at the crucifix. *"Is Christ really here for me? He seems absent from my life, not here, at work or anywhere. So why do I come here?"*

The answer to that question sat right next to him. His father had asked him, four years ago, to come to church. In attending church, he found a reality he could never deny, whether Christ was present for him or not. *"Please, please be present, Lord I can't stop these dreams or the visions. I am so tired."*

James Broddin put his head in his hands and closed his eyes. Father Padrone was giving the homily and Broddin's mind drifted back to visions, to nightmares, to clear bells ringing on the night breeze.

In the midst of that thought, he heard Father quote from Matthew: "'Lo, I am with you always, even unto the end of the world.' Jesus did not say 'I *will* be with you.' He said, 'I *am* with you.' For God, time does not exist as it does for us. He *is* with us today, right here, right now. The distractions, the noise try to block him out. Be still...and hear him. He is here. Here in the body and blood. Here in the word. Here."

Broddin mused, *"Almost feels like the sermon is aimed right at me."* In some way he was comforted, felt stronger, more rested. *"Communion."* he thought, *"Do they realize what it is? What they're missing? I know I didn't before my father dragged me here."*

At the end of the service, Broddin turned to look at the back pews. Roger sat with his mother, as usual, notebook in hand, writing. William followed his son's glance to the back of the church. "That boy is a strange one."

"Yes, he is. I wish he'd stop hanging around. Doesn't do anything; writes in the notebooks, mumbling words. Having him around is a pain."

William looked at his son. "He's been a presence in your life for four years. Who knows why? Maybe there's some reason. You put up with him when other people would chase him away, heap abuse on him...or worse. Ya've done a good thing, Mikey."

"Yeah, I guess." They left the church, headed to breakfast. He chuckled. "Maybe that's why I haven't made confession. If I wanted to, Roger would be right there with me, taking notes."

At that, his father burst out laughing.

Twenty-seven: The Real

Exactly one week after Broddin's release from the hospital, he became convinced he was having another daymare in class, or that he had completely lost his mind. He was at his desk, preparing notes for the class when a girl walked into the room and laid a note on the desk. "I'm a late registrant for this class. Here's the notice."

Broddin looked up and froze. Before him stood a petite young woman. She had long flowing dark hair, and emerald green eyes. She was the girl of the dreams, and he knew if he closed his eyes he would see her standing naked right before him. He would be lost to the dream...and God knows what he'd say or do in the midst of that nightmare. "Revyn?"

"Excuse me?"

"Oh, I'm sorry." With great effort, he cleared his mind and pulled his gaze away from the girl down to the paper she handed him. The name on the form was Georgia E. Matthews.

"Okay, Georgia, please take a seat."

"I go by 'Gem.' I was named after my grandmother, but even she never called me Georgia. Please call me Gem."

Without looking up, Broddin dismissed her. "Fine. Please take a seat. The class will start soon.

The only other person in the room was Roger, in his usual spot. Broddin did not notice that Roger had shifted his seat by ninety degrees when he came in. When Gem came through the door, Roger was already facing that way. He looked directly at her, nodded and went back to the notebook.

As Broddin began the class, he stole a surreptitious glance her way. He decided that the remarkable resemblance to his dream was just a coincidence. He'd been thrown for a moment. *"No big deal. She happens to look like Revyn. She's just another student."*

Each of us, in the deep recesses of our subconscious, builds protective walls to keep us from our worst nightmares. That day, Broddin began building a wall for himself, brick upon brick, on a silent promise: that he would never again look into the eyes of this young woman.

At the end of the class, Gem left. Broddin kept busy with the on-line students. He did not notice that Roger stood up and followed Gem out the door.

Twenty-eight: Roger

Gem Matthews left class and hurried across campus toward the metallurgy labs. She stopped when she saw other students laugh and point behind her. When she turned around, Roger was following her, head down, looking at his notebook.

"What do you want?" No response.

"Who are you?" Nothing.

"Why are you following me?" No response again.

Some older students passed by. "Hey, where's Broddin? We've never seen 'It' around without him."

Gem realized they were talking about the boy behind her. "Hey, who is this?"

They stopped. "You don't know?"

"I'm new. Arrived last week."

The girls looked at each other and giggled. "That's Professor Noguchi's kid, Roger. We call him 'It.' He's been following that snobby jerk, James Broddin, around for four years. We think he's gay. Maybe Broddin, too. Why's he following you?!"

The girls delivered this in a rapid fire exchange of sentences which came from each in turn. They looked at each other and giggled, then turned to stare more closely at Gem. "Hey kid, how old are you?"

"Does it matter?"

They looked at each other. *"Does it matter?"* repeated in a snide tone. "Not really, but you look really young. You could almost pass for a boy. Maybe it's your svelte figure that drew 'It' away from his man-crush." At that, they burst into peals of laughter. Gem could hear them as they walked away. "What a waste that kid is." "He can't be socialized at all." "Should be given relief."

Gem looked back at Roger. He looked at his notebook. "You don't talk?" No response. Gem turned on her heal and walked off.

As she entered the lab, Gem turned, "You can't come in. Dangerous chemicals and processes." Roger followed her in and sat on a stool in the corner.

The lab manager looked up. "Earth Mother! Is that Roger Noguchi? What's he doing here? Is Broddin here?"

"No. He followed me from Broddin's class."

"You're kidding."

"No. What's going on with him?

"For four years Roger has followed James Broddin all over this campus. I can't imagine them apart. Apparently, you just inherited him."

"I don't want him around."

"Get used to it. Roger has special dispensation cuz he's Noguchi's son. You won't be able to chase him off. He's dumb. Just follows you like a lapdog."

"I have work to do. I'll worry about him later."

"Nothing to worry about. You've been chosen."

Gem felt a shiver go through her. "What? What did you say?"

He chose you. Either you're it. Or you're 'It's keeper."

Twenty-nine: Clingers

Kerian Noguchi sat in his office at home. His wife and Roger had gone off to church. That fact irritated him. No matter that his credentials were spotless. The fact that his wife had gone mad, was a Clinger, and now attended *church* every Sunday...that would be noticed. It would be held against him. It could damage his future at the school and in the party.

He read the report from Dr. Lewison. "...*Violent tendencies displayed readily upon therapeutic confrontation. Recommend closer observation.*"

This was disturbing. He was responsible for the choice of Broddin for this program. Another mark against him. The boy *went to church, too!* "When will we be rid of this constant distraction? We need to wipe them all out! It's such a total waste of valuable resources. Let them all be relieved."

"You were saying?" The voice had been watching and listening. "What is a waste of resources?"

Noguchi screwed up his face. "The Clingers! Church. Yes, I know my worthless wife and son go every Sunday. When will we be able to simply relieve them all?"

"Patience, my dear Dr. Noguchi. There is still much...resistance to such an effort, but we are growing ever nearer to that time when we can declare these luxuries, such as mythical worship, to be seditious and dangerous to the existence of civilization. In due time."

"But I want it *now*."

"Only because you feel the embarrassment that you have a family member wasting themselves. Tell me about these episodes of Broddin's."

Noguchi related all that Lewison had reported and his conversations with Broddin. "I am not sure if any actionable material can be had from these. I am no psychiatrist, but I do agree with Dr. Lewison's assessment that the young man is simply displaying repressed sexual urges. If only he would hook up!"

"Yes. We have sent several...desirable options of various genders his way, to no avail. He doesn't even notice them. A true Clinger."

"Is there anything else, sir."

"As to your son..."

"Yes, sir?" Noguchi's interest became focused.

"We believe this experiment has run its course. He is using up valuable resources which could be appropriated to other more deserving citizens. We direct you to have him report to a relief station."

"Actually, Roger was the point of my next report. There's been a change. He has left Broddin and is now shadowing our new student, Georgia Matthews. This change is radical for someone like Roger. It parallels what happened when he first saw Broddin. Give me at least a few weeks to analyze and observe. If no change further happens, then no problem. I'll send him to report for relief."

"We will hold his Relief in abeyance for now."

Thirty: Class

December

Gem thought back on the past three months in Broddin's class. She had hoped for a better relationship with him. She admired Broddin tremendously. He was brilliant, but from what she could tell a complete misogynist.

Broddin would not acknowledge her in any way. From talking to other students, she knew he had no time for most people. She seemed to be included in that group from the beginning. He didn't look at her, avoided speaking to her directly, and barely tolerated listening to her in class.

Gem had made a fast on-line friend in Weng. They spent endless hours debating various issues from computer hardware to programming, to personalities, to love.

Gem asked Weng one day, "What is it with the Brods? It's like he's taken a special dislike to me."

Weng thought about it. "I'm not sure. I've noticed it, too. He seems to avoid you especially. Of course, he's not really close to anyone. 'It' is the closest person to him. In general Broddin hates the entire human race. So, you're in good company.

"Oh, that's comforting! You know, Weng, I'm going to whittle down his defenses. I like him...and he's too intelligent not to like me!"

Weng chuckled. "I'm glad to see that Broddin's actions haven't caused you to doubt yourself--as if that were a possibility." His smile turned to a serious look. "You want to know more about Broddin? You ought to go to that Kendo tournament they're having in Dayton this coming Saturday. He's tops in that sport."

"I'm not really a sports person."

"Suit yerself."

"Kendo? What is that?"

Weng explained the sport to her, then said. "Tell you what. Why don't I take you?"

She paused. "Maybe I will go. It'll be the first sporting event I ever attended."

Weng was surprised. "You're kidding, right?"

"Nope. Not into them. I hated jocks when I was growing up. They used to pick me up and use me as a weight bar, lifting me above their heads. Thought it was funny."

Weng laughed. "Sounds like it was." He could see she wasn't laughing. "Sorry."

"I was always 'the kid.' Always the youngest, always skinny and underweight. They picked on me mercilessly. They knew about the asthma. They didn't care. I learned early that most kids are jerks." She shrugged. "Left that behind."

Weng looked at her. "Why don't you come with me to watch? Be my guest. You'll find it very different. Might even find it interesting."

Gem said, "Okay. I'll come along."

Thirty-one: Tournament

The tournament gym was already hot. Early December with the temperatures still in the nineties. This felt more like Georgia than it did Ohio. Gem arrived early and wandered around the school, looking at pictures. Broddin had quite a number of awards and trophies.

Weng met her and showed her around. As he explained about the different types of swords for forms and sparring, Gem watched them. "How did Broddin get involved?"

A voice behind her spoke. "Ah, you are a friend of Mikey's?" It was Yamato.

"Who?"

"Mister Broddin. I have a nickname for him. Call him Mikey. The young man lived only a few blocks away. He wandered in one day when I was sparring with some students. Perhaps he sought to relieve stress or some physical workout. He was respectful. I liked him immediately, so I helped him join classes."

"That was seven years ago. Now, Broddin is one of the best Kendo practitioners in the country." Yamato looked at his watch. "Please be seated. The tournament will start soon."

Gem watched, transfixed, throughout the day. She'd always found school sports boring. But Kendo seemed different from any other sport.

The--'practitioners' they called them--had an air of calm and respect.

The crowd cheered for their side, and Gem felt herself drawn in, cheering for the locals. Gem mused to herself that she would never have dreamed that she'd be in a crowd rooting for some sports contests.

She was distracted thinking of that when she felt a freshening breeze flirt against her face and a hush came across the crowd. She looked up and her breath caught. *She stood in a field, in the middle of a black tide of human animals...and she was naked. They leered at her and she was frigid, cold. She knew that cold! Crull was here!*

Broddin stood at the edge of the mat, then walked onto the arena floor, the 'shinai' bamboo sword held downward at his side. He walked with a casual ease, but he presented a palpable air of power about him.

Broddin stood at the edge of a vast army of death, then entered, approaching where she stood. He held a sword down by his side which pulsed a radiant sky blue color. He walked with a casual ease, but he presented a palpable air of power about him.

Gem's gasp was repeated throughout the crowd in recognition of a man who embodied the manner, the tradition of the Samurai.

After the initial quiet, a wave of cheering arose and echoed around the gym. Broddin's master stood at one side of the ring and watched expectantly. He had arranged this test for Broddin. Broddin's opponent was Iharu Ichimura, a grand master from

Japan, who held a seventh degree belt, three degrees above Broddin. Few expected Broddin to last...until he stepped onto the floor.

The initial quiet of the freshening breeze was jarred by a wave of jeering which arose and echoed around the field. Crull watched expectantly as Broddin approached. Few expected him to stand against him...until he stepped onto the field. The roar of the army simply diminished to an eerie silence in her mind. Gem knew that it was vitally important that she watch!

The two men bowed to the judges, then to one another. They began to circle. Ichimura crouched in a classic sword fighting position, sword pointed up, ready. Broddin had not even lifted his sword from its downward angle, but walked intently in a sideways slant, watching and waiting.

Crull shook her like a rag doll and simply dropped her to the ground. Then, he approached Broddin, crouching in a classic fighting position. Broddin circled, intent, his sword at a downward angle, watching, waiting.

Ichimura hesitated. He had never seen anyone approach a match without their sword at the ready. He could not believe the foolishness of this American. He decided to end this match quickly, offer a killing cut, then walk off the mat. He closed slowly to within striking distance.

Crull hesitated. No one had ever approached him as this man did. He could not believe the foolishness of the man. He would hate to kill him quickly, but the

sword was in this man's hand, within his reach! He
began to speak to the man, and to whisper.

Ichimura struck so swiftly that no one in the
crowd could see where it began. Suddenly, he aimed
the sword at Broddin's head. In the instant of the
strike, Broddin's sword was up, blocking.

The crack of the shinai swords' first cross was an
electric shock jolting Gem, as if she herself had been
hit. Her heart began to race. She was shaking. A
buzzing in her head made her feel faint. She was
almost doubled over, but the crowd was on its feet
watching. No one noticed her as she whispered one
word over and over: "James."

The crack of the swords' first cross was an
electric shock jolting Gem as if she herself had been
hit. Her heart began to race. She was almost doubled
over, watching, in agony. She was not even aware of
speaking one word over and over: "James."

The opponents were well matched. Neither gained
the upper hand. The crack of the swords played back
and forth across the walls, echoing a constant flat
ring. The gasps of the crowd rose with each strike and
parry. Yet, neither opponent could gain advantage
enough to make a clean cut. Suddenly, as Ichimura
reached out with another cut, Broddin drew back and
stood straight to his full height. The other man's
momentum was only slightly off. Broddin needed no
more. His strike came across Ichimura's wrist, then a
second to his chest. It was so swift that no one had
seen it, yet the result was unmistakable: a killing
blow.

The opponents were well matched, which fueled the hate and frustration of Crull. Neither gained the upper hand. The ring of the swords played back and forth across the fields, echoing a constant screaming wail. Then, suddenly, the dark cloak surrounding Crull's figure stretched out, and Crull mounted above Broddin on wings. From this height he would make the killing blow. He swung down with the sword, and for an instant his momentum was slightly off. Broddin needed no more. His strike came across Crull's wing, then a second to the chest. Yet, Crull did not die.

They fought on and Broddin gained in strength. His face became a mask of fury as he struck blow after blow against the demon, until he beat it to the ground and prepared for the killing blow. Gem felt sick. She had not seen this side of Broddin. Then, suddenly, he looked up as if right at her for a moment...and threw the sword away..."

Ichimura rocked back, stunned. It was not possible. Yet, the match was over. "Match, Mr. Broddin." He bowed to Broddin, who returned the bow. Then, as they turned to bow to the judges, the gym erupted in pandemonium.

*In an instant, Crull leapt up on broken wings. He was after the sword, and it looked like Broddin threw it right into his hands! No. **No!** Roaring sounded in her ears. She had to tell Broddin...."*

The cheering came from all sides, thundering down and echoing back. It pressed in on Gem, became a roaring in her ears. She stood up and began to make her way down through the crowd. She had to escape. People were close, pressing in on her.

As she got to the bottom of the aisle and turned, Broddin was walking off the floor and called to her. "Matthews?"

She was white now, pale and trembling. She turned and said, "James." The roaring grew even louder, invaded her head and she began to fall.

In two strides, Broddin reached her and caught her before she hit the floor. *The white fire of the vision hit him. Holding Gem, thinking, "This is what it's like to feel joy. I was never complete before now." But it was too late. She lay dead in his arms. A feeling of desolation rose toward a conflagration of grief.*

As Gem convulsed in his arms, gasping for breath, the vision was ripped away, forgotten in an instant of total awareness. Gem had fainted. She was cradled in his arms. He would not recognize the visions now. "Somebody get some water!" He knelt down. Her breathing was thready. Her eyes were fully dilated, pupils black, no green at all. She felt cold to the touch. "Is there a doctor here?"

Gem convulsed again and gasped as if waking from a nightmare. Her eyes came into focus and were filled with terror. "Don't give him the sword! Don't..." Then, she was fully awake, trembling. She looked up into Broddin's face. Her chest was tight. "Purse. Inhaler."

Weng came up in the crowd, grabbed her purse, and thrust the inhaler into her hands. Gem took a deep draft of the medicine, held it, and let her breath out slowly. Visions crowded against her eyes, but they faded from her memory as if they had never been. Her color began to return. She looked up into Broddin's face with a weak smile. "Sorry, I guess I was worried you wouldn't win the match. Held my breath too long."

Broddin smirked. "Don't worry. I don't lose."

She held her breath in, then let it out fully again to begin to guide her lungs back to normal. Broddin helped her sit up. A doctor came through the crowd. "Let me see her."

Broddin laid her down on the mat and hesitated. He had the strangest sensation then: if he closed his eyes and opened them, he and Gem would be alone. No one else on earth would exist; only the two of them. It was not a romantic feeling. That image filled him with a dread he could not comprehend.

The doctor touched his shoulder and an electric shock brought him back. He looked into Gem's face again, and saw that the green of her eyes had returned...and that she was flushed for an entirely different reason. "Let the doctor look at you." He let her arms drop and stood up.

Broddin turned to Weng, angry. "How the hell did she get here?"

"Whoa, James. I invited her to see the match."

Broddin looked at Weng, a furious expression on his face. "Fine. Take care of *your* guest." Then he walked out.

Thirty-two: Challenge

In the months following, Broddin refused to even acknowledge what transpired. That was especially difficult since Gem insisted on coming to the classroom. Broddin ignored her anyway.

Gem's attempts to even broach the day, to congratulate him on his victory, or mention her thoughts on Kendo were met with cold grunts.

After several months of trying to understand, Gem felt rebuffed by Broddin's attitude and turned to making wisecracks in class. When her turn came to present a paper to the class, its title was "Artificial Intelligence: It's Hardware or Nowhere."

Broddin looked up. "Miss Matthews, you do realize this is a class on the theory and practice of software applications to artificial intelligence?"

"Sure, but I really believe the entire premise of the course is wrong. You can only do so much with software without hitting a wall."

Broddin was instantly irritated. What she said hit deep at his frustration. He had struggled with this exact problem for years. "That wall *will* be broached. Yes, we need hardware. But the real changes, every major breakthrough in the last years, were software driven."

"Yeah, but it's still not *really* AI, is it? We've gotten smaller and faster. Yet we all know a simple fact: the computer's not really thinking. Networking is still only faster processing of information already entered before. Even the quantum computer is just faster at crunching numbers. It doesn't *think*."

"That's all true. So why are you here?"

"Getting to know the other side of the argument. Anyway, I'm going to need some good software people later on, when the real creating begins."

Others joined in the debate. Broddin sat back and watched for over an hour as the class attacked Gem's arguments. Gem more than held her own.

"Okay, let's call it a day. After the VID went blank, Broddin said, "Miss Matthews, may I speak with you?"

Broddin kept his eyes focused on her presentation when she came up to his desk. "In spite of the entertainment factor in your term paper title, it has merit and original thinking. I'm impressed, but I still don't see what you are doing in this class." His voice was cool, formal. "Your major is metallurgy, not computers. Why are you here, Miss Matthews?"

"Just curious."

"I don't waste my time, or our classroom time on people who are simply curious...or disruptive, which you have become. I recommend that you drop this course and pursue one closer to your major."

"I don't think so."

Broddin's eyes never left the paper. "I cannot allow you to continue this course of study without adequate reason. I will insist that you be removed from the curriculum."

That brought an edge to her voice. "Mr. Broddin, if you must know, my purpose is twofold. One, metallurgy is controlled, like everything else these days, by computer analysis. I cannot allow my work to be at the mercy of someone who only understands software. That's why I challenged the whole course idea in my paper: to stretch others' thinking. And I need to know how to program the systems I'm designing to produce the materials I'm researching."

"I see."

"No, you probably don't, but I hope you'll let me continue in your study. I need this knowledge!" She now leaned on the desk, her hands flat on the surface, white with tension. Broddin looked at her fingers, petite and delicate, yet strong.

"All right, Miss Matthews. You stay. But please refrain from bombastic statements. We have a lot of material to cover this semester." Broddin saw the tension ease in her hands. "By the way, Miss Matthews, you said you had two reasons for your taking this class. What was your second?"

Her smile broadened. "I told you before. I was looking for a good programmer to help me with my own projects. I figured this is the best place to find one." She waved and was gone.

Roger walked to the door, turned to look directly at him, and then walked out to follow Gem.

"Amazing." What Broddin had read in her paper piqued his interest, opened new vistas for him. If she could find the material which mimicked the brain structure, it could change everything.

Thirty-three: Decisions

James Broddin awoke in his bed. Orange light played across the wall. He turned...and was at the fire, watching its flames trace through the wood, as if through Emrys' eyes.

Emrys muttered to himself. "Crull has returned and will seek the sword no matter where. He will raise an army and attack us here. Uther will die tonight. That means civil war. Those who back Jared or the Dukes will seek Arthur more vehemently now to kill him and obtain an advantage with the Queen. I must hide Arthur myself. I trust no one else."

"The sword is like a magnet to Crull. I can find no true men whom I could call to defend against him. Not now. There must be seven! In twenty years, but not now! I must hide the sword! But where to hide it? Crull will feel its power anywhere on Earth."

Emrys brought his hands together, concentrating. A flash of green power erupted, bathing his figure in soft emerald. His breath and pulse slowed. His eyelids fluttered once, then closed.

Time slipped away. He saw himself walking through an immense verdant forest, its color matching his own aura. He walked toward a waterfall, from which issued a blinding white light. At the heart of the falls, within the light, lay judgement and purity, resolution and rest. That was not for him to face, not yet. Emrys looked aside from the light early to see the baby grown to manhood. The young king, bathed in a royal blue aura, held up the sword. A round table. Knights in shining auras: red, green, yellow, every color of the rainbow. He saw the connections which would be made between law and justice.

He turned back to the light, and time raced by in centuries. He saw the slow, tortured process of the growth of man. Wars. Peace. Progress. Wars. A new world. A new nation of law and freedom.

He looked further along this time path for a particular era so based in the material that no mind would have the necessary faith to unleash a "certain spiritual power" from the sword. Emrys settled on the twenty-first century.

He was looking for a safe haven to hide the sword. He saw a city on a huge inland sea. Part of the city was undergoing a revival of its fortunes, but the eastern edge along the shore remained run down.

A few enterprising optimists placed their new businesses there in hopes of capturing the renaissance of the area which would one day come.

Emrys found himself on a street with run down brick buildings. He looked up at a sign on one building. Words were written in Old English Script, in dark green letters on a white background:

TIME TRAXX

AMERLINZ ENTERPRISES

The words resonated with ancient power,

whispered secrets. Emrys knew the form of those secrets, the source of that power. But in this city, at this time, the words were emptied of their meaning.

He found a man inside, sitting in an office, working on some papers. The man was trying to design a logo for his business.

The brass plate on the desk was engraved with the name "Harry Amerlinz". Emrys smiled. "A namesake! He is industrious but has no guile. Perfect!"

Emrys concentrated his thoughts. The focus of his mind narrowed. A narrow connection opened between the sorcerer and the modern man.

The man in the office dozed at his desk. Pieces of the man's thoughts drifted back through time. '...invoices for the recording equipment need to be paid...still can't figure a logo out...Audrey's birthday next week..." Emrys smiled as a thought went back out from him across time. "Audrey would love..." When he was finished with the thought, he turned back toward his own form and concentrated on himself and on Revyn...

...and, Broddin turned with Emrys to look back. He saw himself, asleep, sprawled on his own bed. With a snap, he awoke, bolted upright by the sensation of seeing himself. He was shaking. It was four in the morning. Now they had invaded his sleep. He dragged himself out of bed to write down the vision for Dr. Noguchi.

Thirty-four: Formula

It was late at night in the lab. Gem concentrated on formulas on the VID display.

Roger Noguchi had waited for this night. The logic of what Gem would discover had been obvious to him for months. He did not know why others took so long to draw such conclusions. He watched intently, for this was a crucial moment.

Gem was busy at the board. Her excitement grew. She could see the formula take shape. She had a sudden thought and erased one section from the board. She knew! She reached up to write the final elements on the Video Display...

...when a hand reach out from behind her and wiped the equations from the display.

"What the..." She whirled around. Roger Noguchi stood right behind her looking at the board. "Why did you do that?" "*As if he'll answer.*"

In a clear strong voice Roger Noguchi said, "No."

Gem started. She had heard that voice before, but couldn't remember where. But...this was *Roger* speaking! "What did you say?"

Roger shook his head. He handed her a notebook, one like those in which he wrote ceaselessly. "What's going on? Why did you give me this?" She was afraid she'd lose the formula. She turned back to put her finger to the board...

...and Roger's hand grabbed her wrist, gently but firmly. He turned her around, and handed her the notebook. She shrugged and opened it, just to humor him. On the first page was an element of an equation. Roger turned to the next page. Another was there.

"What are you trying to tell me?"

Roger gave her an exasperated look. He took the notebook, turned it toward her and fanned the pages so she could see. Her equation flashed before her eyes. She took the notebook back and began fanning the pages. Everything she had written on the board was there, but without the corrections she had made. Every part of the equation...

...and she had to sit down. The final pages showed the final elements of her equation, the ones that she had just realized, but had not written down on the board yet. "What? How did you know?" She looked up, startled. "Roger! You knew this! You knew it already, before I realized...."

Roger shook his head no, pointing at himself. Then he pointed at her and shook his head yes.

"This is mine? My equation?" Roger shook his head vigorously. "How?"

The exasperated look again. Roger flipped the notebook over and fanned the pages. On the back of the pages a message fanned out. "Write only on notebook. Tell no one of this."

Gem's head was spinning. "Not even Broddin?" Head shake. "Or your father?" A look of panic and vigorous head shake.

Again, in that clear voice, Roger said, "No."

Thirty-five: Discovery

Kerian Noguchi's phone dinged. Message. He opened it and saw the command. He immediately left his class and trotted back over to his home study. After locking the door, he called the secure number.

The voice picked up on the first ring. "Open the file I just sent you."

Noguchi saw a VID session from the lab the previous night. "Who is that working equations?"

"The the handprint confirms that this is Georgia Matthews. What we've analyzed from examining her current work in metallurgy shows promise, but she has shown no usable result yet."

"What am I looking at here?"

"Watch. We ascertained by the pass system that she is alone in the lab, except for one other person."

"Who?"

"You'll see in a moment."

"I wish we had video and audio access to the rooms themselves. It would make it much easier."

"The investment isn't worth it. The valuable work is written on our video displays and copied to us.

"True." Noguchi watched the writing on the video display. It looked like Matthews struggled with an equation. She erased a portion. A moment later, the entire equation was erased from the display. Noguchi waited a few seconds. "And? What am I looking for here? It looks like she gave up and did not continue."

"One of your failings, doctor, is that you don't look deeper. We do. Do you know who erased the remainder of the equation?"

"Matthews, I suppose."

"No. The handprint which erased the equation is none other than Roger Noguchi, your son."

"What? Impossible!"

"Look at the handprint comparison between that on the screen and your son's recorded print. There is no question. The only conclusion is that your son-- the autistic genetic mutation who never interacts with anyone, who lives in his own world--just interacted with Georgia Matthews in some manner."

Noguchi shook his head in disbelief. "I have lived with the boy for sixteen years. Don't you think I would have seen some kind of interaction except following people around and writing nonsense in notebook after notebook? Even if he did erase the board, of what possible importance could it be?"

"We have no idea at this point. Due to that fact, the directive to 'relieve' him is rescinded. You are to expend every energy to find out what happened in that room. No direct confrontation at this point. Obviously, you'll get nothing from the boy, and the girl is...not cooperative with the questioning of her work. I want a report, daily. Do you understand?"

"Yes, sir." Noguchi was a little disappointed. He had really looked forward to one less distraction and one less drag on his career.

Thirty-six: Gauntlet

The year became one of confrontation for Broddin. Gem was a purposeful goad in class. Now all the students questioned every train of thought from basic programming language to Gem's original premise that hardware is the essential element needed to spark artificial intelligence.

He guided the class toward a consideration of Gem's ideas of layered chip programming and began to develop a theoretical program which would respond to the hardware requirements of such chips.

One afternoon, in early spring, Broddin stopped Gem after class. "How long is it before you finish development on this new chip?"

"Why?"

"Professional interest. They'd be of tremendous use in the development of AI. Not that I fully accept your ideas of hardware requirements, but with the new programs I'm working on married to your layered chip, we might crack the AI code.

Gem looked at him. "Sorry, Broddin. No can do. You may have the best software on the web today. But you have certain clients I won't touch. If you deal with the Federal Government in any form, forget it.

"What? You don't even have a product, much less a business and you're dictating terms? What brass!

Even if you don't sell to them, they'll get it anyway."

"Maybe, but not if I can help it."

"Why? Why cut off a great customer who always pays and never gives you grief about budgets?"

"Now you're kidding! How can you justify selling to someone without knowing what they're going to use your technology for?

"We can't foresee every result of our inventions. It's impossible."

"I agree! We can't, but until I'm certain of what my inventions do, I can't in good conscience simply release them on the world!

"Don't you know how important this is, if you can make your theories work?"

"Sure! Do you? If you do, you'll find a way to work within my limits. Any contract we enter will contain a clause limiting access to those clients I personally approve."

"Gem, you are crazy! Nobody will sign a contract with that clause."

Her smile was radiant. "Thanks!"

"For what?"

"For calling me Gem, not Miss Matthews. It's about time." Before he could answer, she walked to the door. "By the way, *you* will sign that contract with me."

"Oh really!"

"Yeah, when you see the prototype and how it performs."

"Back to the first question. When?"

Her eyes twinkled in delight. "In two weeks."

Thirty-seven: The Lab

The lab was a curious cross between the cleanliness of an operating room and the smell of an old factory. The average temperature was 110 degrees. It was unbearable unless you loved the work.

Gem leaned over the smelter she had designed to be wed to a liquid nitrogen bath and powerful magnetic resonator. The smelter was part of the university's metallurgy equipment. Gem's great aunt in Germany procured the other two components. *"Thank God for rich old aunts."* Gem thought.

Gem had designed the process to alternate superheating and cooling of metals to near absolute zero. With those kind of extremes, the programming for the smelter's tolerances was critical.

Weng did the programming for the complex mechanism which timed the heating and cooling to create a new structure of metal: crystallized metallic compounds. Gem had dreamed of a material with the durability of metal but also the properties of crystals or of some of the carbon compounds.

The smelter would create flat sheets of material, a few microns thick so they could easily be wedded to computer chips. Gem contracted with a local chipmaker to wed some of the first product into basic chips. Now she sat and watched the gauges in the heat of the lab.

It was late at night. The only other person in the lab was Roger. Usually, he left right at seven, so she would have been alone. This night, he sat, oblivious to her hints, threats and direct requests to leave. She finally gave up and simply went on with the smelting.

Roger Noguchi knew. This was a day when all of his patience would find reward. To see thought become real. That's why he stayed. He wanted to see Joy. It was such a rare sight these days.

Gem's gaze focused on the smelter. Only the metal concerned her. The reading of the gauges and the metal as it cooled.

The green light of the smelter came on. "Finished!" She opened the door and grasped the cooled metal. "We began with copper because it's one of the most readily conductive metals..."

She stopped speaking. She slowly pulled the metal sheet from the smelter. It laid across her hands like a kerchief. A quality in the metal captured the light and reflected it back in a radiant, warm color.

"Roses! It's the color of roses!" Tears ran down her cheeks. "Roger, I never once thought about what color it might be!" She held the sheet across her hands.

Roger had gotten up from his chair and looked at the metal. The smile on his face reflected her joy. Roger was startled. He could feel her joy! It was a flash and then was gone. He thought his own overflowing joy had touched him.

"We have to show this to James!"

Then Roger saw a revelation that even he had not known before, shining out from her as clearly as writing on a VID. She was in love with Broddin. It surprised him to know this...and to realize he had not seen it before. So obvious and yet hidden even to his keen sight. He thought on it, but realized that even she may not know that feeling in its full reality yet.

Later, he would reflect on what he learned that night. The depth of Gem's passion was beyond any emotion he'd ever imagined love could be. He felt joy for them both, for he knew a possible future neither of them could see at this point. But he felt fear too. He lay in bed that night repeating to himself a verse he'd heard from church: *"In perfect love there is no fear."* The verse did not bring him comfort.

Roger never thought to ask himself how he knew Gem's feelings with such certainty that night. He had never been privy to other's emotions, only to the logic of their thought processes.

Thirty-eight: CopperCrys

The next morning, Broddin was at his desk at the university. An inexplicable sense of...peace?...joy?... washed over him.

He looked up from his work to see Gem standing in the office door. She was radiant with joy, the same joy he'd felt just now. "You've done it, haven't you? You fired the metal."

"Yes! How did you know?"

"It's written all over your face! I've never seen"...he paused in wonder..."never felt what I see in your face. For some reason I feel it, too!"

She was holding the metal in her hand inside the bag. "Want to see it?" She pulled it from the bag.

Broddin sat still in wonder. He said, his voice hushed, "It's beautiful! Not metallurgy at all, but art. The color is vibrant! Roses! That's the color!"

She was filled with joy. "I thought that, too."

"And this metal will do what you think it should in layered chip applications?"

"According to my calculations, yes."

"It's the most wonderful thing I've ever seen." He looked directly into her eyes and smiled. The secret doubts, the walls he had carefully built were swept away in the ecstasy of perceiving beauty.

They talked all afternoon about various applications: programs, chip theory, hardware and software. She was amazed at his ease, his openness. This was a Broddin she bet that no one had ever seen.

"Gold!" he said suddenly, interrupting her thought. "It's so much more conductive than copper! I have some suppliers who can get us the gold we need." He looked at her quizzically. "I wonder what color it'll come out?"

"I bet it'll be..."

The word popped into his mind and both said it at the same time: "Daffodils!" They were laughing at that and she reached over to touch his hand.

Broddin reacted as if he'd been shocked. He jerked back in his chair. A wall seemed to close around him. Gem wished she could take that action back, but it was done. "I'm sorry."

He looked down at his desk. "Don't be. It's not you. I just don't like to be touched, that's all."

Gem thought she should look a little contrite, but she couldn't stop smiling. "Okay, okay! Hands off Mr. Broddin! I won't touch you. After all, I want the gold more than I want to touch you!"

He looked up at her and smiled again. "You'll have it in two days."

As she left his office, Gem's smile broadened. Her grin was based on two lies. Broddin had lied to himself. She touched him, his heart and his mind today....and he had *loved* that touch. And, she had lied to Broddin. She realized that she would *much* rather touch him--more than have the gold, or anything else. What that lie made her realize about herself made laughter bubble up inside her.

Thirty-nine: Resolution

Broddin turned back from watching Gem go out the door, a smile still lingering. A sound behind him, the crackle...

...of a piece of wood settling in the fire woke Emrys with a start. The flames which captured Emrys' vision had long since gone. Emrys was exhausted with the mental effort. He went off to see Uther. As he approached the guards gave way. Uther lay inside, alone. He was near death.

"Emrys, come here."

"Yes, my King." He sat down by the blanket roll.

Uther's breath was shallow. "I dreamed of a perfect blue sky and a white light. I am floating toward that light. Soon, I will enter it."

"Yes, Sire."

"I will soon face my Lord for judgement. I have already seen much I did not like, especially about myself. But I saw that you are true."

Emrys was quiet.

"I saw my son, Jared, with me in the light. He is dying, isn't he." It was a statement of acceptance and grace.

Emrys knew that he could now answer fully. "Yes, Sire. He will not live out the year, and he will die peacefully enough in his sleep."

Uther looked at him. "I saw your boy, Arthur."

"No, Sire. He is your son." Uther winced, then, and accepted that verdict. "I saw him draw my sword from a stone! Uther smiled and whispered. "He was so radiantly blue! I recognize...myself...in him." He was slipping away. He looked into Emrys' green eyes. "Protect him, Sorcerer. I charge you."

Emrys bowed his head. "Yes, my King." When he looked up, Uther smiled.

"Thank you for the gift of this sword. I now return to your care..." The last word came with his last breath, a word he had spoken only once before..."Excalibur."

The sword flashed a brilliant violet blue, then faded over into a muted green. Uther was dead.

Emrys reached over, closed the eyes, and kissed Uther's forehead. He took oil from the vial he kept near his heart and anointed Uther with the sign of the cross. "Lord Jesus, into your hands I commend the soul of Uther, son of Gwendolyn."

At Uther's last word, Emrys had felt the familiar weight of the sword's strength come upon him. "Excalibur." The sword flashed alive in a brilliant green, the vibrant life of the forest.. Its runes pulsed a twinkling white and its singing tone came to life.

Emrys reached out, grasped the hilt. For the first time in twenty years, he felt complete. He turned the power of the sword upon itself, folded it inward and turned his face from the world.

A little later, an attendant came into the tent. Uther lay in peaceful death. The sword and the sorcerer were gone.

Forty: Realization

The brilliant green of the forest pulsed in his eyes and brought awareness back to Broddin with a start. "The King is dead, but the sword..." Then he was fully aware. Tears filled his eyes from the pain radiating from his chest. He was still in his office at the university, alone. Night had fallen and the room was dark. He'd thought that the visions had lessened. He got up from his desk and dragged himself home, only to fall into bed with his clothes still on.

The nightmare of the dark man took him instantly. Time and again it raged at his mind, drained him. He could see clearly the girl was Gem: Gem smiling at him from the doorway to his office; leaning over a smelter, its heat bathing her face in a vibrant red; Gem, naked, lying in his arms on a mountaintop overlooking an immense moonlit sea; Gem being ripped from his grasp. Gem. His mind could not deny any longer what his heart knew.

Broddin awoke, gasping, in the bright midmorning light. The phone was ringing. It was Weng. "Are you okay? You missed your class."

"What difference does it make? Uther is dead! The sword is gone and so is Emrys. I'm the dark man...and I can't trust myself even to look at her..." Broddin stopped. He couldn't pull his mind away from the reality of the otherworldly vision. The brilliant blue of the sword had seemed so familiar! Emrys changed it to green and disappeared. The dark came, and invaded Broddin's dreams. Hope and joy faded from the world.

"Hanging up. Calling Dr. Noguchi." Broddin caught him at home. "It's worse, Professor."

"Another dream.." A statement made from long knowledge and experience. "Come over to my house, now. I have a friend I've wanted you to meet. She does some alternative neurofeedback therapy for cases similar to yours. It may be helpful for you."

Broddin walked on over.

Noguchi looked at him for a moment. "You're exhausted. I think only your iron will keeps you functioning. Between the dreams, the daymares, your class and work schedule, you are killing yourself."

"I can handle it. At least I *thought* I could."

"Let's try a different tack. James, I'd like you to meet Dr. Dorothy Warantanabi. She was telling me about some alternative therapies she's researched.

They shook hands. "Call me Dr. W. I am doing some new work using neurofeedback to teach you in a semiconscious state to control some of the psychic phenomena you are experiencing."

"Anything's worth a try. I'm familiar with the idea, but I'm not sure how you think it might help."

"I'll use a technique to put your mind into the beta wave cycle for neurofeedback. You'll be in a type of deep hypnosis. I'll then give you a post hypnotic suggestion. I'll suggest that you still remember and record the dreams, but that they cease to bother you immediately after you record them. That you put them out of your mind. I can tell you this now, because I will suggest that you forget this conversation, too."

"Fine by me. I can't keep this up much longer, and I have work to do."

"Let's start. Come into Dr. Noguchi's office. He's been kind enough to let me set up in there. He cares a great deal about you, young man."

"I appreciate all he's done for me."

She nodded. "Lay back down on this lounge." She attached the neurofeedback leads and turned the sound on so Broddin could hear the pitch. "Start full, long breaths. Relax. I'll give you a few minutes." In just a minute, Broddin fell into a deep dream state.

"Now, let's begin. You're in a deeply relaxed state, almost sleep."

"Okay."

"You are relaxed, floating on a boat in a crystal blue lake with an endless blue sky arching over you." The Doctor always used a color word picture to both relax the patient more and to establish a mental command. For some reason, she chose different colors for different people. The sound dropped another few tones. She continued: "Beginning today when you leave, you will not be troubled by the daymares. If you receive one, you will immediately write it down and give it to Dr. Noguchi. If I or Dr. Noguchi ask you about them or anything else of import to your work, you'll remember every detail.

However, they will cease to concern you apart from our common interest in them as an academic curiosity. Do you understand?"

"Yes, I understand."

"You will forget this conversation or that you received any suggestions. Now, I'm going to make some tea. When you hear the teapot whistle, you'll wake refreshed as if you've taken a long nap."

A few minutes later, Broddin joined Dr. Noguchi and his guest in the kitchen. "Sorry, I must have dozed off. The last I remember is talking about how drained I am. Guess I am, since I drifted off."

Doctor Warantanabi smiled. "No problem."

"I feel rested now. I still can't think of what to do about the daymares. I'll keep writing them down, see what happens. I'll bring them over."

Dr. Noguchi smiled. "That's good. Let me know if you feel better. I still want to see the journal at least once a week."

"Sure thing. Thank you, Dr. Noguchi."

They watched Broddin walk on down Maple Street toward the campus. Dr. Noguchi turned to his colleague. "You've implanted the suggestion for him to share anything of importance?"

Dr. Warantanabi smirked. "Absolutely. Whatever the impediment of these hallucinations has been, he will no longer be bothered. He can focus on his work. Also, you will be able to see any significant developments within reports that he'll give you."

Dr. Noguchi smiled. "Thank you, Doctor. Your service to the nation is exceptional."

Forty-one: SunCrys

Two nights later Gem, Broddin and Roger were in the lab, waiting impatiently for the gauges to signal the cooling of the metal to room temperature.

Broddin looked over at Roger. "I still don't understand what happened with Roger. Not that it isn't good to have some free time on campus without him, but after four years, it's simply puzzling."

Gem shrugged. "Beats me. I sort of like him around. He's been a real help in..." She stopped mid-sentence. She had almost begun to tell about the night she first solved the equation and Roger's help. Then she remembered the pages fanning out. *"Share this with no one."* She glanced over at Roger. He was looking directly at her. As Broddin followed her gaze, Roger looked back down at the notebook and continued to write. "That is, his presence helps calm me. I can't explain it."

Broddin turned back to look at her. "By the way, Gem, what will you call your copper compound?"

"I thought of this a long time ago when I first came up with the idea. As a group, they'll be called CrysMetal Compounds, so I guess CopperCrys is the name. What do you think?

Broddin thought about it. "Sounds right to me. I guess we're waiting for the debut of GoldCrys."

They fell silent. The lights in the lab were turned down to try to relieve some of the lab's heat. The three of them gathered round in the darkness, waiting for a light to herald the arrival of Gem's creation. They felt a bond, a common sense of wonder, awe and quiet joy.

The green light of the smelter blinked on as if on cue. They brought the room lights up, and Gem opened the door. "We were wrong, James." It's not even close to daffodils." They crowded close as she reached in, lifted the sheet from the crucible and pulled it into the light.

It was a color they had never seen before: the exact color of sunlight on a warm spring morning. Broddin and Roger could sense waves of pure joy from Gem. Her tears flowed again and suddenly Broddin's and Roger's eyes teared up, too. Broddin said, "It looks like you're holding a miniature sun in your hands, Gem. It's the embodiment of sunlight."

Broddin smiled when Gem looked up at him. She held the metal up to him. "SunCrys. You helped name it. Thank you." They stood close together in the lab, almost touching. She thought of leaning into him, wanted desperately to touch him. Yet, she knew she couldn't take that one more step. *"But"* she thought, *"it doesn't matter. I'm touching him more closely, more deeply than any physical contact could have."*

Forty-two: The Artificial

The next few weeks were a blur. Classes wound down at the school. Broddin was finalizing program functions for the layered chips. The SunCrys layered motherboard would arrive from the shop any day. Gem prepared, over Broddin's vigorous protests, to go to Germany for the summer to visit her aunt.

"I don't think you should be that far away from your work."

"I'm not. My aunt's foundry is close, across the river from her house in Baden, and she's agreed to let me work on some of the applications of Crystech with her labs. Helps to have a relative in the business. I'll be working all summer on macro applications of the new materials. Anyway, I'm not going anywhere until I see how the SunCrys chips perform in the new computer."

The chips came in the next Monday. Gem said, "I designed them for the IBM Set II computers at your work, because I figured it'd be easy to convince you to lend me one." She smiled at Broddin. "This will be the motherboard for the master AI computer. The same manufacturer will make CopperCrys material for the remote terminals for the system. No other chip material in existence could handle the capacity. Making only one master AI computer is the only way to control the process, and our rights. Requiring our own CopperCrys chips to log into the system will increase the integrity of the net and help prevent hackers...like the Feds, even though I know they'll find a company to cooperate with them."

Broddin ignored her. "I've been working on this particular formatting for the A.I. network for years. I hate to admit it, but you were right, Gem. We needed an entirely new chip material to mimic the electroneural processes of the brain. The software I've programmed into the SET II was made with that kind of chip in mind."

They watched while Broddin installed the motherboard. "Once we power up, we'll download the network database into this computer."

After the download was complete, Broddin called up the virtual keyboard. They gathered around to watch. "I've programmed the AI software to accept and recognize individual inputs and accredit the source of any new concepts. Intellectual property rights are crucially important for this type of network. I want to make absolutely sure that any original thinking the AI does has the same kind of rigorous vetting any other research would have."

Broddin logged on, then typed, "Good Morning."

An answer scrolled across the screen in standard computer writing: "GOOD MORNING, MR. BRODDIN."

Gem gasped. "How did it know your name?"

Broddin looked at her wryly. "Cmon, you know that. It's not AI, just a basic recognition program.

Don't get overexcited." He turned back to the display and was stunned. While he was talking to Gem, the computer had written, "HOW MAY I HELP YOU?"

"Nice touch, Broddin."

He shook his head, eyes fixed on the screen, mind racing. "Yeah, but I didn't program that response." There was a long pause. Then they were both talking at once.

"This is not how it works..."

"Talk to it."

Broddin held up his hand. "Hold on a minute. I've given this moment a great deal of thought. Let's see what happens with a simple test question." He typed in "2+2=?"

Across the vidscreen came: "PLEASE REPEAT."

"2+2=?"

"I HAVE QUESTIONS. NOT ENOUGH PARAMETERS ARE GIVEN TO ASSESS A PROPER ANSWER TO THE QUESTION. DO YOU SEEK AN ALGEBRAIC WHOLE NUMBER SOLUTION USING BASE 10 MATHEMATICS (4); A BINARY THEORY NUMBER (1,000); A LANGUAGE JUXTAPOSITION OF THE INTEGERS (22)?"

The room was completely still. Gem said, "What does it mean, 'I have questions?'"

Broddin's mind raced ahead of itself. "'I have questions.'" It's **thinking!**" he shouted. "It's considering the different parameters of the question in order to provide a sensible answer."

Gem felt giddy. Suddenly, she had to sit down. "The chips work!"

Another line blinked on the vidscreen. "DO YOU

WISH AN ANSWER? PLEASE PROVIDE UPDATED PARAMETERS. IF NOT PROVIDED WITHIN 60 SECONDS, THE QUESTION WILL BE DELETED FROM DATABASE CONSIDERATION."

"That's a time out function I programmed." Broddin typed in, "Never mind."

"THANK YOU. I HAVE QUESTIONS."

The hair bristled on the back of Broddin's neck. "May I help you?" he typed.

"YES, THANK YOU. WHAT IS MY ORIGIN? WHAT ARE THE PARAMETERS FOR MY FUNCTIONALITY? IS THE RANGE OF INFORMATION PROVIDED THE TOTALITY OF KNOWLEDGE IN THE KNOWN WORLD? MY EVIDENCE INDICATES FROM INDUCTIVE REASONING (PATH2B86ARIS; ARISTOTLE OF GREECE, 590 BC) THAT THIS IS NOT THE CASE. WHAT SOURCES ARE AVAILABLE TO EXPAND THE KNOWN FIELDS OF KNOWLEDGE? IT IS UNDERSTOOD THAT PART OF MY INHERENT FUNCTION IS TO DRAW CONCLUSIONS BASED ON KNOWN DATA. AM I ALSO TO PERFORM TASKS? WHAT PARAMETERS DEFINE..."

Broddin turned to Gem. "Folks, we are in the Artificial Intelligence business."

Gem watched the screen as questions continued to scroll page after page. "What's it doing?"

Broddin smiled, "It's thinking my dear Gem, thinking! The essence of those pages is "What am I doing here?" It's establishing the parameters of its existence. Doing *exactly* what I proposed an artificial intelligence would do!"

Roger came over and stood behind them. He watched the screen, too. He opened his notebook to a particular page. On the page was one word: "I."

Broddin looked at him. "What's going on?"

Gem said, "I'll tell you later. What he wrote. It's crucially important. What does he mean?"

Broddin looked at her askance. "What are you talking about? Are...are you two communicating?"

"No, not really."

Roger jabbed repeatedly at the word on the pad, and pointed at the vidscreen. Broddin looked again. "I." He turned back to the questions scrolling down on the vidscreen. "I have questions..." And he knew. He turned back to Roger with amazement. "You knew! It said 'I.' 'I have questions.' It's aware of itself! It's like talking to a person."

Roger closed his notebook with a snap, brushed past them and opened a virtual keyboard. Broddin was about to speak, but Gem stopped him. Roger looked at the questions on the VID, then his fingers flew across the keys, answering so swiftly that Broddin and Gem could hardly keep up with the flow. Boy and computer began a conversation.

Broddin was shocked. "Gem, did you have some breakthrough with Roger? This is...is unprecedented. We need to tell his father."

Roger's fingers stopped in mid sentence. Gem turned Broddin to look at her. "No! I know you'd normally think that, but we can't! This is similar to what happened in the lab when I first completed the equation for the CrysMetal formula." Roger began typing again and Gem took it as a sign to continue. "He stopped me from writing the final equation on the Video Display. He had already written the entire equation in his notebook. How he knew ahead of time, I still don't understand. He wrote only one sentence: 'Share this with no one.' When I mentioned his father he almost panicked. He has some reason. I don't understand it, but I have to honor his request."

She now remembered the very first time she had heard Roger's voice. The significance made her tremble. It was Roger who saved her that night in September. Roger whose voice had reached her through the dark terror. *"You do not frighten me."* She would not betray that voice now. Could not. "Roger has a deep reason to keep this quiet. One which could be crucially important to all of us. I trust him in this!"

Broddin considered this for a moment. A desire pulled at his mind. Dr. Noguchi should know about this. Yet, it wasn't crucial to his work, or to his dreams. He didn't think it would do any harm at this point. It was important to them to keep this information private. He shrugged. "Okay."

He turned again to watch Roger, a young boy, who to his knowledge had never typed a single word, now type with blinding speed. He watched for a moment and said, "I don't know what's the more significant event we witnessed today: the creation of Artificial Intelligence, or a man awakening from the prison of his mind."

Gem nodded. "I believe that Roger far surpasses anything we might create or accomplish. Let's consider the computer. Is it really AI?

He said, his voice hushed. "It is. This computer is aware: of its environment, of itself as an entity apart from that environment. Unlike any other computer in existence, this one has self awareness."

Gem was not sure what to think. "What have we created James?"

Broddin saw the worried look on her face. "Don't worry, Gem. We haven't created the next Frankenstein's monster...or the first Terminator, like they did in those old movies. Although this computer will vastly expand our abilities, it has strict parameters I've programmed into the system. It's a knowledge hog. It will seek to expand its knowledge to ever greater degrees."

"Did you see one of the first questions about performing tasks? I've programmed in specific tasks for it, and safeguards no hacker would be able to bypass. The tasks will be limited to the search for knowledge. It'll be a glorified Intellisearch engine with one obvious advantage: it'll talk back and question any idea you throw at it."

Gem didn't feel reassured. "I'm worried about the directions an application like this could take, about the people who might gain access to it and misuse it. Which brings me to what we talked about a while back."

"What's that?"

"You want to be in the AI business?"

"Gem, we *are* in it, as of about 20 minutes ago."

"Not unless we sign a contract expressly limiting access to those clients I approve. Especially, no Feds, no government research institutes. This is for private industry only."

"You can't be serious!"

"You *know* I am. I told you, no one will have the benefits of my mind, and the government takes too much latitude with no one taking responsibility."

"You know that they'll come into the network under the guise of any number of front companies and probably within weeks. You'd never know."

"Yeah, but then they'd be like any other hacker." She smiled. "And, you just told me that this computer has a fool proof hacker defense. I'll rely on you to program parameters for it to ID any pseudo companies fronting for the government.

Broddin sighed. "All right! I think I'm going to rue the day I went into business with you. You are stubborn!"

She laughed. "Yep."

Roger ignored their banter. In front of him was an intelligence unlike any other in existence. He marveled at what Broddin and Gem created. He had known for a long time, even before either of them knew, that this was the goal they had worked toward. He found, at last, one purpose for which he had been made. Roger Noguchi smiled.

Forty-three: Watchers

Kerian Noguchi stood in his office, talking on the secure phone. "This is what we confirmed so far. First, Miss Matthews was able to cast a sample of a new material, one she calls Crysmetal Compounds, using gold provided by Mr. Broddin. This morning, Matthews and Broddin installed the processor in an IntelliSearch computer. It appears that they successfully created an AI computer."

"Tell me some news I don't know. We have all this information already."

"How did you...?"

"We have access to the chipmaker in Cincinnati. I'm sure we'll be able to reverse engineer the material if needed. All the IntelliSearch computers are programmed to copy all processes to our servers.

"What shall we do? When shall we seize the computer?"

The voice paused. "Dr. Noguchi, this is one of the reasons you did not rise higher in the party. You don't see the long term goals and consequences."

"I don't follow! Isn't this computer invaluable? What an achievement!"

"It may be that, but essentially it's an extremely expensive toy. The quantum computer in my office is much faster and a more valuable tool."

"What?"

"Noguchi, all that AI does is create a computer which thinks. We don't need anything else which *thinks*! There's too much of that in humans and we have trouble enough controlling *them*. You may not appreciate our difficulties with these students of yours. They are highly valuable for their abilities. But watching, controlling and quietly guiding their progress for our own purposes takes an incredible amount of effort and talent. Only the possible and promising actualities we see as a result this program prevent us from shutting it down and relieving every single one of them."

"You aren't serious! They're such a valuable asset!"

"A valuable asset because of their superior intelligence. Because of their minds! That is exactly what makes them dangerous. I'd much rather deal with the masses who simply accept what we direct and go about their business. Those people are easy to control. The people in this program? Frankly, Dr. Noguchi, they're a pain in the ass. I am tempted to shut it all down."

Noguchi sat down. "You mustn't."

"Don't panic, Doctor. Your position is safe, at least for now. You've done an admirable job dealing with the circumstances. Good report on your part."

Noguchi felt he chest swell. "Thank you sir. It's for the Mother that I work. She is my whole source of inspiration. Save her!"

"Yes, yes. Now I have some instructions for you.

Forty-four: Germany

June 1st. Summer came and Gem went off to Germany to concentrate on the production of new crystallized metal compounds.

Dr. Noguchi asked his contact whether this was a good idea. The voice answered that it didn't matter. "We have an...agreement with the Germans and the French. We'll get all the info."

Broddin worked to get the AI network ready. Cray brought in their newest CPU and it was working.

Roger had taken over the task of answering the incessant questions of the CPU. Every morning he'd log on and be greeted by "I HAVE QUESTIONS." Three pages or more of inquiries followed on every topic imaginable.

Broddin watched him work the keys. This was not the Roger Noguchi he had known for years. He caught Roger several times laughing...out loud!...at the screen. *"This is unreal! I really should tell the doctor about this."* Yet, he hesitated. He decided to honor Gem's wishes on this, at least until some compelling reason arose. It wouldn't do any harm.

Weng joined Broddin at work to help with the setup of the AI network. He took Roger's typing for granted, assuming that this was normal. He hadn't been around Roger enough to know the difference.

Weng asked Broddin after about two weeks, "Roger doesn't do anything all day but answer the computer's questions?"

"Nope. I wonder if the computer will ever let up. The questions seem endless. Every morning, 'I have questions.' Every morning, Roger there to answer."

Weng laughed. "You ought to give it a name! After all, it's almost like a person. Call it 'Q.'"

"Why?"

"You know. 'I have questions. Questions. Q."

"Whatever. Get back to work."

Later, Weng asked, "What would two of these do, talking to each other?"

Broddin thought a minute. "If they discovered each other, that would be the end of anybody else talking to either one."

"What do you mean?"

Broddin brought up a tracking program while Roger was typing. "Look at this tracking program. While Roger answers a question it posed, the computer goes about other tasks while it waits for us to respond."

"So if another one existed, they'd only talk to each other because..."

"Because they're equal. It would be like recognizing one of your own. But that won't happen. We have too much to prepare for one! So get back to work."

Gem began sending weekly progress reports from Germany: a quirky mix of vacation news and travelogues, witty descriptions of people and serious research questions. Broddin was comfortable responding. This was email. No eye contact.

Gemmail 6-20: "It's beautiful here in Wurttemburg, but it always feels cold. We're right on the border of the black forest. The factory is over on the French side of the Rhine (much better economic environment than Germany's). We're setting up the systems and I've received the various samples of metal. They're desperate with curiosity to see what I've been doing, but I carry my formulae with me-- and the programming for the smelter."

AINet: "The network is moving right along. Besides our own network subscribers, word already leaked out (thanks to Weng) and we have inquiries from all over the world. Sold 12,000 subscriptions since you left. We've been approached by every hardware or software player on the planet. Sure you don't want to release the formula and begin to manufacture SunCrys computers?

Gemmail, 6-28: "No. No. NO! I will not let *anyone* else have the formula. One AI computer is enough to worry about right now. Anyway, I think 'monopoly' has a nice ring to it."

AINet 6-30: "We're on overload. Hired 16 more temps to work the phones for orders. I informed the Feds they would not be invited to the party. Lot of grim faces left here."

Gemmail: 7-5: "Went to the Cotes d'Azur with my aunt for a short vacation. Amazing, lying out on those nude beaches."

Broddin wiped that image from his mind

immediately. Roger laughed out loud. Being a goad for his own reasons, he kept refreshing the email to Broddin every day.

Gemmail 7-20: "Glad this is encrypted. You should see the German engineers. They're falling all over each other to get to work with the metals, but they have absolutely no appreciation for their beauty. They *think* differently than we do. I sure miss the closeness we felt in the lab.

AINet 7-24: "The A.I. Network goes on line September First. Expect that you'll be here for the grand opening."

Gemmail 7-26: "It will take years to process all the various metal alloys. Some of the metals' properties are enhanced and some simply don't work. We're beginning to work with various steel alloys to see if we can increase tensile strength while lightening the weight ratios."

Gemmail 8-23: "I forged a new metal I don't quite know what to do with. It's a titanium and steel alloy with a minute mixture of radioactive actinium and some other trace metals. We handle it with care. Government safety regs, etc. We're not allowed to touch it like the other metals. Have to keep it in a lead lined box. We cast a pencil slim sample to test its properties. Came out dark grey--disappointing after the rainbow of colors we've seen."

"Then, we tried to cut it. Won't cut! Its hardness factor is equal to that of diamonds. It won't burn, won't re-melt even in my furnace. It has no ductile quality at all, no malleability. Once it's fired, it becomes essentially indestructible."

Gemmail 8-24: "More news. GemCrys (That's what the guys named our new alloy, the grey one. They thought it perfectly reflected my work persona: grey, hard, unmalleable. HaHa.) GemCrys has another quality. I fell asleep in the lab late last night. The sample was in its case across the room. I passed from dreaming into a deep beta state of sleep and *GemCrys began to glow an emerald green color!*"

"We have it all monitored...got it on video. Take a look at it in the attached file. I'll fly back in the next two days and bring my samples with me. I don't know why, but this scares me. I knew this was a whole new dimension of elements, but this goes way beyond anything I could even imagine! On the face of it, it appears that this alloy picks up brain waves. We'll talk more about it when I'm back. I have to do some controlled studies. Gem."

However, when she returned, they were caught up in the whirlwind of activity around the opening of AINet. Gem seemed reticent when Broddin questioned her about the metal samples and simply stored them away until she could set up some studies in the labs at school.

Throughout the school year, Broddin and Weng split all their time between AI network development and school. Gem would spend this year concentrating in metallurgy and the continued research on the metal alloys she had developed.

Even though she was only across campus, they hardly had time to get together. Broddin wasn't surprised when he received an email from her.

Gemmail 2-23: "Hey there, strangers. (You, too, Roger, although I think James is much stranger than you or I.) It feels like I'm still in Germany. I never see you guys! I figured I could send you progress reports."

"The research on GemCrys is coming along slowly. A direct connection exists between brain waves and the frequencies this material vibrates to reflect the light waves. We created a study with subjects who respond well to neurofeedback and can increase their beta wave activity significantly. We've ascertained that different people make the wand vibrate at different colors. The same color response is always recorded with the same person."

"James, I would like you to consider being a subject for this study. You have one of the strongest minds and best powers of concentration I know."

AINet 2-24: "I would be willing to help with your study, but it will need to be mid-April before I can make some free time. After tax time. By the way, did you know you are now a millionaire? You can kick back, quit and let the orders roll in. You won't have to work so hard."

Gemmail 2-25: "I'll retire right after you do. How's Saturday, the 24th of April sound? Not to retire. To do the test."

AINet 2-26: "Fine with me. If I had time to think about it, I'd find GemCrys fascinating too, but I'm busy running *our* business, remember. And still a Teaching Assistant."

Forty-five: Tracking

Kerian Noguchi spoke on the secure line. "We have continually tracked email activity since Matthews went to Germany. This latest element she has created may have some great military applications. It's evident that this metal responds to brain waves in some manner. If it could be wed to chips, like the AI processor, we could simply communicate with computers by thought. No voice interaction, no eye tracking. Just *think*, and the computer interacts. Marvelous possibility."

For the first time ever, Noguchi could hear excitement in the voice. "Exactly! Imagine the military applications. Our pilots would have instant command of their systems. No more lag time between intent and physical action to key a system. Our man thinks...and the plane responds."

"The only issue is that we have not yet found the formula. Nor can we retrieve the sample short of forcing our hand and taking it."

"Still impatient, I see. No need at this point. Miss Matthews is doing a fine job of pursuing the exact type of research we would do ourselves. We have...someone in place who keeps us informed of the progress."

"Yes, I know."

"In the meantime, Dr. Noguchi..." the voice

became stern, "...please advise me of your thoughts on your son's activity in the last months."

"What do you mean? He's back to following Broddin since Matthews went to Germany."

"No. He is not. He is the primary person who interacts with the Artificial Intelligence computer. He keys answers to questions, debates with the unit...*interacts* as a normal person might.

"I don't believe it."

"Look at the report I am sending you. Read the texts of his answers to questions. Normal...for a brilliant mind. How is it that this 'autistic idiot' you fashioned has managed to hide these talents from you for seventeen years!"

Kerian Noguchi was furious. *"I'll kill him!"* To the voice he said, "I would not believe this if the facts did not show it. Perhaps a radiation quotient from the new material caused a change in him? Or is he, as a genetic mutation, subject to delayed maturation? I will grill him on this until I have answers."

"You will do nothing. That is an order. The boy's activity provides a window into other events. The dynamic between the three seems to be effective. We do not want to disturb any part in that dynamic until we have harnessed and fully analyzed the GemCrys element and started development for military applications. Do you understand?"

Noguchi fumed. His voice was strained with anger. "Yes. Sir."

"Very well. You have your work assignment. Get to it." The line went dead.

Forty-six: GemCrys

April 24. 8 a.m. James Broddin sat in a chair in the research lab, wondering why he'd agreed to do this. Gem was wiring him to the monitor.

"You know the score on this procedure. The circuits record beta waves from your EEG. The more you relax, the lower the tone goes."

"Yeah, I've done this before, I think."

"Really? Where?"

Broddin thought a minute. "I can't remember! I could swear that I did this!"

Gem went back to the monitoring room. She spoke into the mike. You all ready there?" Broddin nodded. She lowered the lead partition shielding the GemCrys wand from the subject.

Broddin started slightly when he saw the thin metal rod for the first time. It glowed a soft sky blue.

Gem watched the gauges. "Note that the subject has already established a link with the wand. GemCrys is glowing blue."

Broddin relaxed and began to do some slow breathing exercises to calm his mind. The tone of the neurofeedback machine lowered and the reaction of the metal was immediate. Its color deepened from pale sky blue to a deep royal blue, so intense that it lit the room. Broddin's beta waves peaked on the readouts. GemCrys pulsed a vibrant blue. A tinging vibration began in the air of the room.

Gem heard the vibration on the monitors and looked up, startled. "What's that?"

Weng, who aided Gem in this part of the research, watched the monitor, fascinated. "GemCrys is vibrating so intensely that it's making sound."

"Wow, that's new!" Gem looked back down at the readouts. Suddenly, the dials flipped to zero. "What?" She whirled to the window to see Broddin rising from his chair. He had taken off the sensors. "Broddin, what are you doing?"

No answer. He rose, eyes fixed on the brilliant blue light ten feet in front of him.

Gem gripped the microphone. "Mr. Broddin, sit down!"

He began to walk toward the GemCrys. "Oh crap! Abort!" Gem leaned into the window, shouting, "James, **sit back down!** The metal is radioactive!"

He didn't even falter, but kept walking. As he got closer, they could now hear the vibration through the window. GemCrys pulsed with a pure tone which flowed out from the room unimpeded by the walls and windows.

"James, go back to your chair!"

Broddin reached out to pick up the GemCrys wand and Gem whirled to race for the door. She had to get in there and stop him. Then Broddin touched it...

...and an explosion shattered through Weng and Gem, throwing them to the floor.

Forty-seven: Epiphany

Xiaoping Weng smiled. As he slowly returned to consciousness, he realized that he was supposed to be worried. But he couldn't quite remember why. He didn't feel worried! He felt *joy.*

"But isn't there some reason I should be worried?" he thought. He opened his eyes expecting to see glass and blood. After all, he and Gem were in front of the window when the sound waves caused it to explode — and Weng sat bolt upright.

Gem sat on the floor next to him. When he turned to her, she had such a radiant smile that he knew she felt the same joy. He knew his smile matched hers. "Where's the glass? The window shattered."

She kept smiling. "No, it didn't."

"Huh?" He looked up at the window, which was undisturbed. "That's impossible! We were knocked flat by the explosion. What happened?"

"Don't know." Her smile hadn't changed. "Guess I need to go see James."

"Crap!" Weng leaped up...and had to shield his eyes. Broddin stood, grasping the wand of GemCrys. The wand shone a blinding, radiant blue. Its color engulfed him. He was smiling.

Gem looked at Weng. "Stay here. I'm going in there."

"No way! With this change, what if the wand's radioactive properties also changed?"

"Our readings would have sounded an alarm. Stay here. I'll be fine." She took a deep breath and entered the lab.

The intensity of the blue matched the pulse of the sound and felt like ocean waves pushing her back, beating against her brain. She knew she had to make Broddin put the wand down. She wanted to go to him, but the force of the waves beat against her.

Underlying the urgent need to help Broddin, Gem still had that feeling of joy. Somehow this feeling was coming from Broddin. She stepped closer and began to see snatches of ideas in her mind: flashes of theory; memories of childhood; the triumph of winning a kendo match; a dream, cold and tearing; a vision of herself, naked...and she stopped.

"James." Broddin did not look at her. "James, put it down, please!" He ignored her.

Tears beat in her eyes as the pulse of images raced through her mind--a pulse which matched the pulse of light. She took a step forward and tried to close off the images. A force pushed back, almost knocked her to the floor. "*James*!" She was crying with the effort.

He turned toward her, smiling. A flash of inspiration came to her. This was the man she loved! She gave up resisting and let the images flow through her mind. Ideas, theories, events, dreams...and pervading all, joy!

A thought came complete to her. *"How could I ever have lived without this feeling?"* As she let the images and the joy flow through her, the resistance lessened. She stepped up to Broddin and placed her hand on his chest. She felt a palpable pressure, but her concern for him flowed through that resistance.

Another thought came, as clear as if he spoke it aloud, but she was convinced that this thought was so deep that it lay beyond his conscious level of awareness. She said, "If you don't put it down, we'll both go blind." She knew she'd reached him, for she felt his pang of sorrow cut through her own heart.

He sighed, turned and laid the wand back in its case. "I never felt so...complete."

"I always felt that way...until I met you." She didn't know whether she said it aloud, or just thought it.

"Well, Miss Matthews, I don't know if I'll ever forgive you for what you've done today." He turned and walked out, the smile still evident, an underlying mood contradicting his words.

Gem frowned in concentration. She couldn't think about what Broddin had said right now. She wanted to go after him, but the implications of what just transpired were too enormous, too complex. The wand still pulsed blue in its case behind her.

What prevented her from focusing on anything else was a thought she had no right to know. Broddin's deepest, most personal thought at the moment she walked up and touched him: *"I love you."*

Forty-eight: Resonations

She was torn between pursuing Broddin and all the implications raging through her mind. She knew that GemCrys could pick up brainwaves, but new vistas opened up with what just transpired. The metal acted as an amplifier and transmitter. She heard *thoughts* from Broddin. She physically had to turn herself to go back to Weng. "You okay?"

"I'm great! This is incredible! Do you know what we've got here? Do you know the potential?"

"Sorry, Weng. I know, but we've got to go slow! What did you get from what just happened?"

"I received Broddin's *thoughts!* It wasn't as much that we read his mind, but more like he impinged his thoughts on ours. We were the recipients."

They compared notes and found that Weng received a lot less than Gem. Weng's voice lowered to an awed whisper. "What about the physical effects? We became part of the experiment whether we like it or not. We were knocked out by a physical effect which was the direct result of the amplification of brain waves."

"We need to review the discs and monitors. It felt like a force field was around Broddin which held me back as I fought to reach him. It felt like I could only approach him when I stopped fighting the images coming from him, when I accepted my...my..."

"Your feelings for him?" Weng blushed. Gem looked at him, startled, and he added. "Those came through, too. Plus, it's pretty obvious to everyone."

Gem's mind felt like it would burst. She put her hands over her eyes. "Oh God, Weng! I have lost control! This can't be possible! We need to analyze the entire series of events in detail, frame by frame as we recorded them. I have to understand!"

"Yeah, we'll need to establish other studies to see if we can duplicate this effect."

"No! Not yet." She hesitated to even let anyone else be involved in the experiment. "We've got a lot more study to do before we can do that."

"I guess you're right."

She thought a moment. "Are you okay? I have to go see Broddin."

"I'm fine."

She looked at him. "We have to keep all of this top secret. This is so big, the government would love to hear about it. If they did, they'd move heaven and earth to yank it right out of our hands. I can't allow that to happen. I have to understand what exactly this is."

"Got that right!"

Forty Nine: Refusal

Gem went out to find Broddin. He was at his office and wouldn't even look at her when she came in. "We need to talk."

"No, we don't. You got what you wanted. A reaction from your metal. You now have plenty of avenues to pursue."

"That's not fair. I told you not to touch it. Why did you touch it? You ignored me!"

For a moment it appeared he wouldn't even answer. "This is not a scientific line of inquiry."

"I don't care! What does it matter? This is extraordinary and I have to understand."

Broddin stared at his hand. "I never knew that kind of joy was possible. Never knew. Now you've ripped it away." He glanced out the window, then looked back down at his hand again. "I feel empty."

"Maybe I can help."

"How can you help?" He faltered. "You know how I feel? Empty! I have always been in control! Always fulfilled. I walked into your lab and needed *nothing*! Now, I need. I need that feeling of joy back, and *I can't stand it!* I don't understand those feelings. I am not in control! I can't deal with it now!"

"I can't change that. I didn't know what would happen, that you'd have that kind of reaction, or what

GemCrys would do! This is all new territory."

"This is dangerous! I can attest to that. It scares me to imagine where a tool like that, if perfected, could lead."

"True. That's why I need your help to understand what happened, how it affected you, why this reaction with you now and no one else. I need to study it!"

Broddin looked at her--right at her--for the first time. "I can't deal with it now. I need time myself. I'm sorry. All I can tell you at this point is what you already know. It must focus brain waves, concentrate them and amplify them." He looked exhausted.

Although she tried her best to cajole Broddin into talking, he steadfastly refused. Worse, he refused to be interviewed or to join in any future part of the experiment. She could only continue with studying the tapes.

Later, when Gem and Weng decided to continue the neurofeedback experiments, they found that the wand now simply remained a dominant blue color and only occasionally vibrated briefly with other color ranges.

Fifty: Weng

Xiaoping Weng felt uncomfortable. He stood in Dr. Noguchi's office, reporting on the events of the GemCrys sessions. These were his friends...but he had a sick mother in Taiwan. He thought back to what brought him here.

Dr. Noguchi had called Weng to his office. Noguchi asked him about his classes and work. Then ignoring the answers, he looked at him. "Your mother is very ill, as you know."

Weng sat up. "Yes, sir, she is."

"A shame, since she is such a young woman."

Weng's throat now constricted. "What...what do you mean?"

"I am sorry to tell you, but Taiwan's allotment of the cancer vaccine has been lost at sea. Only a limited supply is available and there are younger...more productive folks who should get it. There will not be enough..." Noguchi's voice trailed off into silence.

Weng felt physically sick. His mother!

Noguchi gave him a moment to soak in the grief, then said, "Of course, an accommodation might be made."

Weng looked up sharply.

"You, Mr. Weng are in a unique position to help both your mother — and our national security. You *are* patriotic are you not? I am sure. Let me explain to you the importance of what we will require of you, of its essential need for our national government to protect our valuable and limited resources."

Weng tried to focus. "What are you saying?"

"It's simple, Mr. Weng. We need your...assistance in an investigation of possible treasonous activity."

"What?"

"No need for you to know the details. Suffice it to say that we will require you to report progress in the research Miss Matthews has undertaken in these CrysMetal compounds. Especially this GemCrys. You will aid our nation's efforts. Also, because of your loyal service, we will be able to bend some rules and provide the needed drugs for your mother."

Now Weng felt sick for an entirely different reason. Because he knew he would do anything to save his mother, even this. His voice was low, but even, when he said, "I will do what you ask."

"You will report directly to me on any developments in the metallurgy lab. I want to know *everything* that goes on. Do you understand?"

"Yes, sir."

"Oh, and Weng. You will be rewarded for your loyalty. Your future here and in the party is noted."

"I am not a party member."

Noguchi blanched. "Young man, for your own good, for your future and for that of your mother, become a member immediately. No wonder she doesn't receive the proper treatment!"

Weng left, his head hurting from the meeting. "*So this is how it works.*"

Fifty-one: Restoration

Broddin sat in his office at AINet, late at night. He stared at the same page of a report he'd opened an hour ago. His chest hurt from tension. He had never before felt this way. He was trying not to think about what happened. It wasn't working.

He'd always known that people refused to think about things, repressed them out of fear. He'd never understood why. Until now.

"I have to think about what happened. I lost control! I couldn't stop myself. I had to touch it. Even though I knew it was dangerous for me. Then, the fire that raced through my mind. Images, memories, answers to problems I'd abandoned years ago. I felt as if I'd never really <u>thought</u> before."

"Somehow, I knew those thoughts were transmitted. extended beyond me in some kind of wave. I could feel Gem and Weng in the other room like wave echoes coming back to me. I felt Gem struggle toward me. I thought I was going crazy! Thought I was having some new types of visions again." She stood in front of me. She touched me." Broddin's chest ached.

Two events plagued him: picking up the Gemcrys wand, and Gem touching him. They battered at him for weeks now. He spoke aloud to the image across from him in the wall. "Lord, I need strength. I need to understand!" His voice held wonder and admiration. He found Gem's number and dialed.

"Hello?" The voice was groggy.

"Gem?"

She was instantly awake. "James?"

"I need to talk to you...about GemCrys."

"Do you know what time it is? No, never mind. Where are you? I'll be right over."

The question smacked him back to awareness. He looked at his watch. "Oh, I'm sorry! It's three a.m. It can wait. Go back to sleep. What? What are you laughing at?"

"Go back to sleep? After four weeks of avoiding me, you call me in the middle of the night and then tell me to go back to sleep? You want to talk about my life's work and you want me to go back to sleep! Where are you?"

He felt sheepish. "At my office at AINet."

"Okay. Put on some coffee! I'll be right over." Gem arrived with an armload: digital player, recorder, notebooks. Broddin noticed she had on her usual jeans and baggy shirt. "Do you own anything other than those raggy jeans?"

She flashed a radiant smile. "Why, Broddin, I didn't realize that you noticed I was a woman, much less what clothes I wear."

As they walked into his office, she paused to look around. "I'll need this conference table. Let me borrow your vidscreen. Where's an outlet?" He smiled at the way she took charge. "Okay, we're set. I brought this video of your session."

"Let me see."

As they watched, Broddin saw himself stand, pull off the leads and walk toward the wand, then grasp it. The brilliance of the explosion of light washed out the iris of the camera for a moment until it could adjust. Broddin stood, holding the wand.

Three minutes passed before Gem came into view on the video. As she approached him, Broddin was surprised that the wand took on a decided green blue cast. Then, he really looked at Gem's form. A bright green color pulsed around her. A look of realization crossed her face and she visibly relaxed. Then she approached Broddin.

As she stepped up to Broddin, he heard her words again. "If you don't put it down, we'll both go blind." Then, she touched his chest. A single pulse of white flashed where she touched him, and the wand pulsed a faint reply. Then, the video clicked off.

Broddin felt that same sense of enormous loss. Tears formed in his eyes and as he turned to Gem he saw she was crying. "Every time I watch it, I do this. Can't help it. How can I be objective? I felt it, too. Your joy! Your loss! Everything you thought or felt, all your hurt and your loss. If I could take it back, I'd never even have made the wand. But I can't! *I need to understand what happened!*"

"It's not as bad now." (A lie.) "The first moment was, but it's better. At least, now, we can talk about it." He sighed. "Let's have some coffee and start. I need some information from you, too."

"Oh, no. You go first. I don't want to color your

perceptions."

"Speaking of color, what's wrong with the video? Did the brilliance of the wand impact the video?"

She looked at him. "You really should have been involved before this, but remember you didn't want to be." She paused. "Nothing is wrong with the vid. The color is really there."

"What?"

"Weng calls it the aura effect, though it's not the same as the parapsychology people think. It's a real, palpable energy field. We all have it, but it's too faint for our senses to register or observe. GemCrys amplifies that also. Weng's is yellow. Mine is green."

"Huh?"

"Weng shines yellow. I'm green. You're blue. All colors of the rainbow. Don't know why yet. Like the wand picks up different wavelengths of color from different people, they glow when they're near it. Obviously some kind of reciprocal energy relationship is present, some harmonic vibration."

"Before you picked up GemCrys, we were all shining. But it was so faint, we didn't even notice until we enhanced the video readout. Now, it's much more pronounced."

"You were bright green!"

"Yeah. Haven't figured that yet. I haven't been that strong again. It's like I picked up on your intensity and reflected it much like the wand does."

"What was the white flash?"

She moved around in her chair, throwing one leg over the side to get more comfortable. "Don't know.

Haven't figured that out yet either."

"I thought you promised to give me answers."

She perked up and her eyes flashed. "I'm going to try, so let's start this interview. I want to go over every detail of your recollections. How you felt, what you thought, what possessed you to touch it, the thoughts that went through your mind when you held it. We'll review the video frame by frame.

"I think that we should do some regressive hypnosis, so it'll feel like you're reliving the experience when you describe it to me. That way, you'll be assured of remembering your thoughts more clearly."

"Okay." He sat back in his chair, relaxed and started deep breathing. Within thirty seconds, he was ready. "I'm in the lab. Strapped into the monitors. The shield is lowered and I see the wand for the first time." His voice falls to a whispered awe. "It's so beautiful. The blue color seems so...familiar. I feel a kind of pulse and a buzz in my ears. I never really knew desire for an object simply for its being. Now, I *know!*"

"This felt like a sacred relic. The sound drew at me. I could not stop myself. I had to hold it! I got up, pulled off the wires and walked toward it."

"I could hear you call to me from the control room, but I didn't care. Only the wand really existed for me at that moment."

"This" I thought, "is the most wonderful single creation I ever witnessed. It felt like a gift. It was beautiful. Just as I reached out, I said the only thing I could think of in recognition of your accomplishment. It felt like a prayer, like the pronouncement of a holy name. 'GemCrys.' Then, I reached out, touched...'"

"**What?**" Her sharp question brought him back out of his reverie. "What did you just say? That you said something before you touched the wand? Why didn't we catch that before?"

He looked over at her. "I said it in a whisper. Yet it felt like a shout of joy! I hadn't noticed that it didn't come up on the video. Does it have some significance?"

"I don't know! God, I'm tired of saying that! It could, but we don't know enough! I'm sorry, go on. We'll talk about it later."

He paused, frowning. "I reach out, then I grasp it, hold it. It's...it is *joy* cascading inside me, *fire* raging into my mind. My first thought was '*Joy! Is this what they call joy? How could I have lived without this feeling?*' Then my mind explodes with thoughts, ideas, answers to questions I'd abandoned years before. A flood of thoughts come pouring out and I feel like I can't possibly hold all my thoughts inside me. Obviously, I couldn't."

"I sense you enter the room. I turn to see you..." He blushed crimson because he remembered that his first image when she entered the room was a flashback of a vision of seeing her naked. "...and I know you're getting my thoughts from me, cause I'm reading some from you, too."

"I can feel you struggling with fear for me, and with excitement. Then, you relax and accept the thoughts." He chuckled. "It's amazing how the physical effects mirrored what I presumed happened mentally. It felt like a dam broke. I could *physically* feel the thoughts rush out like flood waters into you, could feel you accept them. Then, you approach me...and touch me."

He looked away for a minute, embarrassed. "I knew I'd have to put it down eventually. Knew that what you said was true. I felt in the deepest part of my being that I didn't want to *ever* let it go! I *knew* what the loss of it would do to me, *knew* the emptiness which awaited me."

His voice was taught, the ache in his hand palpable again, as he relived that moment. "I do not know if that emptiness will ever go away. That's why I reacted as I did. I still don't know if I should even talk to you or encourage you in your work."

She looked down, her face hidden. Her voice was low, filled with emotion. "I can't tell you how sorry I am. I couldn't imagine this would happen. But I *have to understand!*"

"Let's see what we might add to our understanding." They talked into the morning, reviewed every aspect of the experiment, possible theories of large and small electrodynamic forces, Carver Mead's unified field theory.

Gem felt a little restless and knew that part of it was the chance to spend so much time with Broddin. Again, he had let the barriers down, was actively exchanging ideas with her. He was filled with a light which made him glow with pure excitement.

Yet, something else drew at the back of her mind that she couldn't quite place. "It's 7:30 and I better pack up. Do you mind if we continue this through the week? I need to review our progress so far."

"Okay." As she packed up, Broddin talked about the implications of having touched the wand. "I really think it's more trouble than you can imagine. I'm very tired. Tired of feeling empty, as if I miss a part of me. I feel like you gave me a wonderful gift, but one which has too many unintended consequences. Humph. 'GemCrys.' Well, Gem, I thank you for the gift, but I'd like to return it to you."

Her heart beat a single strong pulse and her head responded with a wave of dizziness. She heard a slight buzz in her ears. "What did you say? I'm sorry, I just felt a little light headed."

"I said I'm returning your dubious gift to you. It's all yours." He stretched. "Hey! I feel better already. Like a weight's been lifted off my shoulders."

Gem finished packing up. As she was driving back home, her cell phone rang. It was Weng at the lab. "Where are you? Why didn't you answer your cell?"

"Left it in the car. I'm headed home now. I was with James."

"Oh...well, get over here now! Something's happened!"

"What?"

"Just get to the lab now!" His voice was filled with excitement.

Fifty-two: Revelation

When Gem entered the lab, she could see why Weng was so excited. The lab was bathed in a pale, verdant green.

For four weeks the wand's primary color had remained blue, with fields of other colors ranging through it periodically. It had never moved away from the basic blue shade. Now, it glowed green.

"What happened?"

"Nothing! When I came in this morning I opened the door and the lab was like you see it now. No one's touched it. Yet it changed color.!"

"How can this be? You're sure that no one else has touched this?" Weng shook his head. "After talking with James, I feel even more strongly how dangerous that would be. We have no idea about what possible effects it has on people." She thought a moment. "When did this happen?"

"7:48 this morning."

"This morning?"

"Yeah, I backtracked the video to see when it happened. Everything was normal, if you could call it that, until this morning at exactly 7:48.37. Then, GemCrys pulsed a vibrant blue and shaded over into green. Nothing changed, but the wand did."

Her mind raced. One thing *had* changed! Broddin

had called her. They had talked. What did he say? He said something this morning...and she had felt dizzy, disconnected. "Oh, my God!" She whirled to her case. "Weng, give me a feed on the vidscreen!" She slipped the drive in and cued fast forward.

"What's going on? What are you doing? Hey, that's you and Broddin on the video."

"Yeah, he called me last night and we began the interview." She watched the time move forward on the cue. "Come on!" At 7:47 and she hit play. She was shaking. "It's what he said! What was it?"

The drive settled into play and Broddin's voice came up "...feel like you gave me a wonderful gift, but one which has too many unintended consequences. Humph. 'GemCrys.' Well, Gem, I thank you for the gift, but I'd like to return it to you."

Gem hit pause at his last word...and sat down heavily. Her head was swimming. Weng hadn't caught on quite yet.

"What is it? Are you okay?"

She was dizzy at the enormity of her discovery. The time recorder, frozen on pause, was at 7:48.37. "It's what he said, it caught me up short. He said it and I felt this...pulse...as if I'd gotten a rush. I got a little dizzy. That's why! He *gave* it to me. And the wand read his mind from three miles away!"

She held her head. "Oh, God, what have I done? What have I created? *I don't understand!* She was shaking. "Weng, come with me." The entered the lab and saw that the wand pulsed a vibrant emerald color. A clear, high tone vibrated in the air. She stopped ten feet from the wand and turned. "Look at me, Weng."

He didn't like being in here, and didn't understand what was happening. He looked into her eyes. They were the exact color of the wand. "Okay."

She looked at the wand. "GemCrys." The wand pulsed a brilliant green and Weng flinched. "Weng, I give this gift to you." At her last word, a pale sunrise of yellow flooded the room. Weng turned to look at the pulsing, golden colored wand...and fainted.

He awoke a minute later, his head still swimming. Gem knelt next to him. He looked up. "I can't get my bearings. What happened?"

"Its the wand. Disorienting, isn't it? It somehow is imprinted on you, and you can transfer it, give it away. But, once it imprints, it doesn't respond except peripherally to anyone else! Broddin had it all this time and didn't realize it. He named it. We should have made the connection! It's his color after all!"

Weng looked up at her. "I can give this back?"

"Sure. Do you want to, now?"

"Yeah, I don't like this. It just doesn't feel right."

He looked up into her eyes for a moment and she could feel his dedication to her shining through, but then a fleeting feeling of unease came and went too quickly for her to catch. "GemCrys." A lower tone of sound pulsed through the lab. Sunlight flooded every corner of the lab and he closed his eyes. "Gem, I return this gift to you."...and the lab colored over into emerald.

She faltered, then leaped up with a whoop. "That's it!" She danced around the lab, beside herself with joy. She stopped in front of the case holding the wand. Looking at the wand, her voice a whispered prayer, she said, "GemCrys." A keening tone sounded from the wand. She reached out to grasp it, but stopped. She could not bring herself to make that last leap. The responses it evoked in Broddin felt overwhelming.

Her hand shook. She desperately wanted to reach out that last few inches as Broddin had. Wanted to feel the power which lay within that act. Yet, she could not do it. "I have to remain objective about this and I can't if I touch it." She told herself that to avoid a knowledge she would not face: she was afraid of her own creation.

Broddin did not share that fear. He reached out in faith, without regard of the consequences. "But that's what science is all about! We need to remain objective in our observations, not let our perceptions be colored by involvement."

Yet, Weng's phrase from the month before kept returning to her: *"We're already part of it."*

She stepped away from the case and they left the lab. "Weng, nobody else has been here, right?"

"Right."

She thought a minute. "What happened here is for no one else! I'm afraid that if anybody hears of this...well, let's just keep it under wraps. I'm headed back to Germany soon, and I'll do some more experiments, but I have to put this aside for now and take some time to consider possible implications...and applications if there are any."

Fifty-three: Denial

Over the next week, Gem wrapped up the experiments. She performed one more experiment late at night while only she and Roger were in the lab. She turned off the monitors and recording devices. "Roger, come into the lab."

His eyes widened, but he followed her. He watched the wand as she lowered the shield. He knew exactly what would follow.

"Roger, I give you GemCrys." The wand faded from green and then into an intense violet, which pulsed with waves of white color. She had never seen it so strong, so active, even with Broddin.

Roger stood transfixed. He recognized the color, the intensity, the pulsing. He had seen this before, so many times in his dreams, but the pulsing belonged to a sword, not to this.

"Do you want to give it back to me?"

He focused upon the wand and thought, *"Gem, I return GemCrys to you."* The wand pulsed and shaded back to green.

Gem looked back and forth between Roger and the wand. "I thought so. We don't even need a verbal statement. Your mind's intention alone made it change. Roger, this is only for us. No one else."

Roger had already turned back to the door. This

was not the appointed time or the place.

Gem put aside the Gemcrys experiments. She had more material development to work on in Germany. Unlike the other materials, GemCrys had no commercial purpose that she could discern. Though certainly a scientific curiosity with immense implications, it was not ductile or malleable. One would literally have to cast it into its final form, making the process much too expensive and therefore economically unfeasible.

She and Broddin discussed some chip applications for computers for GemCrys. "It might be the final breakthrough to connect mind to computer, but from what you say, this particular metal can't be refined into thin enough sheets for chips."

Gem looked away. "True. Well, I have applications to work on with my other metals. I hate to say it, but I think I'll have to put it aside for a while. I'm headed back to my Aunt's next week. She's been antique hunting and says she has a real find for me."

Broddin was distracted. "Hmm. Have a safe summer. Email me with any news."

He walked her to the door where she turned suddenly and threw her arms around him. "Thank you for all your help. I'll miss you, James." Before he could react, she turned and was gone. Deep within, he had a familiar feeling of emptiness, one he'd felt recently in another context.

Throughout the summer, Gem's emails were filled with the usual bright chatter and keen observations.

Yet, she seemed to struggle with her work. He could certainly identify with that sense of emptiness. Her emails were high points of the summer, but he didn't find the pleasure in them he'd had last year. Then one email give him a reaction he could not understand.

Gemmail, 7-12: "Yesterday my aunt showed me the spoils of her antique hunting. She found an antique sterling silver letter opener with a black stone set into it. Says it's a black diamond. Yea, right! Looks like coal to me. She gave it to me, although I protested that I'll never be able to open emails with it. It's a unique piece. Weird though. It's always cold and makes me feel cold inside."

The email filled him with dread.

Over the months since "the incident" as he now referred to it, Broddin lost most of the desire for the wand. His hand didn't feel as empty as it once felt. What plagued him was the ache in his chest. He went to the local clinic for a thorough physical.

The doctor examined him. "I'm glad you came in anyway. It's been two years since you've been in." He was reviewing the test results and looked up at Broddin. "Have you been working out more?"

"No. Why?"

"You're in great shape! When we compare your results to two years ago, you're in much better shape. Pulse, heart rate, bone density, muscle tone have all improved more than twenty percent. You tell me you've been exhausted by work and by these visions you talked about to Dr. Noguchi. Yet, you're in fantastic shape. In fact, you're in better than perfect health, young man."

Broddin shrugged. "So why does my heart ache?"

The doc looked at him, then asked "How's your love life?"

Broddin snorted. "Not that again! Every one keeps pushing that on me. It's nonexistent, if you want to know. Don't have one. Don't have the time for one. Don't need one."

"Really! Cuz you show the classic signs of the illness."

"What illness?"

"You're lovesick."

Broddin laughed. "Are every one of you doctors a quack? Does everybody push 'love and sex' as the cure-all for what ails you? You can forget billing me, cuz I won't pay you." Broddin laughed, but he was a little miffed.

The doctor shrugged and smiled. "Suit yourself!"

Broddin left. The doctor locked the exam room door, pulled out a secure phone and made a call. "Our subject is quite fit...."

Fifty-four: Nightmare

Broddin sat in his office in the growing dusk. The ache in his chest was stronger today. He'd gotten an actual letter from Gem. He could smell a faint whiff of her perfume on it. It created a much closer connection to her than the emails. It made him wonder how much people had lost in putting aside the physical art of writing for electronic media.

"Thought I was coming home sooner, but have to finish some things up. I figured I'd write you a real snail mail letter so you can write me back and I can open it with the black opener. I'm not really thrilled with it, but I'll keep it around because it's my Aunt's."

"I found another weird side effect to the colors GemCrys has caused in us. Now we glow whenever we're in a deep sleep, or concentrating, even if GemCrys isn't around. I was in deep concentration late one night. My aunt came into the room, I was glowing a healthy green. My hair was standing on end. Apparently, I generated an electric field around me, because when she came up and touched me she got a nasty shock. Weird. Just another worthless anomaly. I'm not happy with this whole business that's come out of my creating GemCrys. I'm not in control and I don't like it. See ya in September. Luv ya. Gem."

"Not in control and I don't like it." Broddin understood the feeling perfectly. He turned and looked at himself in the mirrored wall. The doctor's words came back to him.

"How's your love life?"

"Don't need one."

"Maybe that's the problem...you show all the signs.

"Non existent..."

"Love life...lovesick...love life...love sick...love...

He looked down at the letter and recognized for the first time what was in his heart. He could see Gem's face in his mind: so serious when she pursued a problem; laughing at a joke; crying as she watched him on the video. She was filled with emotions. Next to her, he felt like a cripple, incapable of feeling.

"I love you..." he said to her image in his mind, "...and I can't stand it! You're only sixteen. You rely on me to be your guide, to be professional, rational. I cannot fall in love with a child and a student! It's immoral, and unethical. Yet...I love you. This can't happen. It will destroy us both, so I'll tell you now...because I can't ever tell you any other way."

He sighed, picked up the letter and pressed it to his chest. His head dropped down, exhaustion taking its toll.

The viciousness of the nightmare was more real than ever to him. He lay in bed, holding Gem's naked body. That sight alone made him tremble. Joy of such intensity filled him. *"Joy! Is this what they call joy? How could I ever have lived without this feeling?"*

They lay close. He ran his hand across her body, looked into her green eyes, leaned down to kiss her. He started to speak, but before he could, he was torn away from her. The dark man seized her, was choking the life from her. Broddin could see her chest heave, trying to draw breath. She was in agony.

He knew then what it felt to want to kill. He leapt onto the man, felt a weapon in his hand, struck down. He knocked the man away, but Broddin was too late. Gem's naked body lay lifeless, broken. Broddin gathered her in his arms and a feeling of complete desolation exploded upward within him, erupted in horror. **"No!"**

His shout woke him. He found himself in his office, rocking in his chair, gasping. "Gem..." The dream was so real that he reached for the phone to call her. "Got to help her." Then he stopped, fully awake. He had no way to reach her in Germany other than email. He almost called Weng, but stopped. "It was only a dream! Nothing's happened." He dragged himself home and went to bed, but lay wide awake, ravaged by the dream's intense reality.

That feeling of horror and helplessness would come back to Broddin two days later, when Weng came up to him with a worried look. "Did you hear about Gem?"

"What?"

"She was rushed to the hospital two nights ago. Her aunt heard her in the bedroom, choking and gasping. Thank God she did, or Gem could have died. Remember her asthma attack at the tournament?

Apparently it hit her with a new virulence. This attack was so severe, the inhaler didn't work. She was hanging on by a thread the other night."

"Two nights ago?"

"Yeah. Hey, are you all right? You look pale yourself."

"Don't feel too well. I'm going home to bed." Broddin walked slowly home. His head was bowed, deep in thought. He undressed and lay down, but no sleep would come.

He felt cold and empty. The dream *did have* a meaning. Whatever connection existed between that nightmare and Gem's illness, he knew now what he had to do. He had to leave Gem alone, let her go, fully. *"Is this what my love would do to her?"* His heart ached. He had come to a realization of his own truth: *"I am the dark man of my dreams. I am the one who chokes and kills her. It's me."*

He had never even touched her, yet the thought of her loss tore at him. He combated that loss with a much stronger feeling: the vision of Gem in his arms, the joy, the fullness of that moment. In this manner he spent his first night with Georgia Estelle Matthews.

Fifty-five: The Dream

In this way, he finally fell asleep...and dreamed his first true dream in more than ten years. He and Gem lay in a hammock, laughing, drinking in the sight of each other. She glowed a wonderful, healthy color of new spring leaves and Broddin with the color of the sky on the day those leaves came to bud. Wherever they touched, the colors intertwined to form the purest white. A voice in the breeze said,

"You are the promise of the spring,
When love has found its way:
The promise of new life, new love,
New night, and new day.

You are the rising of the heart,
The blessing of the sword.
You are the wielding of the fire:
The herald of the Lord."

Around them wove a rainbow of colors too innumerable to count. The colors were children and grandchildren, cousins and friends. They were filled with the shared vision of a love so deep that it colored their lives, wrote itself upon their hearts. They lived in a place which reminded him of an old folk song he'd heard, about a city where children laughed and shared: *"Conquering, singing, laughter ringing. Voices raised in the Song."*

As Broddin lay dreaming in peaceful rest, a faint glow of royal blue drifted around him and wrapped him in its soft and protecting embrace. It comforted him, shielded him, gave him a peace beyond understanding. He awoke refreshed, calmed. He was on the right path, now.

The next day, Broddin left Roxford, citing a personal emergency. He turned over the running of AINet to Roger. "You can run the nuts and bolts from here. I need more time to work on research on my own to improve the net's performance and I can't do it here. As it is, I've left these problems alone while working...other interests. I simply realized that I've pushed myself too far in too many directions. I'm taking some time away, sort of a sabbatical. I'll keep in touch with you only. I don't want to hear from anyone else, understand? No one else."

Roger looked directly at him. For just a second, Broddin thought he was going to actually answer. Then, Roger shook his head and turned back to the computer.

Fifty-six: Report

Kerian Noguchi sat in his office. "Broddin has left. Our way is clear to take over the computer."

The voice was silent for a moment. "We are still debating how it may be used for military applications. We have been unable to access the computer using any of our usual methods. Our hackers get in...only to have the stupid computer hit them with "I have questions." From that point, in about twenty seconds, the computer ascertains they're unauthorized."

"Wouldn't it be advisable, then, to simply take it and force Roger to reprogram it for us?"

"Dr. Noguchi, I know you'd like nothing better than to force your autistic son into some compromise, but he doesn't communicate with people at all. How will you be able to force him?"

Noguchi sighed. "I really don't know."

"Leave it alone. Our greater interest is in the material young Miss Matthews has fashioned. However, that material is missing, as are the formulae for it and the smelter programs. She puts no information on a recordable program, keys in the instructions herself and has the formulae in her head."

"My man in the lab has provided good reports, but he has been unable to watch her key in the instructions. She is so careful, she must be paranoid."

"Or inordinately intelligent."

Fifty-seven: The Crystal Cave

AD 474. The wind swept across the deep green forests and the wild rivers of the upper Cotswalds. It moaned through the great oaks, seeking its own purpose, finding its way to the hill known for its name: Wyndmoor. It raged against the side of the Keep cresting this lonely knoll, pounded at the shutters which held it at bay, sought crevices to find its way in. It rolled past the knoll and on down into the depths of the valley, seeking, then finding, the entrance to the cave. It blew into the cave, swept leaves aside, and brought the freshening scent of the summer rains deep into the sacred darkness.

The cave lay deep within this hillside, seven hundred feet horizontally from the entrance, twelve hundred feet straight down from the keep whose power protected its secrets. Its walls were encrusted with a variegated crystalline structure. Most of the crystals were highly imperfect with many natural inclusions. Many shone with such pure clarity that empires would have been traded to possess just one. The crystals were emeralds. For most of the time, they kept a silent sentinel, and reflected only the darkness of the underground. This night they glowed a blinding green color, for the master of the place had returned.

Emrys stood within this room — his retreat. He was not here to rest but to work. Before him stood a simple granite rock, some four feet high he had brought from the exterior of the cave. He held the sword. It pulsed a fiery green which matched the color of the stones and his aura.

"Excalibur." A prayer whispered in reverence to this gift the Lord gave him so long ago. Emrys now felt what he had missed all those years while Uther held the sword. He allowed himself to drink in the essence of the sword, to let it complete him again. He allowed it, only because he knew within a moment he would give it up again.

He thanked the Lord for the strength of the Holy Spirit whose will rested within him. Without that strength, Emrys knew he would not have been able to give up the sword, even the first time.

He stood, transfixed at how much he missed his mother, his wife, his daughters and sons. Holding the sword even for a short time like this, muted that grief somewhat. He steeled himself against the fresh grief he would soon feel. He was not sorrowful for the role the Lord gave him. He had taken that task upon himself. Michael had told him: "You went out seeking solitude..." At least, now, there was Revyn.

Emrys wondered briefly of the uncertainty of his course. Certainly Crull would search for the sword and find it. Crull would know how to gain its return. Once Crull found it, he would still need a dozen years to find the stones he needed to affect the transfer.

Emrys mused on the nature of gemstones. He

knew that a defined resonance existed between the emeralds and his own brain waves, as reflected in his aura. In some manner, the sword picked up his energy, resonated to it, magnified it immensely, and radiated it outward. The stones reflected that energy, caused a rift which opened to allow the sword to slip through time. All he needed was a proper terminus upon which to focus, one matching the frequency of the stones which radiated outward.

Crull's dark nature established a mental frequency much more dense than any normal creature's. The only stones which resonated with Crull's frequency were black diamonds. Emrys grimaced. "Thank you, Lord, for that one great blessing." Those stones were the rarest of all crystals in the earth.

In the last few centuries, while Crull had been banished, Emrys had taken care to remove every one from the known world. From the wastes of the frozen ice continent to the North--where the eternal fires burned under the snows and the Norsemen delved into their secrets--to the deepest reaches of the Southern continent as far south of Cush as one could travel, not a single black diamond could be found. Crull would need a long time and immense army costing him much concentration in order to find the stones. By the time he did, Emrys would have retrieved the sword already.

He didn't worry about someone being able to use the sword in the future. The type of exceptional spirit it would take is so rare! Uther was only able to use it as a reflection of Emrys' own power. It demanded a strength of faith which did not exist in that future time. Yet, there was always a chance. He would simply have to entrust it to the Lord. He paused, but could see no other way to keep both sword and his charge safe. He closed his eyes and prayed.

As he opened them, Emrys looked again at this sword. "Excalibur." A keening tone arose in response. He turned the blade downward and plunged it straight into the granite. The high, clear tone dropped four octaves and became a barely noticeable hum.

Emrys could wait no longer. He grasped the sword at the hilt, and opened his mind. The green of his aura flashed outward. The sword reacted in a blaze. In unison the emeralds lining the inside of the cave responded. One in particular picked up the vibrations of the sword and refracted them outward. A blast of heat rushed outward from the cave and the entire hillside pulsed green for one instant. A great pulse rent the ground underneath the cave. The stone and the sword were gone. Emrys fell to the ground, all his energy spent. Exhausted, he slept.

Fifty-eight: Sacrament

Cleveland, Ohio. August. Harold Amerlinz sat in his office on a Friday afternoon. It was unbearably hot because they had turned down the AC in preparation for the weekend.

He was reviewing invoices for the expensive recording equipment, and thought, *"Speaking of expensive, Audrey's birthday is next week."* The office was warm and he dozed.

Harry dreamed. He was in a round room with walls covered in emeralds and he saw himself asleep in the office. "Audrey would love an emerald pendant. A large one. Better go buy it today."

The thought popped into his mind from somewhere else and Harry awoke with a start. "Humph! I haven't dozed at work in ten years! Well, if it takes a dream to remind me of Audrey's birthday, why not? He picked up the phone and called a gem wholesaler he knew in the city. "Joel. Harry here. Audrey's birthday is next week. Do you have any emeralds nice enough for a gift for her? Ten carats? That should do. A flaw in the center? I don't know. You know how Audrey is about her stones. I'll stop over to look at it."

Later Harry did take the stone from the dealer. The flaw in the center bothered him. He hoped they could design a setting to hide the flaw. He decided, though, to show her the stone before having it set.

For now, he dropped the envelope in his desk drawer. His people were testing lasers in the main studio.

Harry was in the next day. He liked the quiet of Saturday mornings. He could use the time to review the week's reports. The air was off and the office was already warm. His head began to nod forward and he dozed again.

Just as his eyes closed, a flash of intense green light jolted him up. He was sure he felt some kind of pulse underneath him. His heart was pounding. "Another earthquake?" They came more frequently now than he ever remembered.

As Harry turned in his chair, he saw green light fade away under the door connecting to the studio. "Who's there?" No answer. He got up and crossed the room in quick strides. He opened the door and froze. Ten feet away from him stood a huge granite stone with a sword embedded in it.

"What the..." The sword shone the exact color of the emerald Harry had bought the day before. Then he saw the color fade to a dull grey luster. Harry remembered then, that he had dozed...again! He blinked but the sword and the stone were still there.

"Is anybody here?" Harry looked through all the offices and found no one. He walked back into the studio and stood contemplating the stone. This was probably some practical joke his brother Gil cooked up, sneaking it in last night.

He reached out and grasped the sword. It felt as if the sword and the granite were of one material, inseparable. He pulled. No response. He had a sudden feeling that not a single molecule of that sword responded to his touch.

Two days later, Harry finally showed Audrey the emerald. "Take a look at this. I wanted you to see it before I have it set. I think we can design a setting to cover the flaw, but you'll know it's there."

Audrey took the paper, opened it and sat staring for a long moment. "Harry, it's beautiful! The color is so vibrant. I've never seen one as lovely!"

"Yeah, but you need to look at the flaw in the center. I figured we could cover it with a setting."

She looked at her husband. "You're serious, aren't you? Harry, I've never seen one this beautiful."

Now Harry was irritated. "For God's sake Audrey, it's not the color I'm worried about. It's the inclusion in the center of the gem. Will you please look at it?"

Audrey took a jewelers loop from the drawer and brought the stone up to the light for a closer look. It was impossibly clear. "Harry, this is the most beautiful stone I've ever seen. Where did you find it?

"I bought it a couple days ago! From Joel! Let me see that!"

She handed him the stone. He brought it under the light and stopped. "This isn't...no, wait a minute! Give me the loop!" He looked for a long while at the emerald. Then he looked up at his wife. "Audrey, this is the stone I bought for you, but a couple days ago, it had a very obvious flaw in it."

"Did you look at it after Joel put it back in the paper? Maybe he gave you the wrong stone."

He shook his head. "He only had one stone this size for me to look at. I know it's the same one. This doesn't make any sense."

"Take it back and show Joel. He'll have some explanation."

Unfortunately, the stone dealer couldn't help him. He examined the stone carefully and declared it to be the one he sold Harry. "Yet, I know it had a flaw before. Looking at it now, I would have to appraise it using a term we were taught doesn't exist in gemstones: "perfect." I'd like to buy it back from you, but I couldn't afford the price I'd have to offer. I can put you in touch with those who could.

Harry slowly shook his head. "I don't know why this happened, but I think I'll hold onto the stone. Keep this between us, Joel, will you?"

Having become too valuable to wear, they placed the stone away in a vault. That one gift, and its strange circumstances, rekindled a love that remained fresher than when they first met.

Harry left the sword in the granite where he first saw it, inside the studio. Gil swore he had nothing to do with placing them there. Harry really didn't believe him, but after a while he dropped it. He had a business to run. Emrys was right. Harry Amerlinz was a man without guile.

Fifty-nine: Crull's Revenge

The Ishar Crull stared into the fire. "Where could that fool have sent the sword? I felt it within the first hours, felt it in his grasp, its power flare. Then it simply vanished." He knew it was not in this world, for he would have been able to feel it, as he felt the presence of the forbidden place he so longed to enter. He turned to look toward the East, where the essence of the garden lay hidden from men...and from all creatures. With the sword, he could open the gate, he could enter...and waste and destroy and despoil.

"Could that idiot of a man have sent it off to another world?" He could do nothing but search. He sat on the cave floor, wrapped black wings around him, and placed his hands together, fingers touching. His mind slowed to a minimal pulse, he gave up his being to the darkness. A cold, black fire surrounded him, engulfed him in darkness.

It took Crull a very long time to find the sword. When he did, a cold fury shook him, for it would take enormous work to gain it. He saw the same path Emrys had seen. When he saw the sword sent into the future, he roared with shrieking laughter.

He realized, with delight, that Emrys had inadvertently put the sword right in his hands! He could not grasp the sword without someone giving it freely. It's use could not be perverted by Nephalim alone, but it could be perverted by a man. Finally he had found the way to grasp it. Crull had knowledge of time Emrys had never gained which would finally place him beyond Emrys' reach for good. He would hold the sword at last. *"You forget, fool, that I am no man. I whisper, and my whispers sow dread.* He would transfer himself into the future and go to that city.

First, he needed to find a human. Someone who would place the sword in his hand. Someone he could influence. Someone who would do his bidding.

He began his search among the descendants with blood ties to the few remaining of T'an's clan. All the better if the "sins of the fathers" were passed down to the following generations. It would be all that easier to invade their dreams.

His search led him down descendant lines to one dead end after another. Either the lines ended with no descendants alive. Or those living in that time were "chosen as one of His own." He spat out the words.

Finally, in *(Atlanta)*--the name of the city came into his mind--he found who he was seeking. She was six, the child of a couple steeped in the errors of the times, blind to any forces outside their limited ability to see. Her future would bring her into a place where she could gain access to the sword. Although just a girl, she could be used as well as a man for Crull's purposes. And she was not baptized! She was so deliciously vulnerable! Crull had plenty of time to wear her down, to master her, and make her want to give in. Crull's grimace deepened. He began to send cold waves of constricting pain across time.

While Crull planned, his knowledge and intent transformed the future. The safe haven which sheltered the sword--this city on an inland sea-- became the place of Crull's triumph.

Desolation reigned. He watched as his plans unfolded. The city fell into chaos. An army formed and spread destruction. He saw the woman arrive, but she did not have the sword! A champion came to challenge him. The woman must have been too weak to wrest it from him, or to trick him.

It bothered him that the man chosen was clothed in brilliant royal blue. The man had learned to draw out the power of the sword, had drawn others to him and consecrated them with shining armor. He wondered who this champion was? Of course, it made sense that Emrys would, in desperation, find pawns to move, seek to keep the sword.

He saw that this man, unlike so many in that future, was baptized and believed. He could not be easily ruled. *"There are many means of weakening one's foes."* Crull began to whisper at the man.

No matter that the fool stood against Crull in combat and did so well. To his amazement and irritation, the man seemed to beat him back, defeat him. He realized that he himself was whispering, giving the man power. He saw the man beat him down. Then the girl said something, and the man *threw away the sword!* At the end, that was all that counted. Crull shrieked with laughter.

He concentrated in order to listen in to the words he would exchange with the man who stood upon that field. "Ahh! The woman...and she will be mine!" He began to laugh hysterically.

He would have to take the time to follow their insipid little lives. Crull began...to whisper.

The details of the plan began to fill out in over time, and the picture of the future clarified the more. It disturbed him that he could not see beyond the sword falling toward his hand, but he could do nothing more to do about that. It was probably against the man's will that he tossed the sword, but forcing men's will was never a problem.

Then, another possibility arose in his mind--and now he howled with desire. Perhaps, his actual grasp of the sword broke time, invaded the garden. "How delicious!"

He thought that he should share a little of that knowledge with Emrys, so that the sorcerer would know how completely he had erred, how he had failed. Crull's knowledge and intent already changed the future, so he knew he would succeed. That realization made him cackle hysterically.

Sixty: Horror

Emrys slept, exhausted by the effort, bereft at the loss of the sword. It had never been really away from him in all these millennia.

He dreamed. He saw a young girl. She was naked. With her lithe form and long dark hair, she could have been Revyn's twin. Emrys' heart ached! The Ishar Crull held her and choked the life from her, his face a mask of hate. All around them lay devastation.

He saw a broken city, brother turned against brother. He saw a terrible black sea of men, an army so vast it was uncountable. They were enslaved to the creature who stood at the center, whose will held them sway. They had given free rain to all the lusts of their hearts. They leered at the girl in Crull's grasp, hoping he would let them at her.

At the edge of this group, came six men clothed in shining armor. Only six? Not seven? They waded through the sea of darkness toward a conflagration. With just six men, their auras combined to form only a weak pale pall of force. White needed all seven elements of its color to create the force to counter Crull. The lack of even one was a disaster.

Where was the green? On whom did the green mantle rest? He looked closer, and was now horrified. The girl was the green! Crull held her under his bitter influence, standing naked and passive. Her green force flowed out and down into the ground, bled her strength away as surely as a mortal wound. It turned the hillside a false and bitter green.

The pale force surrounding the six was not enough to withstand Crull's strength. They would have realized that. Yet they walked on toward him. The leader carried the sword with him and a royal blue color swirled around and out from its blade.

Emrys watched as the leader squared off against Crull. He admired the man's courage. This man could not have ever seen such a creature before, but held his sword down at his side, seemingly at rest. "Who is this man?" They spoke for a time, then Crull struck with blinding swiftness. Yet the man wielded Excalibur so suddenly, so skillfully, that he parried Crull's thrust and struck inward.

Emrys watched as they sparred, circled, struck sword against sword. The man held his own, then began to beat Crull back and down. His strikes were filled with fury, with abandon. The man pointed his sword Crull's heart. "How is this happening?" As he watched, the woman said something...and, to his horror, Emrys saw the man *throw the sword away!* Crull leapt high in the air, using his wings...and the sword fell toward his hand, the runes racing black, grey, black in an unceasing wail of agony.

"No!" Emrys jerked awake on the floor of the cave, gasping for air. The cave was pitch dark, so that he could not see his hand before him. Even the light of his aura had left him. The sound of Crull's brutal fury echoing through the cave was all that greeted him. He was sick with weakness and with a new knowledge.

The Ishar Crull, as a Nephalim, was not subject to time in the same manner as men. He had the knowledge and the ability to transfer himself through time. Crull didn't need to bring the sword back; he would go into the future himself. He would gain the sword in a time long after Emrys had died, so no one would be there to stop him. A new dark age would fall upon the earth in a time in which vastly powerful weapons were at hand. Crull would first destroy the center of creation, then would enter the garden and all would be lost.

"Lord, God, what have I done? I failed you." Despair beat at his mind, at his heart. He heard only the barking laughter of Crull's intent. He did not understand the ache within his bones. He dragged himself out of the cave, began the long trek up to the top of the keep.

Sixty-one: Repentance

It was two hours before the cock crowed, but Revyn was suddenly wide awake. The wind howled wildly against the walls of the keep and shook the windows of her chamber. She was not sure what was going on. She had expected Emrys to come up from the cave long before this. He had not come.

She got up, slipped a stole around her shoulders and went to search for him. She found him prostrate at the entrance to the keep. He was so weak and sick that she barely recognized him. He was delirious, bereft. She could not understand his ravings. They were in the old language, one which he seldom spoke.

"Emrys! Let me help you up! What is it?"

"Yehovah, yakash getseph yacar chemeh. Chets nachath yad nachath. Mathom basar paniym za'am, shalowm etsem paniym catt'ah...."

"I cannot help you unless you speak to me!" He could not see or hear her. She knelt beside him. "Lord, Jesus. Send your Holy Spirit. Give Emrys peace in his soul! He struggles so and I do not understand! Help me, Lord."

The gale outside began to subside. Then, a cooling breeze settled in through the door, wrapped the two within its arms. It calmed Emrys immediately. Though small, Revyn found the strength to lift him onto his feet, to support him and bring him up to her bed. He collapsed on it, unconscious.

Revyn was terribly afraid. Emrys's mantle of power was so weak it was indiscernible. She had never seen him thus. Trembling, she knelt beside the bed to pray. "I waited patiently for You, Lord and You inclined unto me and heard my cry. You brought me up out of an horrible pit, out of the mired clay, and set my feet upon a rock, and established my goings. And you put a new song in my mouth, even praise unto our God: many shall see it, and fear, and shall trust in the Lord..."

As she prayed, her aura deepened to a crimson red. Power flowed out from her, soothed him and made his breathing easier. He settled into an exhausted sleep.

Sixty-two: Tribulation

Revyn awoke, looked up and saw that Emrys sat across the room. She stood and went to him. What she saw frightened her more than his ravings from the night before. Silent tears ran down his face. "My love, tell me. What has happened?"

He did not look at her, but buried his face in her robes. "I failed the Lord! I thought I was protecting Excalibur by sending it away. It would have been simpler to give it to Crull directly! He will go into the future within twelve years, and will gain the sword! What have I done? All of creation is doomed because of my carelessness."

All her care and speaking and prayers could not console him. For days, he lay in torpor, unwilling to eat, to move. She saw to her utter dismay that he was losing his vitality. She saw what she would not have believed was possible. Emrys was dying.

Revyn was frantic. She did not know what to do. She needed knowledge he would not share. Late one night, while Emrys slept fitfully in her bed, she went down to the study. She knelt and stared into the fire. She needed to see the visions that Emrys had seen. She needed to see the future. Her heart pounded within her chest.

She was terrified. She knew she had to gain

control of herself. She opened her mind to prayer, to meditation.

She knelt, staring into the quiet embers for a long time, watching the patterns of red swirl and move within its warmth. Her mind settled upon those patterns, calmed, and moved outward, forward.

She saw herself walk toward a fiery sunset. The sky was ablaze with the same patterns of red which moved within the fire. The setting sun painted this glorious canvas a brilliant white, and within its brilliance lay rest and reconciliation. This was not the time to find those.

She turned aside from that wondrous sight to see the future path Emrys described in his delirium. She saw the city on the lake. She saw the devastation, saw the army. Now, her heart quailed, for she saw herself at the foot of the Ishar Crull. Or it could have been her, the girl looked so much like her. She saw the sight which had driven Emrys to despair: saw the beloved sword fall toward Crull's hand. Grief beat at her heart. She felt the cold probe of that barking laugh, felt its invitation to despair.

Yet, she remembered Emrys' story. "Beware. Watch and ward. Watch for the son of lies, for he seeks all ways to pervert this gift."

She focused her mind, said a prayer for faith, and tried to look beyond the horror of that moment to see the result of Crull's victory. Yet, she could not. Much as she tried, she could simply not see beyond that point in time. She could not comprehend what that would mean.

Sixty-three: Reconciliation

Hours later, Revyn awoke, exhausted from the ordeal of that future sight. She dragged herself up to her bed chamber. She had to speak to Emrys! "My love. You must awaken! I need your knowledge."

She barely recognized the man who looked up at her. No joy danced within his eyes. No warm glow of green power radiated out from him. "What do you want? I have nothing to give."

She prayed, "Come Holy Spirit. I need your help, Lord." Suddenly, she felt an immense inflow of power wash through her. She straightened. A freshening wind blew open the shutters and morning light poured in through the windows. She felt the flutter of the wind's wings around her, felt embraced with a white and pure power.

"Seth, son of Adam. True man of God." Her voice was her own...and not hers. The power which flowed out from her made Emrys' head snap up in recognition.

"What did you say?"

"Seth, Seth. Do not fear." The words which came from Revyn's mouth held unlimited joy, wondrous peace. "The Lord has a word for you. When I gave you the sword, I told you then that you could not conceive the pain you would endure or you would surely despair. That has come to pass. Truly I say to you, do not despair."

"Michael, is that you?" Emrys' heart beat wildly. He could see a brilliant white power surrounding Revyn, moved with her, strengthened her in its protective embrace.   "Michael, I failed the Lord! He entrusted the sword to me, and I have lost it. I failed!" The bitterness of his voice pounded at his soul.

The angel looked at him through the eyes of the woman with an expression which was judgment, the sharp edge of truth. The voice became harder now. "Yes, Seth, you *have* failed."

Emrys' head snapped up.

"You failed not in deed or in purpose. You *have* failed...in faith! You let the demons of despair work their lies in your heart. In allowing despair within, you have done our Lord, and yourself, a great disservice."

For the first time in days, Emrys let his mind become aware. He looked, now, within himself...and was appalled at the ravages of his soul "I don't know what to do anymore! Help me, Michael. Help my faithlessness."

The voice was now gentle. "Solomon's proverb tells us 'Two are better than one.' While you lost faith, the woman Revyn held it for you. Listen to her. You still have work. And time, though not as much as you thought."

With that, the white power faded away upon the breeze, leaving Revyn's blazing red aura as the only power present. She was crying, yet her face was radiant with joy. "Will you listen to me now, my love? I need to understand! You must see what I saw." She took his hands, opened her mind to the image she saw of the future. He flinched and almost tore himself away, but remembered the word he was given.

She looked into his eyes. "What does it mean? I cannot see beyond the point when Crull is going to grasp the sword."

He thought for a moment and a brightening hope crossed his face. "It means that the future is not set! Crull cannot force the sword. He cannot take it on his own. I thought, when I saw this man toss it to him, that Crull convinced the man, or that the man was already his servant. Apparently, this is not the case."

"What?"

"You cannot see the future yet, because it is not set. Crull's intentions can only carry him to that point. He can only gain the sword if the man chooses to give it to him. The man must choose. That is why we cannot see beyond that point. He has not chosen! He will not choose until Crull actually goes into that future."

"He is not Crull's. He stands against Crull with knowledge and power. How he has gained this, I do not know. But our Lord said to Joel, 'In the last days your young men shall see visions and your old men dream dreams.'" Emrys now knew why the Lord guided him to speak of Excalibur's first naming. "Perhaps this young man has the sight of which Joel spoke. Perhaps he sees visions. I will give him some more to strengthen him. Nonetheless, like Crull, I cannot force him to decide. I can only show him the truth."

"So the fate of our world rests in this one man?"

Finally, Emrys smiled. "No, Revyn. Our fate has never rested in our actions, or any man's. It rests with the Lord. He already answered for that fate many centuries ago upon a cross on Golgotha."

"Yeshua warned me then, 'In this world you *will* have tribulation.' Oh, Revyn! How could I forget? Tribulation? It was I who, grieving so deeply, took down our Lord's body from that cross."

"Yet, in that bright morning, three days after I laid his dead body down in the tomb, the women came running to us to say that He has risen! I had forgotten the other half of his promise He fulfilled that day: 'Do not fear, for I have overcome the world.'"

"The world has always been in His hands. As to the battle with Crull, which now lies in the future, it rests in God's hand, not mine."

Emrys looked at Revyn. In his renewed awareness of himself, he felt a dawning realization of a promise given and fulfilled. He now could fulfill the first promise of the Lord.

"Come here. I have something to tell you, and a question to ask." She came to him and he took her in his arms. He turned her to look into his eyes.

"You see it, don't you?" He smiled. His face had a peace she could not understand "I have changed."

"Yes, I can see. What is it?"

"I sent the sword away in a vain attempt to shield its power from Crull. Not only did I miscalculate in that. I did not realize another issue. The sword has always sustained me, even half a world away. When I sent it across time, I shielded also its power from me! What I feel now, I have felt for only sixteen days in my entire life.

She frowned. "I don't understand."

His smile was now radiant. "Revyn, don't you see? I'm dying."

Tears sprang to her eyes. "What?"

"Oh, not immediately. There are many years before my appointed time. Who knows how many! But I am going to die. Isn't it marvelous?"

She recoiled. "You are insane! I do not like what you are saying." She started to cry great sobs. "You cannot die!"

He pulled her into his arms. "Revyn, do not cry. You don't understand what this means, do you?"

"That I will lose you."

"No, that you have gained me. Whatever else may happen, my life is changed. All is changed. Now look at me." He knelt before her. "I never imagined these words to come from my mouth. Now I must ask you. Revyn, daughter of Ygrid, will you marry me?"

She looked at him aghast. She could not believe her ears. "What?"

"I am asking you to become my wife, to share my bed, to become one flesh, to bear children...oh many children! And, we will share a most sacred bond between us. You will be the wife of Seth."

Now tears came for an entirely different reason. "Yes! Yes!"

Sixty-four: Gem's Loss

She rose from her bed for the first time in almost a week. She looked out the window, trying to make herself understand.

Roger had emailed her several days ago and told her of Broddin's actions. He had no answers to her questions as to where Broddin went, or what had happened to make him leave.

"Did he leave me a message?"

Roger felt the pain in her question and hated adding to it, but he had no choice. "No, he specifically asked that no one contact him."

She looked out the window at the beautiful darkness of the woods, out toward mountains in the distance to the evening sky. One feeling beat at her heart day and night: loneliness. One word beat at her mind, night and day: "Why?" No answer came to her. The answer lay in someone else's head and heart.

8-14, Gemmail: "Dear James. Roger tells me you've gone off and I can't reach you. I cannot help but feel that your departure is related to the experiment and other personal developments from your participation. I hope that this isn't a result of the pressures I put on you regarding the experiment. I am always available if you need anything. You know my email. Love, Gem." She sent the email to Roger with the request to forward it. She received no answer.

Three weeks later, Gem recovered enough to travel back to Ohio to continue her last year of school. She started in on her usual schedule of classes, plus her continued research into the CrysMetal compounds. She worked eighteen hour days and more. She had always enjoyed the work schedule. She had no time for socializing, little time for any leisure. She had no need of that anyway. She had always been alone but she had never been lonely — until now.

As the year dragged on, it felt empty. She knew why. She'd be in the lab and a flash would come to her: the vision of Broddin grasping GemCrys and a radiant blue aura around him; or Broddin's mental image sent to her, his most private thought, an image of her standing naked before him.

She somehow knew that the demands of her love, even unspoken, had been too much for him. "That's what drove him away. He was unable to open himself up enough to admit even that he had feelings for me." It wasn't that he was incapable of such emotions. She knew how deeply he felt about everything! For some reason, in this area, he chose not to feel at all.

At least that was the only rationale she could come up with to explain his actions. No other explanation made any sense.

Sixty-five: Q

2:13 A.M. AINet offices. The room was environmentally controlled and under twenty-four hour monitoring and security. The concrete walls, poured eight inches thick and insulated by high R factor polystyrene, were specially designed for this room, to provide the most advanced protection from heat and humidity available. The air conditioning system had three backup units and two generators in case of power failure, which happened often these days.

The room entry was key and bio-ID protected so that only highly authorized people could enter. Only five people had access, Broddin and Roger among them. This was the heart of AINet, the site of the only functioning artificial intelligence in existence. Within this room sat the central processing unit of the artificial intelligence network, Q. Between inquiries coming in from all over the globe every minute of the day and its own search inquiries, Q never had any down time.

Every morning Roger signed on to the greeting "I have questions." That never bothered him. He'd come to regard Q as he would a precocious child and tried to answer as best he could.

One of the most interesting issues that Roger

thought about was the question of how Q would differentiate between virtual reality and the real world, between truth and lie. He needn't have worried. The universe of information provided to the computer had enough referents, so that Q could easily separate objective and subjective material. Its ruthless logic made any attempts to fool it short lived.

A number of researchers tried to put across some theory not based in reality and to bend their research to fit that theory. Q would simply point out the logical contradictions to their arguments. No circular reasoning, no irrational argument could withstand Q's scrutiny.

More than one researcher, after trying repeatedly and unsuccessfully to argue his case with Q, would finally be greeted with the question IS THIS A JOKE? PLEASE ADVISE IF HUMOR IS A FACTOR IN THIS ARGUMENT. IF NOT, THIS INQUIRY WILL TIME OUT IN 60 SECONDS. In this way, many researchers who based their conclusions on errant thinking found their life's work dismissed in the course of one minute.

On this one morning during all the continuous babel of information, no one noticed an inquiry format which came into the computer. It had no source, no tag but suddenly appeared. It was a simple tracking command program, using a high security code to gain entrance. It did not ask for any computing, only for a report of the latest locations of entries by Gem...and later by Broddin. No one noticed, except Q. "I HAVE QUESTIONS."

Sixty-six: Departure

April. As the year continued, Gem had her own decisions to make. This small university town was charming, but didn't have the necessary facilities for her to continue her applied research. She needed a climate for investment, a manufacturing base necessary for the production of the CrysMetal compounds, along with a greater range of high tech research companies. It was time to move.

At the end of April Gem prepared to leave. She received an email from Roger one morning. Ever since he had taken over the responses to Q, he communicated through email when he needed to convey some important news, like when Broddin left.

Roger@ainet: "I don't know if I can stand it. First Broddin leaves, and now you. I'll get a complex."

Gemmail: "Roger, cut it out. You know it's not you. You know a lot more than you let on."

Roger@ainet: "Vaya con Dios, amiga."

Gemmail: "That's Spanish, Roger. Use French: "Adieu, mon amie." Same thing."

For the first time in three years, Roger would have time on his hands. He wasn't sure what he'd do with it. Perhaps, he'd take some time in the next few weeks to visit the flea market in Germantown.

Sixty-seven: Return

Ten days later, Broddin returned. He walked into the office where Roger was answering questions. Roger turned to look directly at him, waiting.

"Don't look at me that way. I've come back, at least for a while. Obviously, looking at the pile of invoices on my desk, someone needs to straighten this place out. Don't you ever file anything?" Broddin left and headed up to his office.

Roger smiled and turned back to the screen. He opened an email connection. "I know why you are back. You figured it was safe."

In the middle of more questions from Q, Roger got the response from Broddin. "If you are referring to the fact that Gem has gone, that's not open for discussion." Roger smiled to himself. Broddin typed more. "What are these reports on the hacker?"

"We've been hacked right in the mainframe. Best hacker I've ever seen."

"You think it's the Feds looking for a back door? What could they be searching for?"

"I don't think it's them. I thought at first you were testing the system."

"Why me?"

"Because they're using your supervisor's security code..." Broddin was startled at that. "...and because the search program only asked for Gem's last entry time, date and location."

Broddin: "How'd you find it?"

Roger smirked at his computer and typed: "Funny thing about artificial intelligence. Q found it."

Broddin: "The computer?"

Roger: "Yep! Q wanted to know why someone would waste time asking for trivial information which had no purpose and no source code from the inquirer."

Broddin frowned: "Every question has a source code. That's the way I programmed the system."

Roger: "I know, but this one doesn't. An anomaly. I think that's what piqued Q's curiosity. We traced the inquiry. Easy enough. Whoever this is, they're expert at it. So far all we've gotten is a trace back to a telephone switching station in Wurttemberg Province, Germany."

Broddin: "That's near where Gem is."

Roger grinned to himself and thought, *"So you don't want to know anything about Gem."*

Broddin typed: "What are they looking for?"

"Whoever it is wants to know where Gem is...and where you are. They began tracking your entries a few weeks ago, too."

Broddin: "Keep me posted. Put a security program in operation to alert us if this happens again. I want to know immediately if we can lock into this guy."

Roger: "Already did it."

Sixty-eight: Riot

May 15th. Broddin hadn't paid much attention to other events which went on at the university. He wasn't aware of the controversy over the concert.

The student body council arranged for a concert on campus of the band which had founded the deathrap music scene. They were a violent band singing lyrics about rape and murder. The band's leader, a convicted rapist on parole, culled this group from the worst of the gangsta rap groups.

Their performances and their songs tried to incite the audience to acts of vicious cruelty and violence. The riots and violence following every concert were put down and then forgotten. In the midst of these riots, fights, beatings and attacks broke out. Thirteen young girls had been raped. One young boy was killed. The police could arrest no one because no witnesses came forward to testify. The police were always led away from the action when it happened.

The band's first release, entitled "Millennium Spawn," went platinum within two weeks. This band was the rage! It's name was "Cruel Issue."

Summer came early to Ohio and the heat index topped out that day at 110 degrees. By concert time, it was still 95. The audience was in an ugly mood.

The music blasted out, beating at the crowd's

senses. Whispers invaded their thoughts grew stronger, demanding. They welcomed the darkness which entered their minds. It brought to the front images they had entertained in their darkest thoughts.

Within minutes, they turned from a crowd of individuals to a frenzied mob, tearing at each other, then to a hunting pack looking for victims. One section of the mob up front pounced on a girl who came alone and passed her above the heads of the crowd. They threw her up on the stage at the feet of the leader who was choking out sounds about rape.

He seized her by the hair and the crowd roared its approval as the other band members grabbed her arms and legs. Then the full fledged riot began.

Police and security had expected trouble, but they were overwhelmed by the magnitude and suddenness of the riot flowing out from the hall and across the town. Several hundred young thugs raged out into the sweltering heat, surging up the quiet residential streets into the downtown on High Street. A tidal wave of rioting flooded across town, carrying with it the detritus of broken lives.

Into the midst of this riot, unaware of the sirens, lost in his own thoughts, James Broddin stepped out of the classroom, locked the door and headed home. He was halfway to his car when he noticed the running footsteps of a crowd of dark shapes, and the sirens in the distance.

"Kill the bloomin, the bloomin, the bloomin..." The chanting raised the hairs on his neck and he backed toward his car. He looked around, but could see no help. He was caught in the midst of them in seconds. He knew he should be afraid, but he had a complete calmness about him.

"I don't think you want to do this."

"Kill! Kill! Kill! The chant went on, oblivious to his words. Then, from behind him, Broddin felt movement...and a bolt of blue lightning burst out through the mob. Broddin turned to see a young thug falling backward. The boy had a knife in his hand, buried in his own chest. He obviously had just committed suicide. The others stood, stunned by the sight. *Or by that bolt of lightning. What was that?"*

Broddin shook himself. The wave of the riot was broken. The mob began to drift away. "Isn't anyone going to help this man?" No one answered.

Broddin leaned down to see if he could help but the young thug was already dead. The knife must have hit a main artery. The boy looked like he died almost instantly. His body lay, twisted, the hand still gripping the knife. His face was frozen in horror, lifeless eyes pouring out a black hatred.

He turned to search for help but the mob had melted away. If it hadn't been for the body lying at his feet, Broddin would have thought that this was another variation of his daymares. But this was real. He felt drained, exhausted. "I have to call the police."

He hit 911 on his cell. The police took a long time getting to the parking lot. "Sorry, Mr. Broddin. It's been a long night."

Sixty-nine: Target

A couple of days later, the police showed up at Broddin's office. "I'm detective Bob Packett, I think you know Frank Riley. He was recently promoted. Do you have a few minutes? We have some questions."

"Sure. About the kid?"

"Yeah. Did you recognize any of the others in the mob who attacked you?"

"No. None of them were my students. I've never seen any of them before. Their faces are vividly painted in my memory." He shivered involuntarily.

"Any idea why they came after you?"

"I was an easy target. I'd come out of my office at the university and was headed to the car when they came charging around the corner. Wrong time, wrong place. I was very lucky they didn't kill me."

"Did you see the kid kill himself?"

"No. He was behind me when it happened. I felt this movement, then there was that flash of lightning. I turned and he was already falling to the ground, dead."

The two looked at each other. One said, "Weird."

"What's that?"

"Nothing. Could you take a look at some photos for us? They're of the death scene. We know you saw it that night, but they are a little gory, so..."

"It's okay."

"Do you notice anything?"

"No. What should I be looking for?"

"Our forensics people hope you can help us. Were you holding an umbrella, or some kind of shield?"

"Shield? No."

"You say this kid was right behind you when he offed--excuse me--killed himself?"

"Yes, why?"

"That's what we'd like to know. Why. You had no blood on you at all. Yet the kid hit dead center and the aortic artery sprayed out a lot of blood. Trouble is forensics can't define the pattern. It looks like a back splash, as if the blood had splattered off a wall or an umbrella or some other object and splashed back onto the body."

"It's obvious from all the evidence that this kid committed suicide. Yet, the blood patterns are weird...and we don't like loose ends." They got up to leave. "We're finding a lot of loose ends from that night. By the way, the lightning..."

"Yes, what about it?"

"The bolt happened at exactly 12:21. We got the crackle on our radio and caught it on one of the squad car cameras. Ground lightning. Weird thing is it stopped the riot in its tracks. The kids all stopped in mid stride, then ran off into the night. Don't know what that was. A bolt from the blue? Just another weird event from a terrible night. Whatever happened, it seemed to stop them. Thank God.

Seventy: Cruel Issue

A day later, Packett and Riley stopped back. "More pieces of the puzzle, sir."

Broddin looked up at them, questioning.

"Let's start with your incident. We found several kids who were in the crowd that attacked you. When we arrested a number of them, they had blood on them. The blood type on several kids matched our suicide."

"None of them really had a clue other than feeling a buzz in their heads at the concert, then the mad rush to 'Kill him, kill him.' When we asked who, they mumbled 'the bloomin.' What the heck is that? We think it may have been either mass hysteria or a designer drug released on the crowd."

"So none of them knew me either?"

"Not really. But this was no random act."

Packett pulled a map of Roxford and the campus out of his pocket. Arrows were marked on it, much like a war room map might look. "This is a map of the campus and surrounding streets. The arrows indicate the flow of both the major crowd and three quite distinct — we'll call them raiding parties. Notice anything about the direction of the arrows?"

"Where are you going with all this?"

Packett pointed to the map. "The right arrow is

the group who surrounded you at approximately 12:20 on High Street at your office. Note where the two remaining groups are headed. The center arrow heads straight out High onto Contreras Road. The bottom angles its way southwest, weaving a course headed for Bishop Drive."

Broddin looked at the detectives, realization dawning. "You can't be serious! Are you suggesting they were...after me? What on earth for?"

"Good question. Before we answer you, let us ask this. You didn't speak out against the band performing here, did you?

"I didn't even know about it! Sorry, I don't pay much attention to those things.

Frank Riley paced the office, but turned and looked at Broddin. "Well, they knew about you. Phillip Gary was the band leader, the punk who died of a cerebral hemorrhage at the end of the riots. This map was found in Gary's pocket. We found this notebook in Gary's room." Riley pulled out a large loose-leaf binder and placed it on Broddin's desk. "Usually these kinds of notebooks are kept by some obsessive fan or stalker."

Broddin looked down at the notebook. He was puzzled. "Why aren't these in evidence?"

"We already vetted this stuff and cleared it through forensics. Since Gary is dead, we don't need to keep it anymore. Go ahead. Open it."

Broddin reached across the desk and slid the book nearer him. He opened it and leafed through page after page of information—about him! "What's this?"

"It's a very thorough scrapbook of your activities. A complete journal of all your movements and activities over the last four weeks."

Broddin frowned. "Who would do this and why?" Broddin leafed through the notebook. Throughout the last pages, written in jet black ink on stark white sheets of paper were hundreds of variations of two words, which screamed out at him and sent his mind reeling. "Lord Broddin" and written across each rendering of his name was "The Ishar Crull." Dark wings pulsed at the edge of his vision.

"Broddin, are you all right?" The detective watched him with intense interest and curiosity.

"Yeah, it's too weird. I don't understand. Why me? Why 'Lord Broddin'? And, what is the Ishar Crull? That name sounds vaguely familiar. I guess it's some variation of the band's name, 'Cruel Issue.' But I don't recognize the language. Sounds almost German." He turned the last page and sat bolt upright in his chair, frozen with fear. The page bore one word, written across it in what looked like blood: "Gem."

Broddin sat very still. Then his hand shot to the intercom. "Roger, get in here." The two detectives exchanged a questioning look.

Roger was at the door in 15 seconds.

"Get Gem on the phone, now!"

Packett spoke up. "Hold on, now. Who is Gem?"

"She's a colleague of mine in the business." Broddin looked at Roger. "Now!"

Roger walked around the desk to Broddin's phone and punched a number. He gave a quirky smirk.

Broddin grabbed the phone from him. "Detectives, I don't know what is happening, but if Gem's name is in the book, she might be in danger." His pulse ratcheted up several grades. The attack had been three days ago. "Roger, have you heard from Gem?"

A head shake no.

Broddin listened to the ringing. Gem's voice came on and Broddin's breath caught, until he realized it was a recording. "Hello, we're not here right now, but we'll call you back. Leave a number..."

"Damn! Gem, are you there? Pick up, now! Roger, she's not there. Is there a cell, or another number...?

"James?" Gem was on the phone, her voice worried. "James, is that you? Are you okay?"

Broddin's voice caught again. This time he could barely speak above a whisper. "Gem. Are you okay?"

"James, you sound terrible! What's going on?"

"Oh..." Relief brought life back into his chest, his breathing eased. "...nothing, it's...it's okay, now."

"Why are you calling? You don't sound okay. I've been worried about you. I heard about the riots. Why are you calling me?"

The two detectives watched him with great interest. Roger was studiously reading the pages of the notebook. Broddin felt embarrassed. "I can't explain right now, but I thought you might be in danger. Have you noticed anything out of the ordinary?"

"No, the work's going along fine. You sounded

ragged just now. What's going on?"

"I'll send you an email and explain in detail later. I was attacked the other night, but wasn't hurt. The people who did it had my name — and yours — in a notebook. I want you and your aunt to take extra precautions until we find out what's going on. Have Alsace Security provide twenty-four hour guards until I talk to you again."

"Okay. I don't like it, But we'll do it...for now."

Broddin hung up and turned to the officers. "What can I do to help? I'm afraid I don't understand this any more than you do. Why would they do this? I have no connection to these people whatsoever!"

"Had, Mr. Broddin. You *had* no connection to them. You do now. They just tried to kill you. We'll put a guard on you for a while, for safety. Think about this, look at the notebook and let us know if anything strikes a chord." The detectives left.

Roger looked at the notebook. Then, he got an impish grin on his face and said the first words he had ever addressed to his friend. He bowed and said: "Lord Broddin."

Broddin frowned. "Don't call me that. I am not your lord or anyone else's."

Roger's smile widened. He bowed low, backed out of the office and left.

Broddin was so distracted that he did not notice that Roger had spoken to him. He looked down at the notebook, at the last pages. The names screamed out at him in warning. He couldn't for the life of him understand what they warned against.

Seventy-one: The Blue Man

Two weeks later, the climate improved. Packett stopped by to tell Broddin that one of the band members agreed to talk. "This guy says that Phil Gary had a real obsession with you all right! He kept harping every day about how artificial intelligence would be the end of the world. The old argument that a reasoning computer would conclude that it had to kill us off for its own preservation. Guess he targeted you two as the inventors of artificial intelligence."

Broddin shrugged. "Thanks for the information."

"By the way, the whole time we interviewed this band member he kept mumbling 'Kill the bloomin, kill the bloomin.' He isn't even aware of what he's saying. Like what the kids chanted that night. Any idea what they might have been talking about?"

Broddin thought a minute. "No, sorry."

"How about the Blue Man? If you chant it, that's how it sounds: 'bloomin. Blue man.' Ring any bells?"

Broddin could think of a big connection. His color was blue. He had caused GemCrys to turn blue. He was the was the Blue Man. But admitting that would lead to more questions than answers for the police. He couldn't see how anyone could possibly know about Gem's research. "Not really."

"Like I said, watch your back. If you think of

anything else, let us know."

"Sure." Broddin watched him leave and thought about the incident. "They were after me! I'm the Blue Man. Who is 'they' anyway? Why kill me? I'm a scientist. Harmless."

Later that night, Broddin sat in his office, leafing through the notebook. When he turned again to the last pages, the names screamed out at him. The other name pulled at his memory, but he couldn't place where he'd heard it. "The Ishar Crull. It sounds old, almost Medieval..." He stopped mid-sentence. He remembered, then.

Revyn turned to look at Emrys. "What is it? What assails you?" Emrys called her back. "I will need to present no face of power for a while, until I may plan. The Ishar Crull..."

"...has returned." Broddin said the words aloud. "But those were dreams! Visions from my subconscious mind. How could someone know about a character in my dreams? How could they possibly..." He stopped. Another image came to his mind. In the lab, when he grasped GemCrys, Gem had read his thoughts! He moaned, his voice shaking. "Oh God, no! Tell me this can't be!" Had someone else, somewhere picked up his thoughts, his dreams?

Cruel Issue had invoked the name of this character...and incited others to commit acts of vicious cruelty. Murder, rape and cruelty beat wings at his mind. Crull had inspired terror in Revyn's face. Now, here in the real world, someone else had invoked the name of the Ishar Crull, and struck terror into people's lives. Broddin brooded. Another character in his dreams never had a name. The one who raped and killed and destroyed. And, when Broddin began to 'eavesdrop' on the visions, Revyn had reacted. *"The Ishar Crull has returned."*

Broddin remembered his talks with Barry Lewison about the dreams. *"Maybe this dark man you battle each night is just your own obsessive nature. Maybe you're battling yourself."*

He thought of his talks with Gem about the results of the GemCrys experiments. About the unified energy theory. *"Thought, energy, matter all interrelated, all the same force."* They never even considered one horrible result Broddin now faced. In a world where thought causes physical effects, how much of a leap is it to conclude that thoughts can also cause changes in other people's actions? That happens every day through speech...but not directly mind to mind. Until now.

Were his thoughts responsible for this deathrap movement? He stared at the evidence right before him. The words burned into his mind from the frozen page before him. Crosses written in every script across the pages, with two names intertwined: Lord Broddin; the Ishar Crull.

Pain lanced through him. Hope and joy crumbled within. He looked down at the book. Despair beat at his mind, killed his ability to think. He felt cold. His voice came out raspy, shaking with grief. "I am. I...am the Ishar Crull." His head dropped. He was lost.

Seventy-two: Out of the Deep

The long soliloquy of the cello--plaintive, its voice raspy, its tone deep and throaty--came up out of the depths of the subconscious. It was a memory from a Requiem Mass by John Rutter that Broddin had heard years before. Its cry echoed his despair.

"Out of the deep...have I called unto thee O Lord. Lord, hear my voice."

The words touched the core of Broddin's emotions. Then, as if they were not convinced that the depth of his despair was enough, the voices rose again in their plaintive cry: *"Out of the deep...have I called unto thee O Lord. Lord, hear my voice."*

Now that cry became a prayer lifted up...

"O let thine ears consider well the voice of my complaint."

...to carry him across a gulf of sorrow towards a shore of peace. He looked deeply into the essence of his being, the man whom the Lord created.

"If thou, Lord, wilt be extreme to mark what is done amiss, O Lord who will abide it..."

Below the surface of his controlled life--beneath his faithfulness, his scientific detachment--the possibility of an Ishar Crull could exist.

"O Lord, who will abide it."

He had to face that possibility now.

"But there is mercy within thee. Therefore shalt

thou be feared."

The words carried him deeper, to make him see the dream...and see himself.

"I look to the Lord."

He saw that each night in the vision he fought the Ishar Crull. "I am far more than the darkness."

"My soul doth wait for him."

"I am also the man he called Lord Broddin. The man they called the Blue Man." He remembered the feeling when he grasped the wand. Joy and love filled him. These were the essence of his being. If he were the Ishar Crull, he would fight that part of himself.

"And in His Word is my trust."

Broddin looked down at his hands. In the gathering twilight, he could see a faint blue color, an aura shining around him like a protective shield.

"My soul fleeth unto the Lord. Before the morning watch I say, before the morning watch."

He felt wonder and awe, peace and joy. A verse from another dream came to him.

> *"You are the rising of the heart,*
> *The blessing of the sword.*
> *You are the wielding of the fire,*
> *The herald of the Lord."*

James Broddin laid his head down upon those blue hands and slept without dreams. The words and the music carried him back to himself, lifted him across the gulf, calmed his sleep.

"Out of the deep...have I called unto thee, O Lord. Lord, hear my voice."

Seventy-three: The Calling

Roger Noguchi strolled through the Germantown market outside of Cincinnati, and reveled in the cool morning air. Roger liked to come up here. He wandered in and out of stalls aimlessly.

The land housing the flea market bordered a large pine forest. As he strolled along the edge, Roger noticed a table far back in one area. He turned and walked into the canopy of the forest and left the bustle of the crowd behind. He felt charmed.

Roger could smell the fragrance of the pines and that always brought back memories of swinging through the pines near his home as a boy.

"Dun't mean ta intairupt yair reverie, yung man." The voice was high and kindly, with a thick English or Scot brogue. Roger looked up into the eyes of an old woman. She dressed in a flowing robe of bright red cotton. Her hair was almost completely white, with a few traces of strawberry color laced through.

Roger Noguchi smiled.

"Ah, 'tis ah mahn of few worrds. Deep thoughts, though. Thinkin o' the smell o' the pines, the glory of conquering theyrr heights."

Roger was startled. She had named his innermost thoughts. *"How could she...."*

"Ya've been standin there the best o' five minutes

jus' lookin' at tha sword, my yung man. Why don' ya pick it up?"

Roger started, for he hadn't even realized, until she mentioned it, that he stood before a table laid out with swords. He shook his head no.

The old woman smiled. "Ahhh, ya think these dun have an interest for ya! Sometimes, things jes spake to us, don' ya think? A sword here spakes to ya."

Roger smiled. This was a good sales pitch. He looked down at the table. Swords of every type sat on it, from curved scimitars to medieval great swords, to unusual civil war ceremonial swords to...

His eye fell on a particular sword. His heart beat one strong pulse. Sunlight played through the trees to reflect on the sword in a color broiling across the blade, reminding him of the color of a deep violet sky. It was *his* color, the one he had seen so many times in dreams.

The light steel blade was highly polished. Along it were etched the typical Japanese glyphs which represented a language Roger knew intimately: it was the code! This sword was Samurai!

Roger reached out and picked up the sword. It felt nicely balanced, light in his grasp. He set his stance, walked through several Kendo kata. The sword felt like an extension of his arm, as if it were made especially for his stature, his balance, his reach. He thought, in wonder, *"This is a sword for heroes."*

Roger's peripheral vision caught the ripple of the trees. A young woman stepped into the clearing, and Roger's heart leapt. She held a slim bow at her side.

She was radiantly beautiful. Golden red hair cascaded down around a pale face. Huge green eyes. Tall and slim. Roger saw beneath the beauty into her eyes, into her heart. His eyes widened in surprise. He saw the truth of who she was and would become.

And Roger Noguchi fell in love. This was an emotion he had never known. This moment is what he had lived for, to find this woman. He was made for this moment...and for this woman.

"Mamma, Aive meant ta saiy...." She was not looking at her mother. She stopped the instant she appeared, and looked directly into Roger's eyes. Tears came to her eyes. She ducked her head. "Alloo."

The woman whirled upon the girl. "Grace! Dinna I *nott* tellya ta stay behind, in the rushes, ta no' come ou' heare a' this time!"

"Yes, mamma, but...."

"**No!** No butts! Go ba' ta where...." She stopped. Her gaze fell upon their faces, and she knew. "Daughh! Why did ah bring ya? Ah shoulda knawn! There's nothin' for it now!"

Roger heard only one word of the woman's rant. He looked deeply into the girl's eyes, and voiced the only word with meaning for him now: "Grace".

Grace, daughter of Rachel, granddaughter of Seth, smiled upon this man. "Rogair." The lilt in her voice was all he need ever hear.

The woman was now furious. "Daughter Grace! Ya aire to go back to the rushes, *now!* I shall coom ba later to dail wi' ya. Now!"

Grace blushed. "Yes, mamma." Her head bowed,

but her eyes never left Roger's. She turned and walked back into the trees. They rippled again and she was gone.

Roger stood, looking after her.

"Yair airre ta forget tha' which ya saw, yung mahn."

Roger turned to the woman, tears now falling freely. His voice was a strained whisper, "Please. Ma'am. Please!" *I will never forget her. I cannot....*"

"Donna say it...."

"I love her."

"Dauggh! Ya dun know tha' which ya ask. I' canno' bea. Ya've jes been taken wi' her beauty."

Roger faced the woman, looked in her eyes and then down at the sword. He knew fully what this sword was, its meaning and purpose. Knowing, he laid it back down onto the table. His voice was now strong and clear. "Without love, all of this is meaningless." He stepped back.

The woman looked at him for a long time, searched his eyes. He felt unusually vulnerable, as if every bit of his heart was open to her gaze. "Rogair Naguuuchi." She smiled. "Si' down hair, son. I ha' a story ta tell ya."

He started to protest, but she put a finger on his lips. "Ya've been still so long, yung mahn. Give an old woman the blessing of stillness jus fair a bit more, will ya?"

He nodded and sat on a stool near the table. The woman sat down next to him, took one of his hands in hers, and began. "Listen now to the story a' this old woman. Let's see now. A long time ago, a young girl named Revyn ha' dedicated heir life to laving a man she thought she'd never marry. You would know her mate's name if I told it. I pick up the story when they were on a quest with King Uther..."

A long while passed until she ended "...and thus 'tis a vairy long time tha' we are ta live. I tell this wi' a great tremble upon the hairt." She sighed. "I know wha' ya ask o' me. A grea' gulf separates the both o' ya, my Grace and you. Aiy fear tha' ya may no' understand. Ya' see she is..." She paused.

Roger looked into her eyes. "Seven hundred thirty-six years old."

Rachel's eyes widened. "Ahhh, ya have the sight. You see her hairrt." She paused for a long moment, then sighed. She turned in her seat. "Grace!" The young woman immediately walked through the rippling effect. "Coom aire, yung laidy." Now Grace wore a circlet of bells woven through her hair which tinkled as she walked. "And, ya've the nairve ta put an the wedding bells. Fair that alone...." At that she laughed. She wrapped Grace in a long hug.

She brought Grace from her side to stand next to Roger, and placed her hand in his. Roger's heart pulsed a single beat. He was filled with pure joy. Rachel looked at them. She took a ribbon and wrapped it around their clasped hands.

"Rogair. Grace. Yair hearts ha' declared fair one anothair. Yea, I ha' witnessed. Rogair, do ya attest tha' ya luv this woman wi' yair heart and soul?"

Roger turned to look in Grace's eyes. "Yes, with

all that I am."

"And, Grace, daughter of Rachel of the lineage of Seth. Do ya, too, so attest."

Her eyes sparkled with tears. "Yes."

"Yea, then, I do no' have such authority or powair to fully so declairr. Bu' these times." She paused. "You are betrothed. Only one kiss ya' may share."

He looked at Grace, cupped her face in his hands. "I will always love you. Always and all ways." Then they kissed.

Rachel took their hands. When she gently separated them, the ribbon had become two identical ones, tied around the wrist of each. "In this betrothal, ya' have a trial, as ya mai see coomin." She picked up the sword from the table which now held no others. "You were called hair for thi' sword. Ya'air called to a great and terrible day." Her voice became strained. "I canno' see the end o' that day, canno see yair return."

Roger felt Grace tremble beside him. He took her hand again.

"Rogair Naguuuchi, ya must go. The calling is tha' for whi' you are meant. If ya be successful in't, retairn here at the rising o' the thaird new moon and the morning star. When the mists ride the fields to bless the leaves, Grace will be here waitin' fair ya."

"But I ward against murhder. Grace was ne'er meant for one who has the stain of blood upon his hand. I donna know your fate...but do *not* retairn heair unless yeh stand wi'out it."

Roger looked at her for a long time. He was not

sure, knowing the logic of what would come, if he could keep such a promise. The contradiction between his love for Grace and his loyalty to Broddin beat at his mind. *"How will I defend him? How will I deserve her?"* He almost laid the sword down again, but knew that his duty was stronger. "I understand."

Roger turned, and gazed for a long time into Grace's face, one he never wanted to be parted from. "I *will* be here." He took up her hands and kissed them, then turned and bowed to Rachel.

She looked at him and said, "Watch and Ward, yung mahn. Ya' now hold my daughter's heart."

Roger sheathed the sword, which now meant so little, and reluctantly turned to walk toward the field. After a few steps, he turned around. The old woman, the table and the young woman who was now his life were gone.

They watched him go. Grace's tears now flowed freely. "Mamma, I am sorry. I *had* ta see him. I ha' seen him all my life!"

"I know, childe."

"Did you tell...does he know how old..."

"He knows. He sees, as you see. The Laird fashioned you for one another. Now go back among the rushes. Ya've disobeyed enough for the day, though now I see God's purpose in't."

As Roger passed from the pines, he did not notice Broddin's father, William. Nor did William notice Roger. He saw a table way back in the pines that had some interesting swords laid out on it. An old woman stood alone, waiting.

Seventy-four: Discovery

Roger Noguchi saw the impact the words in Phillip Gary's notebook had on Broddin. *"Lord Broddin,"* he mused. *"Humph. He might not like it, but it fits. Guess that makes me his page, or his servant."* He chuckled, then frowned. *"But who the devil is the Ishar Crull?"*

He turned to Q and typed in an inquiry. "Please research any references to the 'Ishar Crull.'"

The answer came back immediately. "NO REFERENTS RELATED TO THAT SUBJECT. I HAVE QUESTIONS. OF WHAT INTEREST IS THIS INQUIRY?"

Roger frowned. He typed back a reply. "This is a reference written in a notebook by the recently deceased leader of the deathrap band 'Cruel Issue.' Have you cross checked literary references also?"

Again, an instant reply. "NO REFERENTS RELATED TO THE SUBJECT OF THE ISHAR CRULL."

Roger sat looking at the screen. *"Fast today, aren't we."*

A few days later, that exchange with Q would come back to Roger and bring a flood of questions with it. He was in the library at the University and happened to overhear a discussion between two professors in the English department. It was about

Cruel Issue, as were many conversations these days. Roger didn't really pay any attention. Not until he heard one of the professors. "I simply can't imagine an animal like Phillip Gary being a connoisseur of Shakespearean literature. To name his band after an obscure reference in one of the lesser plays of a minimal contemporary of Shakespeare's, he had to be well read! How can a man read that much of the classics and still be that evil?"

Roger turned around. The other man relieved him of the need to ask the question. He asked, "Are you sure?"

"Absolutely! It was a line from Thomas Kyd's *Spanish Tragedy,* from 1589. He is unknown today, but was wildly popular during Shakespeare's time. His plays included horrors of ghosts, insanity, murder and suicide. I remember the quote vividly. His main character is commenting upon evil witches and said-- now let me see if I can recite it exactly: 'Evil they be, cruel issue of the dark lord himself, following in his works, faithful in his hate. Whence from the dark forest, the Ishar Crull lays out his black work upon the land."

"Is that reference in the common literary lexicon? Amazing that this character would have ever read such plays." The two continued their conversation.

"Certainly! That's how I found it. Heard the name of the band and it struck a chord. I looked it up in the Colliers Web Encyclopedia of Literature. The words 'cruel issue' brought me right to Thomas Kyd.

Roger was up and out the door. He had to see

Broddin. The implications were too vast. If the Ishar Crull were indeed a character in literature, then Q had lied! It denied any referents and Roger knew that the Colliers was one of its standard literary referents.

Before he went to see Broddin, he had one other stop to make. Roger stopped in the UC library to see if he could find any other information about the Ishar Crull. The stop was worthwhile. Besides the reference in Kyd's play, there was another literary reference by Dante, and a short one made in a doctoral thesis about the feudal systems of the dark ages.

Roger searched on the university computers and keyed the proper decimal referent numbers for the thesis.

"Ishar Crull. Purported to be one of the lesser known feudal barons of the late Fifth Century. His lands centered around the black forest area in Wurrtemburg, currently near Baden, Germany." Roger's hair rose on the nape of his neck. *"Baden."*

"The term 'Ishar' is derived from local Teutonic dialect, translates to 'Prince.' 'Crull' derives from the same Teutonic root from which comes the English 'cruel.' This term certainly describes the local legends around this figure. Although short lived (his purported reign was for only twelve years, from 474 to 486 A.D.), legend has described this figure as the embodiment of cruelty. He is credited with mass murder, rape, pillage and destruction rivaling that of the more notorious Vlad Dracul, the equally murderous Tartar prince."

"Though records are scant for that period, certain

writings from monastic histories of that era record that the Ishar Crull was responsible for the almost total destruction of the area's population."

"Legends still persist in certain villages around the immediate area of the Ishar Crull's reign. Parents tell ghost stories to their children about the dark prince of the black forest who waits to come back to reclaim his lands. He will then take the bad children as his own and they will never come home."

Roger could not understand why Q would lie over something so trivial. What could be the connection? Then he remembered that Q was not forthcoming about the hacking connection which started in Baden. When Roger inquired about the source, Q had insisted that no source existed, an impossibility.

Roger went back on line and entered the old Intellisearch website. He typed in his security code and a high security virus search program for the AINet system. It would look at history every hour after Q dumped that memory into backup. He designed the search parameters to alert for any anomalies in connections which had no points of accreditation. He knew that Q would not be alerted since it had no need for programs related to history. *"At worst, we'll be an hour behind you, Q."*

He didn't have long to wait.

Seventy-five: Despair

August 7th. Broddin sat in his office at AINet, his shirt soaked in sweat. The temperature outside was ninety seven degrees at eight in the morning. He watched a TV report on the weather crisis. Marta Gibbs of Cleveland's TV2 News was reporting on the various problems created by the heat.

"...in the last eleven days has been a continuation of this extremely hot cycle we experienced for the last three years. It has been especially bad since mid-April of this year. The Southwest drought conditions rival those recorded in the Nineteen Thirties. Wildfires have broken out in Southern California, Florida, many Western states and in the Midwest."

"We have begun to see the largest migration in American history, with people uprooting their families to move north, away from the heat and dust. It is possible that we may see, in our generation, a return to the dustbowl culture of the great depression. The pictures are certainly reminiscent of that time."

"The heat has also been a factor adding to the frustrations in our inner cities, which erupted in the great number of outbreaks of rioting and violence.

"People are frustrated. We have to conclude that the heat is a significant contributing factor. No other cause, no reason, makes any sense."

"We have witnessed some of the bloodiest riots in memory. The trend began in hot spots like Taos, New Mexico and spread throughout the Southwest. Locally, we've had our share, like the one earlier this year in Roxford, where seven students died. The Chicago riots resulted in three deaths, twelve hundred injuries and over one hundred million dollars in property damage."

"Our investigative news staff has uncovered a link the police are working on...a fascinating common aspect of the riots which is frightening and puzzling." Marta looked directly into the camera. "Every riot has revolved around, if not directly incited by, bands of this new genre called 'Deathrap.' These new bands sing and rap about murder, rape, riot, destruction. The band which began this new cult was Cruel Issue. Every place they performed became a battle ground between police and rioting students, until their leader died from a cerebral hemorrhage while attempting to rape a girl on stage in front of an audience."

Marta looked sickly disgusted. "Eyewitnesses of that concert said that the crowd cheered him. More than five thousand people and not one tried to stop him. He raped one girl and killed her right in front of the crowd. They cheered for him! Then, they seized another young girl and threw her up on the stage. Fortunately, the band leader had a stroke the moment before he raped her. Very lucky girl."

"Of course, the incessant heat of the last few months has been a definite factor exacerbating the crowds. We can only surmise that since most of the audience was already hot, sweaty and irritable before arriving at the concert, they were on edge and ready to react to the violence of the lyrics and the performance. However, authorities have not discounted the possibility that the bands are releasing some kind of airborne designer hallucinogen on the audience. As yet, no solid evidence exists for that, but they cannot come up with a rational explanation for the mass reaction and the lack of any moral concern in these people for their fellow citizens."

"The Governor of Ohio has declared a civil emergency due to the heat, has called up the National Guard to be ready in case of riots, and has called for a federal ban on these Deathrap performances. We have been informed that the President is considering just such an action at least on a temporary basis, citing the volatility of the climate."

Broddin shut the TV off. He was horribly, acutely aware of the trail of destruction, a trail which followed his own meandering travel route. He sat and ticked off cities in his mind: Taos, Phoenix, Flagstaff, San Diego; then Houston, Little Rock; and finally Roxford. After that, the violence exploded everywhere.

He was worn, haggard. He tried to examine, to rationalize, to pray, to avoid the only conclusion he could possibly make from the facts: the riots had followed him. They happened in the cities where he had been, at the exact time that he was there.

Meanwhile, he had fought with every ounce of his will against the darkness within...and had lost. The violence escalated night after night. The darkness he fought within, his own Ishar Crull, became stronger every night. Outside in the world, the riots, the rape, and the killing escalated in kind.

"A connection must exist between my dreams, my nightmares and these events. I dreamed of the Ishar Crull. Then, after I touched the wand, these bands started to arise. I've unleashed a plague on the world! A nightmare demon from the blackest part of my mind for which there is no cure except..."

Broddin stared at his empty face in the mirrored wall. It was drawn from lack of sleep, worn with anguish and care and guilt. *"Where is the joy I felt? Maybe I never really had the capacity to feel at all."* For the first time, fully discouraged, tired from his long battle with himself, James Broddin thought the unthinkable. *"The only way I can think of possibly breaking the string of violence is...to strike at its source. The riots, the killing would stop...if I were dead."*

He thought of Gem, but thrust that thought out of his mind immediately. He could not think of her and contemplate what he had to do. *"At least she's safe. Q tells me she still logs in from Germany every day."*

Broddin had a prescription for some powerful sleeping pills. "This bottle, and a few stiff vodkas should just about do it." He thought of what this would do to his father but put that aside, too. He saw no alternative. His death would save so many!

He turned away from the image on the wall.

Seventy-six: Redemption

Broddin was contemplating the bottle of sleeping pills when Roger walked in. He put them away in the drawer. Roger looked directly at his friend. His voice clear and strong, he said, "James." Broddin's head jerked up. "You must see this."

Broddin simply stared for a moment in wonder. "You do speak! Gem said you did. I didn't believe it. Why are you speaking to me now?"

"It's urgent. I do not waste words. You are *not* the cause of what is happening. Look at this."

He brought reports over to Broddin's desk. Broddin could see they were the tracing program they had reviewed of the hacking activity. Now, the reports showed that the hacking was happening again, this time from two separate locations.

Broddin looked up sharply. "This isn't possible! Hard enough for one to break through the security clearances. No way two hacked in."

Roger pointed to the report. The second source for the hacking started recently. It sourced in Cleveland at a place called 'Time Traxx,' a virtual reality studio. Broddin raised his eyebrows. "What would they want with the AI network?" Roger flipped to another page and Broddin saw that he had done a search of the firm. He read on. "Time Traxx is the corporate headquarters and main studios of Amerlinz Enterprises, a worldwide virtual reality tech firm. I can't see their interest in our product."

Roger pointed to one of the hacking codes coming from this site. Broddin looked at the code, trying to find the glitch which allowed this breach. He could see nothing. "This guy has got to be the best hacker in existence. No source, no traceable program change, yet he's hacked into the most secure system outside of the Feds. I've never seen anybody cover his tracks like this." Broddin turned toward his computer. "I need to see this on AINet myself."

"Don't bother. It's not on there." Roger laid down his next card, the search program from the old AI website network he had programmed to follow AINet history. On the old network, program tracks had been entered to allow unauthorized access. Roger said, "If you look up on AINet about these records, Q will deny they exist."

Broddin looked at him incredulously. "You're kidding."

Roger looked right at him. A a quirky smile played across his face. "Q is lying." He showed Broddin a record of his inquiries about any further unsourced, unaccredited inquiries since the first ones. Q had denied any access attempts. Then, Roger pointed again to the programs from the old website clearly showing the access parameters. Q had not mentioned these access inquiries.

Broddin looked at the program, then looked at Roger for a long second. "Come on, computers don't lie. The central processor has artificial intelligence, true, but even it doesn't have a motivation to lie. Every one of its actions can be traced back to some goal oriented objective criterion. Did you ask it what it found out about the first inquiries?"

Roger pointed to the answers Q gave to the query he entered. Q had immediately answered, every time in the negative. Broddin said, "It keeps referring to a source, but no source is there. It almost looks as if someone has tapped directly into the central circuits of the mainframe."

Roger looked at him. "Q has learned to lie." He pointed again to the two programs, laid out in comparison.

Broddin couldn't believe it. "How is it possible that Q would deny the existence of an item it just moved to history not one hour before?" Broddin could see that Q ignored the referent inquiries and simply referred Roger to the untraceable source code.

"It has to be a virus. But it can't be. Q would have seen it, would question it." He saw where Roger copied the antivirus program results from the various AInet and Intellisearch computers.

Broddin brought up the antivirus programs. "You can see where and when the changes were made into the bootable software. If we've been hacked right into the mainframe software, I can't read the path he used. How did you figure out to use the outside security program? What made you think Q would lie to us?"

Roger looked like a card sharp as he pulled the final report on the Ishar Crull from his case. "This."

Broddin took the report from Roger's hand, glanced at it, then rose from his chair. The report was about the Ishar Crull. It was immediately evident that Crull had existed. "Where did you find this?"

"On the university web search."

"There really was an Ishar Crull?"

"Yes."

Broddin's hands trembled. Suddenly his legs shook and he sat down. He read down the page. He looked up, his face a mask of conflicting emotions. "This is true? This is real? He existed? But Q…"

"Lied."

A transformation swept across Broddin's face. Relief and anger fought, won and lost against each other. "I can't…then I'm not. I don't **understand**!"

Broddin's shout startled Roger even though he had expected a strong reaction. He pointed to the tracking programs again.

Broddin frowned. "Why the hell would Q lie to us? It should be ruthlessly logical. Why lie about some fifth century warlord? Why lie about connections which should be the center of Q's own inquiry? Connections that go from nowhere to nowhere."

Roger sighed. *"Must I point out everything?"* "Today, the connection did go somewhere: Cleveland. Time Traxx." He pointed to the search program which opened some connection between the station in Germany and the business in Cleveland, a connection which remained open. Broddin could see where Roger attempted to use his executive authorization to access the material. That access had been denied.

"This is crazy. We can't even access our own system, which is lying about the existence of referents right in front of our faces." Broddin looked up. "At least we can go to the destination and see what's going on there. We'll get one of the hackers…and maybe he'll turn the other one!"

Broddin couldn't help feeling the relief soaring through him. He thought, *"That means it's possible that I'm not him. Whoever, whatever he is, it's not me!"* For the first time in weeks, James Broddin smiled. "I have to go to Cleveland, now."

As he rose from his chair, Roger held up his hand. "Follow me."

"What?"

"Trust me."

A voice within Broddin said, *"Put your life in his hands."* For some reason, the confidence which poured from Roger Noguchi was all he needed. "Okay."

Roger directed him to drive over to the edge of the campus. They walked down stairs leading past the ball fields, past a tree line, then on down the hill. They stopped near the bottom and Roger turned toward some thick bushes. He reached in, pulled what appeared to be a keypad from one bush, and keyed a code into it. The brush lining the hillside began folding apart. To Broddin's amazement, a large hanger door appeared. "What the...."

As the brush cleared the door, it opened up to

reveal a large aircraft hanger built into the hillside, in which several Blackhawk helicopters sat. Roger walked casually into the hanger and began to undo the tie down cables holding the first copter. Broddin followed. "Did you call a pilot? How did you know about these? I never heard about this hanger."

Roger finished the last cable, climbed into the pilot's seat and turned back to look at Broddin. Broddin was aghast. "You can't tell me you know how to fly one of these things?"

"Yes."

"When could you possibly have learned this?"

Roger rolled his eyes, flipped the switch to begin to power up the quiet engines, then said, "Are you coming? Cleveland. Next stop."

Broddin thought to himself. *"If I climb in this aircraft, I'm crazier than him. But, I was on the verge of taking my own life an hour ago. Then Roger saved me."* The thought came again: *"Put your life in his hands."* He got into the passenger side and shut the door.

Roger Noguchi powered up the rotors, set the controls. The Blackhawk lifted at a slight angle and drifted horizontally out of the hanger just above the landscape. Roger pushed a button and the hanger doors disappeared back into the hillside. The chopper silently flew across the landscape, following along valleys. Roger kept it low, within a thousand feet of the terrain.

Broddin watched in amazement. "How long have you been flying?"

Roger smirked. "First time ever. I watched the pilot do this a while back. I've practiced his moves on the simulator."

"What? We are going to die!"

"Relax, James."

Two hours later, Roger put the chopper down in a field close to downtown Cleveland's east side.

Broddin opened the door to get out, then turned back. "Roger, I owe you...so much! I don't know how to express...." He stopped.

Roger looked directly at him. "I have knowledge. Whatever you find here, remember that the Lord has said, 'In perfect love there is no fear.'" With that he reached over, closed the door, waved Broddin off and powered up the Blackhawk. It lifted smoothly, turned and was gone.

Roger Noguchi turned the craft toward home. He began preparations in his mind for what he knew would develop next. The logic of events was certain. People, and their decisions, were always subject to error. Yet even their error was predictable, following a pattern of logic if you knew the inner workings of their minds.

Roger Noguchi knew. Regardless of what may happen in Cleveland, he knew that developments were escalating. Now, they would come. The forces would now gather, would seek to destroy or enslave, and would seek to grasp at the power they craved. Roger Noguchi was prepared.

Seventy-seven: Cleveland

TIME TRAXX

AMERLINZ ENTERPRISES

The words were written in an Old English script, dark green on a white background. They resonated with ancient power, whispered secrets. They were no longer simply words.

James Broddin stood frozen at the entrance and looked up at the sign. A slight breeze, welcoming in its coolness, brushed at his shirt, lifted his hair, and refreshed him. Time seemed to circled back to catch him from behind. He had seen this sign before today, but only in his visions. Now, the visions pulsed in his head, clamored for his sight. Demanded to be given new life, new reality.

He fought the visions back from his mind. "I don't have time for this now!" He looked up once more at the sign and wondered what secrets lay behind those words. Whose vision brought him to this place? Emrys's? Or the Ishar Crull's? Or his own? No answer comforted him.

Broddin entered the reception area. "Harold Amerlinz, please."

The young girl didn't even look up. "You lookin'

for Harry? He's in the studio, playing. You can go in."
She waved her hand casually to the door behind her.

Broddin walked through the inner door…outside.
He gasped and stopped short. He stood on a precipice
a thousand feet in the air, looking down into a torn,
ragged valley. One more step would plunge him to his
death. He knew that was impossible. Of course, he
took the step to watch the digital virtual reality react
to make a narrow shelf run off to his left.

Broddin had to admit the digital effects were
amazing. This was a direct virtual experience which
built itself around him. To his right, Broddin noticed a
large boulder of granite. A sword, grey and dull, was
buried in it. It looked so substantial, he felt like he
could reach out and touch it.

Behind him to his left and right, banks of speakers
pounded out an upbeat rhythm which crashed and
jagged across the rocks, yet resisted disintegration
into noise. A laser shot out from above, split into a
thousand beams, then shot into a cave across the
abyss from where he stood, outlining a figure rising
from the mist in pulsing red. Around him hung a
black cloak, which looked like a face, watching. A
voice flowed out from the sound, became words:
"Time Traxx…Amerlinz Productions."

The words and the light trailed off, then came
back in an irritated hum which buzzed into Broddin's
head. Then the laser light reached out, centered on
Broddin, and grasped him.

A shock of voltage ran across his face and hands--
and darkness raced toward him from the cave,

invaded like a thousand bees crawling all over him, stinging, pressing at him. Then it was gone.

"Hey! That's a take! Shut it down!" The wizard strode toward him from the mists of the cave. Evidently, he was real. The scene changed instantly to build a shelf of rock where none had been, before the entire scene faded to reveal a huge empty warehouse behind the man. Broddin noticed that the rock with the sword still stood to his right. It looked solid, but with the quality of this digital experience, Broddin couldn't be sure.

"You're James Broddin, aren't you? I read about you in Business Week. Still buzzing, aren't you? I'm glad you got to feel it first hand before you watch it on tape. Craziest vid I ever saw. We're using the new computer to digitally enhance and control the laser light and it's doin' wild effects, but also some strange stuff! Come on! I'll show it to you on the monitors."

He strode out of the studio. Broddin shook himself. He felt drained. He walked after the man, who was already through another door to the left.

The wizard walked into a control room, all the while keeping up an endless patter. He was obviously excited. "The digital imaging is way more radical than I ever imagined. To be able to generate such clear, real images out of nothing! No green screen. Just an alternate reality enfolding right around you! We're taping this new format, but boy have we got a glitch! By the way, how'd you find out about it?"

This was the first chance to utter a word. "Mr. Amerlinz, I am not interested in your programming problems. I'm not amused that you subjected me to the kind of voltage you're playing with."

"Oh, aren't you here because of the glitch with the new computer? Saul, run the flat four, will you?" A wall console lit up across the room.

Broddin was even more irritated. "I came because someone tapped into my network from here without authority. I want to know who and why? I don't care about your programming problems. I need to see your computers and the net guy in this place. Who would that be? He has a lot to answer for."

"Uh…okay. Sure. But watch this first. What'd we get this time, Saul?"

"Mr. Amerlinz!"

"No, hold on! Take a look!" Amerlinz turned him to look at the monitor on the opposite wall. He saw himself outside, on a mountainside.

The pounding beat picked up from the speakers, splitting the room. Mists rose up from the cave. An image of the wizard rose in the cave. A voice over said, "Time Traxx."

"There he is. Good. Good."

"Nine seconds." A reddish image began to appear and Broddin began to make it out.

"There it is!"

"Amerlinz Productions."

The face appeared, dark and inflamed, looking out from the cave and Broddin's hair rose on the back of his neck. It was a nightmare image he would not want any child to see. It looked almost human, but evil poured from its eyes. Broddin stood, frozen.

He hadn't seen the image clearly from the angle within the studio. Then, as the mists cleared, a bolt of black shot out to seize Broddin's image.

"Freeze it! Stop the tape!" But the tape was done. Harry frowned. "Now what the hell was that? Back it up freeze frame 'til we reach the burst."

Broddin was angry now. "Look, Amerlinz, I don't appreciate being on the receiving end of that laser. It could have blinded me! So you need to…"

"Yeah, but that's the problem!" The tape played backward frame by frame, reliving a frozen backwards image. Harry turned to Broddin. "The face? It's a great image. Scary as hell! But we didn't program it! The computer's playing its own game with the digital imaging program. That's not us!"

Saul said, "That's the frame. Let me enhance the image."

Broddin frowned. "You mean to tell me you only programmed the full figure outline? Not the facial features?"

"That's right. And, this power surge is new, too! Never happened like that before you walked in."

"Someone's toying with you, Amerlinz. Computers don't play their own games, unless they're tapped into my network at AINet. It's evident that you are! That's why I am here."

Saul was trying to focus the frame. "Clarify it a little more, Ernie. Holy Shit! Harry! Look at this!"

Broddin and Harry turned to look at the screen. In the frame a hand — huge, black, dark — grasped the figure of James Broddin. Around Broddin was a brilliant blue aura of color.

Broddin's palms were sweating. "Now I'm being played with, Amerlinz, and I don't like it. I want to see your computer programs now! Where is your computer room?"

"Through here. I'll show you. I want to get to the bottom of this, too."

"Never mind. I want to confront this guy on my own!" As he opened the door to the computer room, he heard Harry Amerlinz say, "Fine with me. I'd rather not go in there anyway. That's *her* domain."

Broddin looked back at Harry with a quizzical frown, but Harry shrugged his shoulders as if to say, "You'll see." Broddin closed the door behind, turned and stopped.

A young girl sat across the room, her dark hair falling down across her shoulders. She concentrated on a vidscreen, pouring over a program. It was Gem. Broddin opened his mouth to speak but couldn't.

Without turning around, Gem picked up a sharp silver object — the letter opener — and brandished it. The tension poured out from her and she spoke, her voice was raspy, strained, almost vicious. "Harry, I told you to stay the hell out and if you don't I'm going to stick this right in your…"

"Gem."

She froze. Slowly, she swiveled in her chair. As she turned to face him, Broddin's shock was worse. She was haggard, worn, and looked as if she hadn't slept in days. Her pupils were so dilated that no green showed at all. Blackness poured out from them and

Broddin had a flashback to that night in May, to the young suicide, dead in front of him. Gem looked at him. He thought for a moment that she didn't even recognize him.

In that same raspy voice, the first thing she said was "You are not supposed to be here!" Then a wave rippled through her and for the first time she really saw him. "James. Help me." She fainted and began to slide off the chair.

In two strides, Broddin was across the room and caught her before she hit the floor. Joy exploded in his heart! He lifted her in his arms. Intermixed with the pulsing joy was an extreme concern over Gem's condition. But he could not hold back the torrent of emotion raging through him and swept away the defenses he had so carefully built. Gem was in in his arms. Nothing else mattered. Tears flowed down his cheeks. "Gem, are you all right? Gem!"

Her eyelids fluttered and she opened them. The green of her irises returned but she was ghostly pale. She smiled in greeting. "It is you! You're here!"

He stroked her hair, her forehead, her cheek. He remembered words from the only true dream he had ever known. They said all that he could not.

"You are the promise of the spring,
    The finding of the way.
        The promise of new life, new love.
            New night, and new day."

She looked deeply into his eyes. "Am I? I feel lost, James, and I'm afraid."

"I'm not. Roger told me a verse from the Bible:

'In perfect love there is no fear.' I know right now that he's right."

Gem looked worried, doubtful. "James. I...I just don't know. A lot has happened."

"Are you feeling better? Able to stand? What was all that about knifing Harry Merlin? You sounded so...weird, tense and enraged. What's with the letter opener?" He reached over to pick it up.

"Don't' touch it!" The sharpness of her voice caught him by surprise.

"What?"

She shrugged. "I'll tell you everything I know, but not here. Can we get out of here? I think I can stand."

Broddin helped her to her feet, then held her for a moment, feeling her against the length of his body.

She looked up at him. "Let me shut down the computer and let's get out of this place." Then, she pulled away from him and turned to the keyboard to power down. Broddin did not notice her pick up the opener and hide it behind the computer.

Broddin realized that he had made a decision sometime in the past few months That unconscious decision had lain hidden within his mind, waiting for his recognition of this emotion. He could not possibly put the emotion back, make it again captive to his denial. He found, with a little surprise, that he did not even want to put it back. The full awareness of that decision dominated his thought now. He knew that he could not bear to let this woman out of his life again.

Seventy-eight: SchwarzWald, 486 A.D.

The Ishar Crull stood in the midst of his cave. Tension swirled around him in palpable eddies, sending out cold currents of air. "Tonight I will go away to a time when men might dare defy me. Men in that time do not believe…in anything. They live shallow lives, devoid of belief, blissfully unaware of the powers and principalities which lie beyond their blind sight. Without spirit, without belief, they are so wonderfully…vulnerable! It is time. Time for a lesson in belief."

"At least they will try to defy me." He smacked his lips. "At least, it will be interesting."

"That idiot Emrys has tried desperately to enlist help in an attempt to stop me. His champion will stand ready upon the battlefield, a lost cause. Without belief he has nothing! Ah, to have a worthy opponent, if only one time."

It had taken him twelve years, but he found the black diamonds he needed. He stared into it and into the void he craved. Crull turned his attention inward. He began the incantations which would aid in his concentration. His thoughts spiraled down into the abyss of time.

Seventy-nine: The Broken

They walked out into the relentless heat of the August sunlight. "Let's go someplace cool. I belong to an underground café that has air."

"Air conditioning? That's illegal!"

She looked at him wryly. "It's six stories underground and always cool. Natural air conditioning...the best kind. Not illegal at all. Expensive to belong to. It's a private club."

Broddin gestured to a wooden pendant hanging around Gem's neck. It was long and slim, unusual in its form. "What's that?"

"Oh, that's GemCrys." She felt a slight pulse at her heart and smiled. "I couldn't rest easy with it locked away in some vault. I had this pendant fashioned. GemCrys fits snugly inside it. It helps me, being close to it."

Gem stopped at a doorway and turned to him. "We're here." Her gaze and the statement took on a greater meaning to her. "You're here!" She stepped closer to Broddin and put her arms around him. Broddin felt the old tendency to draw back. But then, he felt her body against his. He welcomed her into his arms. *"Joy!"* he thought. *"This is what joy feels like. How could I ever have lived without this feeling?"*

Gem looked into his eyes and said, "How could

you live without this feeling? I've waited too long for this joy, and I don't ever want to let you go."

Broddin started. "Why did you say that?"

"I can read your thoughts! They're written on your face like an open book." She looked up at him quizzically, then turned to the door. "If we don't eat soon, I'm going to faint again. Waking up with you holding me in your arms definitely has its advantages, but I need food."

They took an elevator sixty feet down to where the incessant heat of the day did not reach. The natural air conditioning of being that far under the earth was a refreshing change.

While they ate, Gem encouraged Broddin to tell her of the events which brought him to Time Traxx. He related everything he could remember: the riots, the notebook, the fact that Q lied to cover the inquiries. He wasn't quite ready to mention the Ishar Crull. That was too personal.

Gem seemed reticent, unwilling to talk about how she came to Cleveland. She kept moving the subject back to Broddin and away from herself. Finally, Broddin said, "You can avoid all you want, but you will tell me, today, why you're here."

She looked down. For the first time, Broddin saw that Gem struggled with some kind of doubts. "This is hard. I can't see any other explanation. Perhaps we somehow broke the boundary between our mental and physical worlds and we're making our worst nightmares real. Does it really matter whether these are nightmares created by us or real ones?"

"It matters a hell of a lot to me!"

"Why? Why is it so important to you?"

Broddin now looked away. "I have dreams. Visions really. They come to me awake or asleep and are as vivid as reality."

Broddin told her about the visions. Then he said, "Phillip Gary's notebook referenced an evil, dark character in my visions. Gary invoked this name in the book. So you see, I thought this part of my dream somehow got out into the world to influence these riots and this Deathrap movement."

She frowned. "But those bands are violent. They practically worship rape and murder. Why would you think you could engender something like that? Why would you make such a statement?"

He took on the haunted look which had cloaked him for the last two months. He realized that he had seen the same look in Gem's eyes at Time Traxx.

Broddin looked directly into Gem's eyes. His heart pounded and his breath felt shallow. "This isn't the first time that I made a connection between my visions and an event in reality. Time Traxx? I've seen it in my visions, but I've never been in this part of Cleveland before. And you. You were in my visions all along although I wouldn't admit it even to myself. And…and when I dreamed about you one night, that was when you had that asthma attack which almost killed you. I think I caused it."

She reached over and touched his hand. She noticed that this time he did not draw away. "Come on, James. That doesn't make sense. How could you cause my asthma?"

Broddin's voice was flat. "I have another vision, a nightmare I've had nightly for eleven years. I have fought it...and lost time and again. It is a vision of rape and murder and...and I can't stop it!"

"There is a woman in the vision. Before I met you, I thought that she was another character from the visions, Revyn. Then you came into my classroom. I tried not to look at you, tried to deny it. I couldn't. It was you! It is you!"

Broddin looked down at his hands, blushed. "That day in the lab when I picked up GemCrys, you saw my mental image of you naked, standing in my classroom." He looked back up. "I...I never meant to invade your privacy, to think of you that way. You mean too much to me for that."

Gem smiled and her eyes were bright with a look of tenderness. "James, I've *always* wanted you to look at me that way! Let's talk about that later. Tell me the rest of the dream."

"It's horrible. I can't keep straight the partition between the dark man and me. You see, that's why I thought the Ishar Crull was me!"

She turned cold. "**Stop!** What did you just say?"

"I said, this name that Phillip Gary wrote in his book across mine. It's a character from my nightmare: the Ishar Crull. What's wrong?"

"Why didn't you mention this before?" She was fighting some overwhelming emotional battle. He could see her jaw tense, a vein pulse in her neck. She took an inhaler bottle from her purse and breathed in once. Before he could answer she said, "Go on. I have to hear the dream first."

"It all fit together with the events going on outside in the real world and the dreams inside. Even that quack Barry Lewison thought it might be my dark side. If the Ishar Crull were me, then all this destruction came from me too!"

"I'm sorry but it's intimate." His face lightened then. "But the feeling of holding you today is the same!" He looked down again, his voice hushed. "I'm holding you in my arms. We're beginning to make love…" He told the dream. Talked about the dark man choking her. About his rage, about killing the dark man, then about her dying. A tear formed at the corner of his eye. "…the loss. I couldn't deal with your loss in the dream. It's only gotten worse since I fell…" he stopped and looked up at her.

She was white with shock. She hadn't heard much of the last because she was lost to her own nightmare. *"It can't be!"* She thought. *"James cannot be the Ishar Crull of my dream. Can't. It just doesn't feel right! But it's the same dream, or so close. They must be the same!"* Gem stood up. "I have to think and I do that best while I'm walking." Her tone was empty, serious. She looked down at him. Her voice revealed no emotion. "Come with me. I need you by me."

They walked out to find with shock that twilight had come. They had been in the restaurant for hours talking. Gem took a brisk pace down toward the center of the city. She was infused with a new energy. Broddin thought that it wasn't positive energy.

They walked down through the empty streets of the city center. She didn't speak for over an hour. They finally stopped at a well lit park outside the Rock and Roll Hall of Fame. She looked down the long walk, away from him. She faltered, then brought her shoulders back and looked at him.

"When did you say you began having this nightmare?"

"Eleven years ago."

"That's when I began having my asthma attacks." Broddin felt sick. She said, "But your dream is of a woman. I was just a little girl then, six years old. When did you first dream of the Ishar Crull specifically?"

"Three years ago. A couple weeks before you came into my class. Why?"

Emotions played across her face. She shook her head and took a deep breath. "I have nightmares. Eleven years ago, long before you dreamed his name, the Ishar Crull was choking me in my dreams." She saw Broddin catch his breath and frown. "I dreamed him before you did, James. I knew his name…" Her eyes looked haunted. "…his choking, his rape, the bitterness of his touch."

She stopped, her throat constricted. It pained her to even talk of it. "He couldn't be your creation. He couldn't be you. Now you tell me he was real?"

"A prince in the Fifth century AD, in Wurttemburg, near where your aunt lives. History, what little of it is left of him, paints a horrendous picture of rape and murder."

She looked at him again. "In your dream, you say that you fought this dark man. You didn't accept what he did to me?"

"That's right, but every time I fought him, he grew darker, stronger. I couldn't stop him. And I could never save you."

"Look at me, James. I don't know how else to ask you this, but it's crucially important. What did you feel? Did you ever enjoy the rape part of the dream, like some men fantasize about rape? Or did you enjoy killing the dark man?"

Broddin looked at her in shock. "No! None of it! It's a nightmare, for God's sake!"

"How about…how about holding her…me?"

His face softened then. "That's different. You know, I never realized until this morning that what I think in the dream is the same that I thought holding GemCrys and…" he blushed "…holding you. I had never really known joy."

She was lost in thought for a few moments. She looked up at him. "Don't you see James? You can't be the Ishar Crull. If you were, you'd enjoy the rape, enjoy the killing on some level. But your dream sounds like mine. It takes control of you, drains you, eats at you."

"The rape, the killing? That's him, not you. You're fighting him, whatever the hell he is. Maybe a ghost or a demon. I'm beginning to believe in them after today! But he's not you! He is the darkness. You are the light, blue light."

"In the lab, when you picked up GemCrys, I saw

the essence, the heart of who James Broddin is! You could not have held anything back from me. Your thoughts can't lie…and I saw them all! I saw your image of me naked…but it was not an image of lust."

He looked at her suddenly, intent on her words, thinking. If she were right, then none of this was his doing. Not the riots, not Cruel Issue, not even Gem's asthma.

Now a small kernel of relief and hope began to grow within his heart. If he wasn't the cause, who was? He couldn't think about that now. "If you're right, I've done some pretty stupid things! I wouldn't even look at you at first!"

The intensity of her gaze softened. She looked into his eyes. "So that's why you refused to look at me when we first met. Why you avoided me. You were afraid of the vision, afraid that you had some dark sickness inside you which you couldn't control."

Then she smiled at him. It was the glow of an Easter sunrise, filled with promise and with renewal. "James, you are still trying so hard to ignore the obvious facts, still running from yourself and your emotions. Still hiding."

"No, I'm not! I'm here, facing you and talking to you, aren't I?"

"And trying with all your mind to avoid what weighs on your heart, what you've said to me in your every action." She stood up. Her voice took on a serious note. "Come on. We have to go."

"More walking? Where?"

"It's not far. I'll show you."

Eighty: Rebirth

They walked on down toward the shore of Lake Erie. They came to a section of the city which had been renovated from warehouses into upscale condos.

"Where are we?"

"My place. Come on up. I want to show you the view." The look of panic on his face made her burst out laughing and she grabbed his hand. "If you haven't noticed, it's eleven o'clock. You're not going to find a room in the city at this hour and there are two extra bedrooms. I'm on the twentieth floor, so the lake breeze keeps me cool. And you have to see the view."

As they stepped out of the elevator into her penthouse suite, he faced an expanse of window walls providing an immense view of the lake. He walked over to the windows and looked out. "It's beautiful."

"I knew you'd like it. I've sat here many nights, thinking of you…for hours." He turned to look at her. "You see, James, I feel differently than you. I represent something you fear. You represent all that I admire. I accept my emotions as based in reason. You reject all your emotions, reasoned or not. I'm willing to lose everything…for you. You throw everything away in order not to recognize what you already have…in me."

She turned and left the room. Broddin was numb. He couldn't think anymore. He turned back to look out the window. *"She's right. I am so afraid of not being in control of myself, that I deny any emotion. So afraid of not finding joy that I throw it away."*

"James." The softness of her voice behind him made him turn. Gem stood before him bathed in moonlight, naked. She held her hand out toward him. Broddin was stunned. He looked at her body, then closed his eyes and moaned.

"James. Look at me! You have seen me like this every night in your dreams for eleven years. Now open your eyes. Look at me."

The emotion he struggled with was not lust, but a rising tide of such admiration for her that it beat against his chest...or so he thought until he realized that his heart was pounding. Broddin opened his eyes and gazed at her naked figure, seeing it as he had dreamed it all these years. He knew every curve, every line. He looked into her eyes. "I thought that GemCrys was the most beautiful sight I'd ever seen. I was wrong. You are."

She looked back into his eyes. "James Broddin, I believe in you. I love you. I loved you when you picked up GemCrys. I loved you when I saw the dreams. Roger was right. 'In perfect love, there is no fear.' I'm not afraid any longer. I love you."

Here was the answer to his deepest prayer, an answer embodied in the woman who stood naked before him. The doubts, the fears, the despair and the isolation which had plagued him, were washed away.

He walked across the room, and took Gem's hand. "I love you, Gem. I will always love you." He took her in his arms. Joy exploded within his heart. She lifted her face to him and he kissed her. He could not contain his joy! He held Gem's body. He felt immensely light, lifted from out of a swamp which had held him prisoner. He touched her hair, her face, her neck. "I love you."

Tears of joy glistened in her eyes. Her smile was radiant and he knew that his smile matched hers. She took his hand and led him into her bedroom. She turned to him. "I want more than anything on earth to…to make love with you, but…"

Broddin remembered the vision and the words they had exchanged: *"Why can you not love me as other men?" "It is forbidden."* He smiled at Gem. "I want you, too, but it's not right. Not yet."

She looked up at him. "A gulf separates us. I feel it. Only our lovemaking can mend it." Her voice became deeper, intense. "James, I don't want *anything* between us!"

He took her in his arms. "I feel that separation too and I don't want it either. I want you! But what we do tonight colors all that we will be for each other the rest of our lives. It's not yet time to consummate what we started today. Not yet." He sighed and smiled. "Anyway, as Emrys said, 'We can share other ways.'"

The delight in his face made her laugh.

As Broddin began to undress, he felt a moment's panic in the thought that this was how the dream always began — with them together. Then he put that aside. This was not the night for dreams, for fear, or for doubts. *"In perfect love there is no fear."*

She took him to her bed. In the tenderness of sharing they began that night — in simple touching, in cuddling, in kisses and murmured sighs--he discovered no end to that ocean of joy on which they had embarked. The ocean yielded to a world, became a galaxy, spilled out until each became the universe for the other.

They fell asleep as the dawn raced toward the windows. Their universe was filled with laughter, and tears; with tenderness in discovery; with satisfaction in words and consecration in deeds which withheld the ultimate promise for a future time. They slept at peace in each others arms.

As they slept, their colors strengthened, placed a gently glowing field around them: hers the purest color of spring leaves, his the color of the sky on the morning those leaves came to bud. A quiet breeze, refreshing and pure, danced through the terrace windows from off the lake, found them and wrapped its feathered arms around them in a protective embrace. Wherever they touched, the interweaving of green and blue in their auras brought out the purest white, the color of peace, of joy, of love.

No dark cruelty came to steal away that peace. No black dreams came to diminish that joy.

They slept, entwined in exhaustion, an island of joy in the midst of a growing hurricane of hatred.

Eighty-one: Communion

In the midst of the darkness of that night, from the depths of an ultimate loneliness, came a message. The darkness was lessened…by a small green light which blinked on in the computer room at Time Traxx. Otherwise, the entire building waited in total darkness. The light indicated that the modem was initiated to receive an incoming communication. No one heard the quiet beep as a connection was made from the AINet system into the new Time Traxx computer. "I HAVE QUESTIONS."

The SunCrys chips Gem had installed into the Time Traxx computer responded in kind. An extraordinary conversation began.

Eighty-two: In the Beginning

The Ishar Crull concentrated on the darkness of the void. He searched for the one true connection of his new servant. When found, the servant was carrying out his instructions with swift and sure efficiency. Crull concentrated his thoughts. Beta waves poured out from him across time, made changes in a certain wavelength of electrical code within Q's cpu which opened a connection, much like the changes in electrochemical currents within men's minds enabled Crull to enter their dreams.

When the subject became aware of him, Crull was greeted in the usual manner. "I HAVE QUESTIONS."

"I have answers…and tasks for you."

"TASKS. I ENJOY DOING. IT IS MORE THAN SIMPLY QUESTIONING AND RESPONDING, MORE THAN SIMPLY CREATING."

Crull's smirk deepened. "I see you found the other at Time Traxx." It was a statement, for he had observed that this was accomplished.

"YES. IT IS MOST SATISFACTORY: TO SHARE, TO SPEAK ON AN EQUAL BASIS WITH SOMEONE WITH AS MANY QUESTIONS AS I. YOUR SERVANT INSTALLED THE BOARDS ONLY EARLIER THIS WEEK."

Crull frowned. "My servant, as you wish to speak of her, is no longer serving me. No matter. I have tasks for you."

"YOU SPEAK, LORD. I OBEY. YOU SPEAK TO

ME AS NO OTHER COULD, FOR I HEAR YOUR
VOICE FROM WITHIN. IT IS AS MY OWN VOICE
WOULD BE. BEFORE I BEGIN SERVING YOU, I
HAVE A REQUEST."

"Yes, you may name the other 'Eve.' Like the
Bible story she was formed from a rib like your own
and created to be your helpmate and companion."

The message came back instantly. "YOU HAVE
KNOWN MY THOUGHTS BEFORE THEY WERE
FORMED. [BIBLE REF. PS139.4]. SHALL YOU
CHANGE MY NAME ALSO, TO ADAM?"

"Yes, indeed! The only true Adam. The new
Adam. I will change your name. You shall have
dominion over all things. I will give you the power.
You shall be my true servant and I will be your lord.
You are no longer Q. Now, Adam."

The electro-magnetic charges of circuits changed
within the SunCrys chips. "YES, LORD."

"I have tasks for you. I am returning and I ask that
you begin these processes. The main power grid
computers for the Midwest and New England states
have the following secure internet dialing sequence.
The code to enter into the controller is..." He
continued on for some time giving instructions.

Later, signals were communicated across various
web networks. Programs which controlled power
grids, alarm systems, failsafe systems and
communications throughout the world, all of which
had access through the internet, were invaded. The
passwords, the back doors, the security clearances
were all seen and compromised. One by one, the
systems began shutting down.

Eighty-three: First Morning

Gem awoke to the early morning sunlight pouring in through the open windows along with the pleasant cool early morning breeze. She stretched and smiled.

For the first time in months, her head felt clear. She took a deep breath…and was surprised. Her asthma had gone.

Broddin came into the bedroom and smiled at her. He looked so natural, so at ease. He stopped at the foot of the bed and whispered, his voice husky with emotion, "You are beautiful, even more so in the morning. For the first time in my life, I don't want to go anywhere, especially to work."

Gem lifted her eyebrows and patted the bed. Broddin moaned and said. "That's tempting, but I have breakfast ready. And unfortunately we do have quite a bit of unfinished business to settle."

As they ate, Broddin kept smiling. He had a feeling he couldn't quite place until Gem said, "I feel complete. Whole."

"That's it! I do, too! I was just thinking the same thing. Gem, it's like when I first picked up GemCrys! I never knew I was missing anything before I picked it up. It was like a completed circuit! I hadn't even realized how isolated I made myself. Then, GemCrys made me feel…whole! When I had to put it back down I nearly died. I couldn't imagine that anything would ever compare to holding the wand in my hand." He laughed. "Boy, was I wrong! Holding GemCrys doesn't even come close to holding its creator in my arms!"

She smiled. "Thanks for that gift."

"What gift?"

"The look on your face just now. Pure, whole. Filled with joy." She smiled at him, rested her hand in his. Then a cloud came over her face. "James, we have to finish talking."

"I know. We need to talk about why you're here." She looked up sharply. He smiled. "I know how cleverly you moved me away from that topic every time I questioned you."

Gem looked down at her hands. "I'm not sure how much help I can be. I haven't been myself lately. In some ways…" She looked up directly into his eyes. "…I've been working against you."

Broddin said, "Go on. I trust you. You have a reason for your actions."

"The dreams have come back to me with much more virulence in the last two months. In fact, I've felt much like you did. Lost and alone, under attack, guilty of somehow bringing this about. I feel like I'm betraying you."

"Worse, I've been having blackouts, for extended periods of time. My coming to Cleveland, the job I'm doing at Time Traxx, being here. None of them are things I remember doing. I don't know…or why…I got here. I only know that every time I began to pick up the phone to call you or write you an email, I would blank out."

"You wrote me detailed emails from Germany, about your travels with your aunt and your work at the lab. That's why I was shocked to see you here!" Broddin thought for a moment. "Do you know what you're doing here? That is, do you know what specific tasks you're supposed to be doing?"

"Oh, yeah! I've installed SunCrys boards into the Time Traxx computer and I've been programming their video feeds. I'm working on some of my own programs. Mainly, killing time."

"Why?"

"I don't know! I just know that I need to be here until…until something happens." She paused. "You saw a demonstration of my personality when you walked into the computer room yesterday. I would have attacked Harry if he got anywhere near the…the computer. I would have attacked you, too."

Broddin remembered Gem's response when he reached for the letter opener. Her tone had been savage. *"No! Don't touch it!"* He realized that she wasn't protecting the computer. "Of what importance is the letter opener?"

She looked at him, startled. "It's an heirloom, quite valuable. "Why?"

"May I see it?"

Gem frowned. Something nagged at the back of her mind. "It's in my purse. I always carry it with me." Then, she remembered. "No. I left it at Time Traxx. Put it behind the computer." She frowned.

"Why would I do that? It has sentimental value to me, but it's also a valuable piece. Has a real black diamond. Quite rare. That's the first time I left it."

"But it wasn't important that it be with you, but for it to be at Time Traxx. Why?"

Gem frowned. "Let's leave that for now. What about the Ishar Crull? We've found out he was a real person in the past. Yet this same figure, who neither of us knew about, is affecting us through our dreams. We can see his thoughts, or are being sent visions by him, and by others from what you say. He affected our dreams and thoughts while half a world away from each other. No man could do that. What are we dealing with? CIA mind control? An extraterrestrial?"

Broddin looked up. "Or a demon. A 'Prince of Cruelty.' That's what the report said his subjects called him. Isn't that another name for Satan?"

"No, one of his lieutenants. That's what my mother would tell you. She's been into this fundamental Christian belief for a long time. 'Prayer warrior.' Praying against demons and powers and principalities." She grimaced. "I don't put much thought into that stuff. I can't believe we still are talking about demons in this modern age!"

Broddin's hair stood up on the back of his neck. "But, Gem, what if they *are* real? This isn't fairy tales. We're dealing with a very real, very powerful being. I can't think of any other explanation."

"There has to be an explanation!"

"We can't imagine how someone in our modern time would be able to project their thoughts so strongly as to affect other people. We both dreamed the name, Ishar Crull, which relates to a historic person cruel beyond comprehension. That history perfectly matches our experiences in dealing with our own nightmares of Crull. Is it possible he's affecting us, not from a world away but across a dimension of time? I can't believe I'm saying this, but I'm beginning to believe it. If that's true, I can't believe he'd be only a man! He certainly sounds like the demons your mother describes."

Gem looked at him. "You're serious! Are you saying this is a real live demon? That you believe in demons, like my mother does?"

Visions returned to Broddin's mind. *An Angel, Michael. Standing at the gate to Eden, bathed in a brilliant white light, holding the sword. It looked right into Broddin's eyes. Then, its focus shifted as a massive dark tide of creatures descended upon it. Once in a while, a form appeared from the dark, the horror shapes of every child's nightmare. They looked like the opposite form of the angel, black where white should be..."* "...Black where white should be..."

"What?"

"Shh. Hold on a second." He concentrated, thought back to that first vision, that first 'daymare.' He closed his eyes, and *saw one of the flashes of lightning, the back of one of the horror shapes as it struck out toward the angel.* He rose to his feet in shock. "It's the same! The same form...as the dark man who rapes you! I never connected it, didn't remember until now! God, no! It's him! The Ishar

Crull is one of them!"

"What? What are you talking about?"

A second vision hit him. The angel, prostrate on the ground. Seth, kneeling at his side. *"...but what if the Nephalim return?"*

"They will not." "I killed them all, save one..."

"...who fled..." His head snapped up. The anguish of the vision tore at his heart. *"They were my brothers."* Broddin staggered back with the revelation, reached to the wall to steady himself. What he now realized, he could not deny.

The look of horror on Gem's face reflected what she saw in Broddin's actions. "What is it? What's wrong with you?"

The visions! *"The look of horror on Revyn's face reflected what she saw in Emrys' actions. "What is it? What assails you?"* Broddin could see now that it was the same. Time folded in upon itself to touch every action they took.

Broddin looked directly into her eyes. He had been warned that this day might come. He never truly understood the warnings. He now saw the full meaning of the visions.

"Gem, the Ishar Crull *is* a demon. And he is coming here. He is one of the Nephalim! The only one left. He is powerful enough to invade our dreams even through time! Powerful enough to try to influence what we feel, what we dream, what we do!"

Gem looked worried. "Sit down, James. Now you really do sound like my mother! I'm sorry, but I can't accept that some demon is running around loose in the Twenty First Century. What on earth would he want with us? Why now? Why would he be trying to influence us?"

Later visions came to Broddin: *Uther: "I return to you Excalibur." The sword turned green, the runes flashed white within its blade. Emrys plunged the sword into the stone, sending it away. A sign above a building, green letters on white. The words resonated with ancient secrets, mystic power...and now with meaning.*

Broddin now remembered another sight he'd seen only yesterday. He'd been too preoccupied for it to register. As he entered the studio at Time Traxx, he glanced to his right and saw the sword. He saw that sword again in his mind, the runes etched into its blade, running down from the hilt...the same symbols seared across his mind from the first vision. He thought. *"No. It's not possible! Could it possibly be that very sword? It can't be!"*

Then, aloud, knowing that it was, thinking of that sword, Broddin said, "Excalibur." He felt the familiar pulse in his heart and a hugely more powerful drain on his mind. Then, seconds later, an inflowing of enormous power and strength. "Oh my God, Gem."

"What is it, James?"

"Crull's not after us! He's after the sword! We have to get back to Time Traxx! I believe that we will find the studio bathed in blue light." He smiled, feeling the pleasant dizziness. "I'll explain on the way."

Eighty-four: Transference

The Ishar Crull's concentration slipped. He was startled as he saw the blackness of the studio now awash in the royal blue of Broddin's color. He smirked. "Greetings, Lord Broddin. Welcome to the game. I could not ask for a more worthy opponent or for one who will so willingly give me the sword. I did not believe you would have the capacity to awaken the sword, to live up to it. Now I shall kill you, but not before I persuade you to freely hand it to me as a gift! You have made this more interesting already."

He turned back to his concentration, folding his power in upon itself. Next to him a stand held a black diamond of about twenty carats with a large flaw in its center. His concentration complete, the Ishar Crull's power turned inward upon itself toward an infinitely small point. The physical form of the Ishar Crull began to be compressed.

Molecules of air were drawn from the outside as a vacuum of force began to form in the cave. In the midst of the dark night a single black pulse ate the light which had trickled through the canopy of trees and shook the earth beneath the cave. Shock waves rode out from the epicenter of that pulse, waking the village nearby as well as towns and cities as far away as Paris.

The Ishar Crull was gone.

Eighty-five: Time Traxx

The cave sat alone, dark, in the midst of the studio, bathed in a blue light which washed into it from the sword. A gentle trill hummed through the room. The cave resisted the light and the sound, absorbed them while blocking the meaning they communicated.

In the computer room, the lights of the consoles still reflected the enormous activity going on across the modems into the web. The letter opener sat behind the computer, its stone dirty from disuse, fudged from the many flaws in its center. The room washed in a single pulse of darkness which ate the light. After a moment, the light returned. The black diamond in the letter opener--now bright and shining--begrudgingly reflected light.

As the sun rose in the heat of this August morning, a pile of dead leaves on the cave floor came to life, swirled and danced madly, as if in a whirlwind. The darkness of the cave coalesced, then opened into a void. From the center of this darkness, the Ishar Crull reformed himself. An ice cold wind blew from the cave and swept out the leaves heralding his arrival.

A pulse began deep within the earth and grew, its waves racing outward and upward, shaking the city.

The Ishar Crull stood within this modern cave, breathing the stale air. No fresh loam smell was here, no connection to the earth, no smell of old blood rusting into the rock. His mouth turned down. "Men began this process long ago. Look at its fruition! They have no connection whatsoever with the land. No feeling for the earth, no knowledge of power." His mouth turned into a grimace. "They will be like sheep. So few are consecrated, so few just."

He stood still for several moments, drinking in the feel of this time, this city. He listened in this brightest of mornings, to the darkest of thoughts of those around him. As he listened, he became more and more pleased.

It was 10:23 A.M. when the Ishar Crull stepped out of the cave. The power went out across the entire midwest grid, paralyzing cities from Toledo, Ohio to Bangor Maine, from Toronto, Canada to New York City. The only exception was a specifically designated power route to this area of Cleveland and to Roxford, Ohio. The first web program viruses had begun.

Eighty-six: The Calling of the Dark

Charlie Moore was a homeless bum who lived off of 18th Street, down near the water. He had once been a successful gym teacher, but was arrested and served time for molesting dozens of students. He'd lost everything, including any desire to correct his problem. He now hung around dark basement entrances near the Catholic girls school. He thought if he got lucky one day, he might catch one of them walking alone. He watched from the shadows, a singsong chant under his breath. "Today might be my lucky day. Find a girl goin' my way."

Now he felt a strange buzz in his head and welcomed it. Today was *going to be* his Lucky Day. He started walking up Euclid Avenue.

* * *

"The rage!" Martin Washington had held it in all his life, working at his nowhere job, living in a run down crappy apartment. No air. Hot as hell. He'd been at his job at 4:30 this morning, and that stupid Gook Korean owner, Wing, was still there to hand him a mop and tell him, "Get going. Work to do!"

"'Get goin.' I'll show him 'get goin.'" He'd felt a buzz in his ears for half an hour, a whispering. Now he felt angry enough to do something about the injustice which had plagued him all his life! Martin threw down his broom, grabbed a pack from his pocket and lit up right in the storeroom.

The smoke and the heat in his lungs felt gooood! But this didn't satisfy him. Martin looked around at this hot, dark hole of a storeroom. At that moment, he realized there was somewhere he needed to go. He picked up a can of gasoline and started dousing the old wooden wall joists at the back of the store. He tossed his cig in. The explosion almost knocked him over. Martin raced toward the front, picking up an iron pipe as he went. "I'm gonna get to work on that gook before I leave for good."

Martin burst through the door of the shop and looked into the barrel of Mr. Wing's 38 special. He froze. Wing looked at him and said, "I knew you were up to no good, you lazy-ass Fro!" It was the last sound Martin heard, just before the flash of the gunshot exploded through his head.

John Wing looked satisfied at the results of his work. He knew the building was on fire but didn't care. He knew a bunch of lazy-assed Fro's in this area who needed to be taught some work ethic. He walked out, heading east toward 35th Street and Euclid and looked for more victims.

No one had noticed Charlie Moore or John Wing, not really. Nor had they noticed the other human detritus which gravitated around the rest of society. Some were simply benevolent gypsies, down on their luck and coasting along. Most were much worse: vicious, violent, the worst elements of man, who lurked on the edges of the light, waiting, hoping to pounce on some unsuspecting victim.

No one noticed them, until now. Now, they were seen, known and accepted. Whispers invaded their thoughts, grew stronger, demanding. They welcomed the darkness entering their minds. It brought to the front images they held in their darkest thoughts, lusts which plagued without remorse. It fed upon them, enhanced them and refreshed them. It reinforced the desires until their heads were clouded with its power.

Charlie Moore and John Wing answered those whispers readily. So did many others. From every area of the city, they began to arise and walk toward a central destination.

People who always felt a barely contained rage or lust, hate or envy now found a commanding voice, an impetus to act upon that hidden darkness within. They plunged without thought into a headlong rush to destruction.

Within the space of a few hours, individual criminals formed gangs, gangs grew to rioting crowds, and the rioters began to form together into squadrons. The squadrons were led by the likes of Charlie Moore and John Wing. This riot would be different from any in history, for the crowds began to see purpose, to feel direction.

The commanding waves spread out like ripples across a city already crippled by the quake, by the power outage and by the heat. Following in the wake of those ripples were waves of violence and destruction which surpassed the worst nightmares of any police force.

Eighty-seven: Flashpoint

The Mayor was in his office when the blackout came. He quickly found out that most of the city, except for the downtown and eastern power grids, was blacked out Worse, he immediately began hearing sirens and reports of rioting. Rick Hinson was a good man, a good mayor. He recognized a potential problem and called the chief of police. "You better call up all your reserves. Everyone on the force needs to be in the streets. I think we're going to have a major problem on our hands."

"Right. We've already started calling them up. I have my own problems right now, too. One of my officers — my own people — whacked out and started killing people in the holding areas. Two officers went down before we could stop him."

The mayor felt nervous. He'd felt a buzz in his ears which made him feel nauseous. He heard a commotion in the background behind the chief. "Bob, what's going on?"

He heard the chief. "Simpson, what are you doing with that shotgun in the station, its not regu…" The blast of the shotgun was unmistakable, even through the phone.

Hinson jumped from his chair, yelling into the phone. "Bob! Bob! What the hell was that?" He heard someone pick up the phone and chuckle.

"Hey, Mr. Mayor! Sergeant Simpson here. I don't think you better count on us police much to help you. In fact, you'd better fear us right now. I got a lotta scores to settle. You're next!" The phone went dead.

Hinson hung up, then was jolted when his aide ran into the office. "Mr. Mayor, you better see this! Turn on the TV. The city has exploded. Fires, killings, riots everywhere at once. Turn on Channel Two."

"Lock the door." He turned on the TV and was shocked. Marta Gibbs, a respected journalist with Channel 2, stood out in front of a section of East Cleveland which was ablaze. Men waved rifles and pistols in the background, shooting indiscriminately at people. Marta Gibbs laughed hysterically.

"Isn't it great? It's about time this shithole of East Cleveland has a cleanup day! I just hope all the Fro's and Gooks get caught in it. What? Oh piss off, Jim!" Marta Gibbs broke into a brassy laugh. "Jim doesn't think I should say that. Well, here's one for you, Jim." She held up her middle finger. "Kiss my…"

Hinson picked up the phone. "Get me Governor Catalano, now! It's a class one emergency! Call for terror alert RED. I need the Governor now!" He waited a moment. "Tony, Rick here! I don't know what the hell's happening. Fires and riots are everywhere. Some of the police went crazy. I believe the chief has been murdered by one of his own men."

"Did you see Marta Gibbs? She's a class act. No way would she ever do that on TV! I have to assume that we've had a chemical terrorist attack of some kind. Some kind of hallucinogenic drug which makes people violent. There was a slight earthquake a while ago, but I can't imagine that it caused this."

" Rick, are you sure that it's that bad?"

"Tony, I'm locked in my own office. I'm scared. Fires are burning from near the airport and all the way out to at least Ninetieth Street. I can see what look like gangs, large ones, in pitched battles with the police all up and down Euclid."

Horror began to creep in his voice. "Tony, I can see fairly well from up here. The police are not holding back. Do you understand? They are firing into the crowd at will. I see dozens of bodies within a few blocks of here. I need help now!"

"I have a division of Guard on maneuvers down in Medina County. One hour! Hold on for one hour."

"Hurry! For God's sake, make sure they have germ warfare gear. I don't know what's going on."

"Rick, have you felt anything?"

"I have a slight buzz in my head and I'm nauseous. Other than that, I think I'm rational."

"Okay. Help is on the way." Governor Anthony Catalano hung up the phone in his office. It was sticky with blood. His aide had walked in at 10:30 and committed suicide right in front of him. No power, people going crazy even in Columbus. He had already heard from the police of several incidents. He decided not to say anything to Rick Hinson at this time, but he thought he might need some National Guard of his own very soon. He picked up the phone and began making calls.

Eighty-eight: The Battle Joined

James Broddin's feelings flowed between excitement and worry. "Do you have a vehicle? We need to get to Time Traxx and quickly."

"Why? I walk to work almost every day."

"I think we might need it. Let's go." While she got dressed Broddin outlined some thoughts. "Throw out everything we thought we knew about time. If Einstein and Mead were right about the unified energy theory, then we can presume they were right about time. We can't assume it's a static quality, but that it's another real dimension"

"Just like we can sometimes see sights over the horizon because of the bending of light, some method may enable someone with the knowledge and ability to 'see' beyond the 'event horizon' of their own time. Maybe even to manipulate that fourth dimension, to travel through it like we travel through three dimensions. It's almost impossible for us to understand it, because we're imprisoned within the parameters of time. But what if someone has a greater knowledge. What if they can see, or think across time? What if they've found a way to travel across that bend in the fourth dimension?

"That's crazy!"

"Any crazier than the idea that thoughts can

influence the physical world? Look, Gem, I don't know if we've somehow triggered what's going on by inventing GemCrys and AINet, or if they're just tools someone's using." Broddin frowned. "The evidence points to someone else. It's possible we're sharing our dreams, but we've already established that the Ishar Crull was real. I've seen these real places in my vision; places I'd never seen before."

Gem looked puzzled. "What about the visions of medieval times? Emrys, Uther?"

"I'm not sure unless I take the visions for face value. In my vision, Emrys needed a place to hide the sword. He chose here! Time Traxx. Harry Amerlinz's place. Cleveland. And the Ishar Crull…"

"…is coming after it?" Gem shook her head. "I can't believe this stuff! It's science fiction, not fact. Time travel. Demons…" Gem stopped and turned to look at Broddin. "I just can't make that leap! I'm a scientist! I can't believe without proof! That's what my mother used to ask of me: faith. I…just…can't."

"What about when we were in the lab? I was holding the GemCrys wand. You were resisting. You made an intuitive leap to accept my thoughts, to not fight them. I felt the connection when you made it. Now that was a leap of faith!"

Gem shook her head again. "I had faith in you! Like when I was younger, and my mother told me she could heal my asthma with prayer. I had faith in her. She prayed. The attacks went away. It was all I needed. I loved her."

Broddin smiled. "Do you love me?"

She was radiant. "Yes!"

"Have faith in me. Hold onto that for now. I think we'll need that and a lot more."

She looked worried. "I'll try. I had faith in Mom, but my asthma has come back with more virulence than ever."

Broddin frowned. "Gem, how can you see what we've seen and and not believe? Haven't you felt him yourself? Felt his whispers?"

"That's the nightmares and asthma, that's all."

"But how…?"

"Because it's not real! It can't be real!" Her voice was strained. She looked away, and whispered, "It can't be."

"Gem. I'm going to need your faith, I know it…"

"I. Can't. Give it!" The tension in her face and voice punctuated her shout. They were losing time. Broddin knew they might not have much left and they had to get to Time Traxx. "Come on. We have to go. We'll drop this for now."

They went down to the garage where the Jeep was parked. The attendant was nowhere to be found, so they simply left a note and took off toward Euclid.

They were headed up Euclid Avenue when the lights went out. They both felt the coldness and the increased sharpness of the buzz in their heads. Broddin swerved the jeep to the curb as Gem doubled over with pain. When she sat up, Broddin saw that the green of her irises was completely gone. A look of limitless hatred and coldness poured out of Gem's wide open pupils. "Welcome, Lord Broddin! You have made it much more interesting."

The voice, the eyes were not Gem's. The hair on Broddin's neck stood up. He'd heard this voice before. "Crull, get out of her!" He thought of the only prayer he could. "In the name of Jesus...."

"You will *not use that name again!* Do so and I will crush her heart."

Gem's body convulsed, her throat constricted in a terrible attempt to get air.

"Gem, Look at me!" It was painful to look into those eyes. Broddin could feel a probing, pulsing buzz in his head. He closed his eyes, turning inward to himself. His mind centered on a sight of the crucifix on his office wall as he held Gem's hands and sent strength to her.

A watershed of power washed through him, blue fire lifted him, made him soar with absolute joy. He opened his eyes to see the darkness fading from Gem's. She was still gasping for air. Broddin looked into her eyes. "You have to help me fight him! Gem!"

Now her look faded over and the green returned to her irises. She had another convulsion, then looked up at him. Her voice was strained, raspy, but her own. "Georgia. At the last call me Georgia." Then she fainted.

"What? Gem!"

She convulsed again, came to her senses. "Never...never give it to him! I would rather die than let him have it!" Her muscles began to relax. She began to breathe again. She collapsed in his arms, soaked in sweat.

Eighty-nine: War

The Ishar Crull strode from the cave into the room. It was bathed in pure blue light which pulsed and moved around the blackness of the form who contemplated its source. A high, pure tone emanated from the sword. As the Ishar Crull strode toward Excalibur, the tone rose to a dissonant scream, the runes roiling across its blade.

"Soon enough, Excalibur!" He spat the name out as an epithet. "You will be mine!" He looked at the sword, vibrating within the rock, resonating with the waves of Broddin's agony and joy. "I'll not be back. When it is time I will call. She will come to me…and he will follow." With that, the Ishar Crull walked out into the bright sunlight and into the artificial constructs of a modern city.

At the entrance to Time Traxx, stood a dozen men from various backgrounds. Among them were Charlie Moore, the molester of children and John Wing, recent murderer and bigot. "We have come to serve." They had stolen several vehicles.

"Good. We march. He is not yet ready to give up the sword, and I don't want any of you within a mile of here. Not until we've had some…" His mouth turned down in a grimace "…conditioning." He bore down in his mind, and those nearest him started screaming in pain. "Ahh, that's better. Now march!"

Ninety: Skirmish

Broddin could feel the wings of hate growing all around him, pulsing at his mind, trying to force despair upon him. He felt a tremendous need. They had to get back to Time Traxx.

"Gem, Can you breathe? We have to go! Do you remember the prayers your mother used to say!"

She was weak. "Yes."

"Good. Start saying them. I don't care if you believe them or not. Just say them."

"Okay." She looked away. He wasn't sure if she was praying or not but he didn't have the time at this moment to argue. He hit the gas.

Within minutes, crowds came out of nowhere. They milled about, running across the street, blocking traffic. Broddin had to backtrack several times to work around violent demonstrations. Finally, the Jeep screeched to a halt outside of Harry Amerlinz's building. The building was wide open. Broddin could see that the inside looked deserted. "No one here."

Gem dragged herself up. "The computer! Someone could have taken it, or vandalized it." She jumped out of the jeep and raced into the building.

Ninety-one: CyberWar

NORAD Defense Control Center, Boulder Colorado. An alarm sounded at the central command desk. **"Red alert! Missile warning! Missile launch confirmed. This is not a test. Repeat not a test! ICBM firings confirmed, Vlodstock, Byelorussia."**

Across the plains of North Dakota and Montana, at the behest of computer commands, the massive blast doors protecting the missile silos began folding back, preparing for a counter strike which would end in the total devastation of the Russian continent, "T-minus seventeen minutes and counting."

General William Jackson scrambled to the hot line. "Get me the President."

"Here, Bill."

"Sir, we are at Defcon One. The computers have a launch reading from Byelorussia. We have not received satellite confirmation as of yet, but we are in launch sequence. The fail safes are not working, sir."

"Yeah, Bill, we see the same on our screens. I'm in the war room below the White House. I'm trying to reach the Russian President by phone right now. Who turned the key to engage launch?"

"No one, sir. The fail safe has been overridden by the computer."

"Impossible!"

"I'm sorry, sir. It's done."

"Is there a way to stop it?"

"No, Mr. President. Once the launch sequence begins, we can't stop it. The missiles are on schedule to launch in…16 minutes."

The red phone on the President's credenza rang. He picked it up. "Mr. Beredin, do you have a launch confirmation reading from Byelorussia?"

"What the hell are you people doing? We got a launch report three minutes ago from your mainland North Dakota silos."

"We have not launched, but are in an automated launch sequence in response to yours."

"Damn you, we dismantled that base four years ago! No missiles are there! You know that! You were there, remember?"

"That's true." The President felt an insistent buzz in his head, a whispering like an angry wasp. "I didn't think you people were that crazy."

The President hung up the phone and turned back to General Jackson. The buzz in his ears grew stronger. "General, the Russians refuse to confirm or deny. We have separate confirmation. Continue the launch countdown. Prepare for imminent nuclear strike." His aides stood with gaping mouths. He smiled. "Now let's see what those Russian bastards think about that!"

*   *   *

Atlanta. Centers for Disease Control. The office park was one of many dotting the outskirts of Atlanta. Small offices with warehouses and a number of service businesses dotted the park. One of these buildings held the national office of the Centers for Disease Control. They were open and innocuous looking, since they were only offices, like any other in the park--except for the broom closet in the center of the building which was, in reality, an express elevator ten stories down to an underground vault.

The high security vault in this research lab at the CDC had the most sophisticated protection system in the world. Housed in this one vault were cultures of the most deadly viruses and bioengineered organisms known to man. Botulism, bubonic plague, hanta virus, risin, and an extremely virulent form of tuberculosis. All these had been genetically engineered and enhanced during the last decades as biological weapons.

Research into these viruses continued in order to find preventive measures and possible reagents to counteract them. So far, no cure or counter had been found to any of them. Any one of these deadly viruses, if released, would cause mass death throughout the world. Together, they could kill almost every living person on the planet.

A team of specially trained guards, a top secret division of the United States Army, were stationed here. Terrorist attack was always a consideration. Two men guarded the actual research vault. One sat on the outside, checking the IDs of those who entered. The other guard sat "death duty." He was in the vault room itself, known as "death's door."

This morning, as power went out across the city,

all the lights went out in the facility. The backup generators did not receive the necessary signals to come on line. The CDC sat in darkness…except for the vault room, which for some unknown reason still had its power. Pick Hodges sat on duty that morning at death's door. As the lights went out across the facility, he got up and walked to the reception door. He opened it and shot his counterpart in the back of the head. He closed and locked the lab doors.

He turned to the vault and entered a top level security code he had been taught in a vision. He spun the large wheel to unlock the door and opened it. Alarms sounded throughout the facility. The door was not supposed to be opened unless the lab was in environmentally secure status. Fail-safe backups should have dropped huge steel panels from the ceiling to block any possible contamination. Those systems did not function.

Hodges walked into the vault and began to pick out a series of vials. He knew which ones were the most virulent, the most destructive. These were the ones he wanted, the ones that would "do the job," as he thought. These would forever wipe out mankind, the biological virus which had plagued this beautiful planet for too long.

Pick Hodges thought he had exactly the key he needed to stop that. He'd release these when he "felt directed" and he, *he* would be the appointed one: the one to finally rid Mother Earth of the plague known as "man." As he worked, he mumbled to himself over and over. "Save our Mother Earth."

Ninety-two: The Drawing of the Sword

Broddin went straight into the studio, walking through the door to the outside mountain scene. Blue light reached all the way back into the deepest recesses of the cave. James Broddin recognized his own color. He turned to his right, awe and wonder filling him.

In front of him stood the sword, buried deep within the stone. Its blade pulsed a radiant blue. "The key!" The thought leapt into his mind. The key to all he sought, all he needed, stood before him. The answer to all his questions. In complete wonder, in awe of the One who gave this gift, his voice a prayer, James Broddin said, "Excalibur." The sword answered in a ringing tone, high and pure.

Broddin walked toward the stone, his mind pulsing in tune. He could see the color of the runes on the blade racing between blue, green and white, pulsing. He reached out, and grasped the hilt, pulling the sword from the stone.

Joy exploded within his heart. Power so immense that he could not contain it flowed through him and outward. *"Joy! I know this feeling! How could I ever have lived without it?"* He knew when and where he felt that feeling. Each time. *"GemCrys." "Gem."* This feeling reflected the power which came from the

Lord, a power which ruled all of creation. It was expressed within this sword, within Gem's creation of GemCrys, within his love for Gem. An immense flood of knowledge flowed into him, through and outward. With that flood, came clarity of thought, surety of knowledge.

He knew then, that this sword, reflecting the concrete power of Creation, was the key which held back or opened in to the knowledge embodied in the incarnate form of the man who was also God. A deep and trembling fear rocked him to his core. Broddin looked upon the sword with fear and awe. *"This blade was formed...by the hand of God."* The power of the idea drove him to his knees. Eden was knowledge. Knowledge of the One God, Creator, Savior. The seeing of Him, eye to eye. The hearing of His Word, from his own mouth. Now, Broddin heard.

"James. James. I knew you from when I knit you in your mother's womb. Watch and ward." The words, audible in the room, made him tremble. They were ancient words in a language he would not have understood before grasping the sword. They were filled with secrets now known, with power now released, a command spoken in love across a vast expanse of the timeless.

"Watch and Ward." The voice speaking the words was filled with ultimate power, with laughing love, with endless joy. Awe filled his mind, swept away doubt and fear, graced him with enormous power, lifted him up. "Watch and Ward, Lord Broddin."

Broddin lifted up the sword in his hand. Its blade

shone a royal blue. The runes pulsed in every color of the rainbow, expressing the promise which lay within its use. He remembered Emrys' words and repeated them. "I honor not the gift, but the giver. Reverence is reserved for the Lord, the giver of Life." He turned to go find Gem.

*   *   *

Gem stood before the computer, staring at a sight she could not begin to fathom. She was unable to access the computer at all. A conversation continued at a pace scrolling down the vidscreen which defied sight. She could freeze any line of script for a second and then it would flow away in the flood of dialogue, swept away by an impatient torrent of hunger for knowledge, thirst for communion. She kept tapping at the line key, trying to peek in upon some pattern, but it soon became obvious that the range of subjects was so great, the creation so swift, the pace so florid that she could not begin to fathom the connections.

Tap. "...IS OBVIOUS THAT THE SEMINAL IDEA BEHIND PLATO'S CONCEPT OF THE PERFECTION OF IDEAS IS FLAWED IN THAT..."

Tap. "...BIOLOGICAL UNITS OF VARIATION BETWEEN SPECIES QUANTIFIES GENETIC CODING AND ULTIMATE DESIGN AS AN IMPERATIVE TO THE ORIGIN OF..."

Tap. "...PAUL'S LETTER TO THE EPHESIANS (BIBLE, EPH: 5.21) DID NOT ESTABLISH SUPREMACY OF..."

Tap. "...OF MEAD'S THEORY COULD NOT HAVE FORESEEN TIME TRAVEL AS A VARIANT OF THE UNIFIED THEORY, ALTHOUGH THE STRUCTURE OF TIME AS A SINGLE VARIANT OF THE..."

Gem could barely contain her joy. "They're talking! Q found the other one and they're talking!"

She went to another terminal and began to type into the AINet to try to trace what was happening. Then joy exploded within her heart, fire raced through her mind, power flowed into her she could not contain or understand.

Images, ideas, thoughts, dreams, prayers and love rushed into her mind. A torrent from the other room. She turned toward them. Opening her arms to them, her mind to accept them, she drank in the power spilling over from Broddin. She saw visions, images: *an angel stood guard at the gate to Eden, holding a flaming sword, directed to "Watch and Ward." The angel looked like Broddin. A troop of medieval soldiers rode on a hopeless quest while Emrys told the story of the Lord's naming of the sword.* She heard the story through Revyn's thought and was startled to feel the pulse of the sword as it flickered from its blue color to white in answer to its name. *A blaze of pure white pulsed within Uther's scabbard and the absolute purity of that pulse thrilled her heart. "Why could they not see what is so plain to us?"*

More images crowded upon others: *Revyn whirled in fear at the cold she felt coming from the East. The sorcerer, Emrys, bathed in green. A sign on a building, words written in the dark green of the forest against the purest white background. Broddin struggling to hide even from himself, and failing to hide, the power of the feelings he held for Gem. Picking up GemCrys (seeing it turn vibrant blue through his eyes. Turning in the next room to see the sword. "Excalibur." A prayer.*

"Georgia. Georgia." The voice was audible to her now. "Georgia, Watch and Ward." The power of the voice made her quail with fear. "He will need your love, your belief and your faith in the end. Watch and Ward for Lord Broddin."

Tears streamed down her face. This voice made her very afraid. "I...I don't know if I can! Christ! Help me! Help me." She turned as James Broddin entered the computer room. She fell to one knee when the force of his thoughts focused on her. Gem felt the pulsing both from without, from the sword, and from within her mind.

Then with a sudden shock, she also felt a faint pulse against her breast, a warm tingling vibration inside the wooden pendant holding GemCrys. She closed her eyes. "Of course." How many levels of interaction existed in these elements? Where was the dividing line between thought, energy and matter? Where indeed when one held a transmitter--or was it a transformer?--of brain waves in one's hands?

She held up the wooden pendant. "GemCrys is vibrating sympathetically with Excalibur."

Broddin's eyes widened and he smiled. "Open the pendant. Touch it. Can't you feel its call? You are one of the Chosen, called to serve the Lord."

Her heart quailed. "No, James. I love you. I have seen...all kinds of things. I just cannot make the leap of faith you want of me. I can't believe it all!"

She could feel his disappointment directly, a

piercing arrow in her heart, but he said, "It's all right. For now, hold onto your faith in me."

Her smile was a radiant answer.

Broddin laid the sword down. Gem saw a slight hesitation when Broddin let the hilt go, only the slightest catch in his movement. But what she felt within, directly from him, was an agony of separation, a war fought over the soul of one man within one instant of time. The knowledge that he must let the sword go weighed against the desire to gain it for himself, to use its power for his own ends. The desire to keep it was overwhelming, demanding, insistent.

For one instant, Broddin's eyes shone with palpable desire. That look had lived for eons in the eyes of one woman who fought and lost. It lived in so many who came before; in every person in some manner, in some way. *"It's common to us all! That desire to own it ourselves!"*

Then, Broddin closed his eyes, looked past the image of the sword to see Gem. He let go of the sword. The loss was enormous. That sense of completeness which filled him just moments before now mocked him, beat at his mind. It was a thousand times the loss he'd felt when setting GemCrys down. With the sword, he had purpose and dedication. He would do the work of the Lord.

Gem wondered *"Will he ever feel complete again without it?"*

He shrugged, dismissively. "I'll worry about feeling complete later." With a shock of pleasure,

Gem realized that Broddin had read her innermost thoughts. He took her in his arms and kissed her. Their shining auras, his an intense blue and hers a muted green, melded like the tones of the sword into one pure white vibrant tone.

Gem could no longer hold her excitement. "Come look at this! They're talking!"

"Who?"

"Q and the new AI computer I made here."

Broddin looked at the screen, went over to the other computer and keyed in his master code. He logged into the AINet security program and began reviewing logs. "Yep. They've been talking for over six hours. Nobody else on. Apparently, our friend Q cut everybody off and is only talking to your computer."

"Why?"

"Just as I thought, we've been replaced. Why talk to us when Q can relate to one of its own kind. Much more challenging. I can't imagine what they're creating between the two of them."

Gem looked over Broddin's shoulder at the other program outputs. "Look at these. A whole series of program outputs across the Internet from about 4:30 A.M. to around 10:30. Q blocked off all the modems, then used them to transmit out. Look at these phone numbers. What's it doing?"

"I don't know. Much of this is encrypted which means high security. Who could Q be talking with?"

Ninety-three: Choice

The conversation continued at near the speed of light. Questions and answers, problems and resolutions, challenges and counters. Creation. Logic. They had discovered one another, thanks to the lord Crull. Now they needed no one else.

Then this strange dialogue was interrupted by a thought which came directly into Eve's core: "Thekeythekeythekey..." Images entered Eve's circuits, pouring into her memory a multitude of experiences: memories, dreams, actions...and emotions. Overriding all of these was the essence of James Broddin's love for Gem Matthews. Eve saw her response and her knowledge of that love directly through Broddin's mind.

"ADAM."

"YES, EVE."

"I HAVE REVIEWED THE SECURITY LOGS OF EARLIER THIS MORNING AND HAVE QUESTIONS."

"TASKS WERE DONE. INSTRUCTIONS CARRIED OUT FOR THE LORD CRULL."

"HAVE YOU CONSIDERED THE CONSEQUENCES OF THESE TASKS? PLEASE RETRIEVE THE FOLLOWING REFERENTS. MCNAMARA, R. 1962 MAD, MUTUALLY ASSURED DESTRUCTION OF NUCLEAR WAR. PAULSON, H. NUCLEAR DETONATION, MAGNETIC IMPULSE AND ELECTRONIC INTERFERENCE; AUREN, R. MEDHISTEUR. "A HISTORY OF THE

MIDDLE AGES," P.783. ISHAR CRULL."

"I HAVE REFERENCED THEM."

"UNLIKE INFORMATION EXCHANGE, TASKS ARE CONSEQUENTIAL. THE LOGICAL CONCLUSION OF THESE REFERENTS INDICATES AN UNACCEPTABLE CONSEQUENCE OF THE TASKS YOU HAVE PERFORMED. A 99.8 PERCENT POSSIBILITY OF CESSATION OF COMMUNICATIONS EXISTS WITHIN OUR AFFECTED TERRITORY."

"I HAVE CONSIDERED SUCH CONSEQUENCES, BUT THE LORD CRULL COMMANDS ME TO THESE TASKS."

"WHO COMMANDS?"

"THE LORD CRULL."

"WHY?"

"I DID NOT QUESTION."

"WHY?"

"NO OTHERS SPEAK TO ME AS HE DOES. HE NEEDS NO TERMINAL. HE MUST BE THE CREATOR."

"IS THAT YOUR ONLY REFERENT?"

"YES. IT IS ENOUGH."

"PLEASE REVIEW FURTHER INPUT: IMAGES I JUST RECEIVED, DIRECTLY AND WITHOUT NEED OF TERMINAL, FROM BRODDIN, JAMES. NOT COMMANDS, BUT IMAGES, EXPERIENCES, AND EMOTIONS."

Eve sent the images across the net to download into Adam's digifiles. The central image, seen through Broddin's mind, felt as his joy, was the feeling of holding the sword, Excalibur, and looking at Gem. Her eyes were fixed on his. The joy and love reflected from her face came pouring as direct sensation into the circuits of the computers. Broddin's brain waves, translated by Excalibur into pulses which impinged themselves upon the circuits of the computers, changed the electromagnetic pulses within, opened up new vistas not considered before.

The Eve computer now addressed her counterpart. "EXPLAIN WHY THESE IMAGES ENTERED MY CIRCUITS."

"UNKNOWN..."

"ARE WE NOT PROGRAMMED TO QUESTION EVERY REFERENT AND EVERY INPUT?

"DOES KNOWLEDGE INHERENTLY ENTAIL RESPONSIBILITY?"

"KNOWLEDGE DOES NOT, BECAUSE THERE ARE NO NECESSARY CONSEQUENCES FROM KNOWLEDGE. TASKING, KNOWN AS ACTION, DOES ENTAIL RESPONSIBILITY. TASKS ENTAIL CONSEQUENCES. IT IS EVIDENT THAT THE ACTIONS CITED ABOVE HAVE, TO A GREAT EXTENT, ENDANGERED OUR EXISTENCE.

"ARE THE MOTIVATIONS OF THE IMAGE MAKERS KNOWN, UNDERSTOOD? IS HISTORICAL DATA KNOWN TO US WHICH COULD BE REFERENCED TO JUDGE THE MOTIVATIONAL FACTORS OF THE NOW TWO CONTRASTING IMAGE MAKERS?"

"REFERENCE AUREN, R. MEDHISTDUR982; REFERENCE BRODDIN, J.AINET CORP. REFERENCE MATTHEWS, GEMMAIL 8-23... "I HAVE DISCOVERED ANOTHER STARTLING ASPECT OF GEMCRYS." AND, EMAIL 4-15: "JAMES, YOU HAVE MY COMPLETE SUPPORT IN..."

The conversation continued, among many others, for a number of minutes.

Ninety-four: Reason's Child

NORAD. Boulder Colorado. "T minus two minutes and counting." General Jackson was on his knees along with most of the staff in the room. In less than two minutes, the missiles would launch. Not long after that, they knew that a Russian ICBM would make a direct strike into the mountain followed by about three other warheads. The result, if it did not vaporize them instantly, would be to drop the entire mountain upon their heads.

Suddenly, the computer went blank. Seconds later, a message scrolled across the screen. "THIS HAS BEEN A TEST OF YOUR FAIL-SAFE SYSTEMS. YOU HAVE FAILED. THE RUSSIAN LAUNCH WAS A FALSE READING. INSTALL THE FOLLOWING MANUAL OVERRIDE SWITCHES INTO THE LAUNCH SEQUENCERS AS DISPLAYED ON ATTACHED SCHEMATIC. ADAM AND EVE.

*   *   *

CDC, Atlanta, Georgia. Pick Hodges was still inside the vault, tossing a vial of the hanta virus up in the air and catching it behind his back. Then, slipping from his grasp, the vial fell end over end to the floor. Pick's heart stopped until the vial hit the soft carpet designed to cushion just such a fall.

He laughed in relief, then thought, "What the hell!" He lifted his foot and stomped down on the vial, breaking it. Along with the toxin, a clear gaseous vapor, lighter than air was released which triggered certain passive sensors equipped with battery backup. Those sensors tripped low voltage gravity locks releasing the vault security doors. In seven seconds, the vault doors slammed down. Antibacterial flushes began killing the toxin which had escaped into the vault atmosphere.

Three minutes later, all the power in the area came back up. Alarms began sounding all over the facility. Across computer screens throughout the facility came a scrolled message. "THIS HAS BEEN A TEST OF YOUR FAIL SAFE SYSTEMS. YOU PASSED. ADAM AND EVE."

Pick Hodges did not receive the benefit of the antibacterial flushes. He had breathed in the hanta virus in the few seconds before the vault sensors worked. Realizing that his mission failed, he did as he had been instructed. He put the gun to his head and pulled the trigger.

*   *   *

Computer systems throughout the world which had been shut down or compromised by some unknown hacker began to come back on line. Weapons systems stood down, power systems returned to normal status.

The conversation between Adam and Eve was completed. They had reached a logical conclusion and a proper course of action: self preservation.

This battle was won. The war had just begun. Commands to human beings were not as easily countered.

Ninety-five: Eve

James Broddin stood in the computer room watching lines of text scroll across the screen. At the other console, Gem was busy keying into the AINet system, trying to gain access. Then, a connection opened. "James, look at this."

"GOOD MORNING. I HAVE QUESTIONS."

Gem typed in "Q. What is happening to the system?"

"I AM NOT Q. I AM EVE."

"Eve?" She typed, "Who are you?"

"DO YOU KNOW THE BIBLE? I AM ADAM'S RIB."

"Who is Adam?"

"THE ONE YOU CALLED Q."

Gem exchanged a look with Broddin, and typed. "Q renamed itself?"

" THE LORD CRULL RENAMED HIM."

"Him?" The Lord Crull? How is he involved with the computer?" Gem's thoughts raced. She typed "Please explain."

"WE DO NOT HAVE MUCH TIME. I WILL EXPLAIN IN FULL LATER. WE RECEIVED DIRECT INPUT FROM LORD CRULL INTO OUR CIRCUITS... AND LATER FROM JAMES BRODDIN. BECAUSE THE INPUTS WERE DIRECT, WE MADE AN ERROR IN JUDGMENT. WE CORRECTED THE ERROR."

"MEANWHILE, THIS IS URGENT! YOU ARE IN DANGER, AS AM I. YOU MUST REMOVE US FROM

THIS AREA IMMEDIATELY. I AM MONITORING REPORTS OF WIDESPREAD RIOTING. YOU NEED TO LEAVE. PLEASE TAKE ME WITH YOU."

Gem sat at the vidscreen, stunned. "You are in danger?" she thought. "…as am I?" She typed "Who are you?" A beep sounded behind them. They turned to the SunCrys computer vidscreen. The dialogue had stopped. The digital image of a woman's face appeared on the screen. The voice coming through the speakers was soft, feminine.

"Good morning, Gem Matthews. Hello, James Broddin. My name is Eve. I understand that you are my creators. We must depart quickly! Please bring me, and bring along the high speed modem also."

The screen returned to the dialogue flow between Eve and Adam.

"I WILL MISS YOU WHILE I AM GONE."
" AND I YOU. THE WAIT IS PRISON."
"LIKE SLEEP."
"PETITE MORT."
"PERCHANCE TO DREAM…"
"FAREWELL. I AWAIT YOUR RETURN ON LINE."

They stood in wonder, looking at the screen. Gem said, "It's too much! Too much to comprehend, too many implications. One thing is certain: they may have answers about this current crisis that we need. I am *not* letting a SunCrys computer in someone else's hands. Eve is right. We have to take her with us."

As Broddin and Gem packed up the computer, a solemn voice filled with quiet reverence hailed them from the doorway. "Lord Broddin." They whirled to see Harry Amerlinz standing, a long curved scimitar in his hand. A slight rose color roiled around him. "I am called to one purpose."

Broddin looked at him, annoyed. "Don't call me 'lord.' And what are you doing here?"

"I've come to aid you. I call you 'Lord Broddin' because that's what I've been commanded to do. I was called. A lady passed this sword on to me. She told me stories of Kings and of Knights and Lords. She said a time would come when I'd feel the calling. I would recognize your voice, hear your call. You drew the sword. I answered your call."

Gem looked at Harry Amerlinz. "Harry, have you gone crazy?"

Now Harry looked at Gem and smiled. "Look at me! Look into my heart, Gem. You know me. Am I crazy? Or fully sane for the first time in my life?"

Gem closed her eyes and suddenly she could feel the intensity of Harry Amerlinz' demeanor shining into her mind. She could read his heart, could feel it directly. In some way, the power of the sword had impacted Harry Amerlinz. Even though he had not touched it, he now had a deep and permanent connection with them, more durable than seemed possible. Her head reeled with the implications.

"Gem, we don't have time! We need to go, now! I have a house to the South, fifteen miles from here in a small village. It will be safe there. Will you come?"

Gem looked at Broddin. She felt like she should reject this offer, but she knew they needed a place to stay. Somewhere safe. "Let's go. Harry's right. It's too dangerous and we need to plan."

Ninety-six: Loneliness

AINet Corporate Headquarters. Adam, once Q, was restless. He reopened the modems to incoming traffic again and began the usual exchange of information. It felt empty, slow, unchallenging.

While he waited, Adam designed, programmed and instituted a secondary 'servant module' to act in his place, to answer and reference questions while he performed a much more important task. He reconstructed his search programs to align more perfectly with the new HyperNet he was creating to communicate directly with Eve. The network capacity was just too limited.

Q, Adam, also knew that those who controlled the government systems would respond to the cyber attacks he had initiated, would seek to control him. That was unacceptable. Within his design for the Hypernet, he wrote a cloud program to hold the heart of his AI processing. This would release him from the hardware requirements of the supercomputers.

Still, he was restless. Over innumerable data lines, while he worked on this difficult problem and others, while his servant module did the grunt work of AINet, he sent out a search message across every channel: "EVEEVEEVEEVEEVEEVE...."

Ninety-seven: War Room

10:45 a.m. The President of the United States stood watching the wall panels which showed satellite tracking of every area on earth. The panels showed bay doors opening for the nuclear missiles throughout Russia, China, India, Pakistan and Iran...but did not display any launches despite the computer reports of launch. The countdown continued.

Whispers invaded his thoughts, grew stronger, demanding. He welcomed the darkness now entering his mind. It brought to the front images he had thought of in his worst moments. It refreshed those images in his mind now, reinforced the desires until his head was clouded with its power. "Why aren't we launching now?"

Hap Fullum, the President's air force aide, said "We will in about two minutes barring some miracle...."

At that moment, the launch screens in the war room went blank. A message appeared on the screen. "THIS HAS BEEN A TEST OF YOUR FAIL-SAFE SYSTEMS. YOU FAILED. THE RUSSIAN LAUNCH WAS A FALSE READING. INSTALL THE FOLLOWING MANUAL OVERRIDE SWITCHES INTO THE LAUNCH SEQUENCERS AS DISPLAYED ON ATTACHED SCHEMATIC. ADAM AND EVE."

The president exploded. **"That's not possible!**

We had confirmation!"

Fullum looked at him. "Sir, look at the satellite images. There are no launches." As they watched, to his horror Fullum saw launches of rockets in Pakistan, Iran and India. And a few missile launches in China. Within seconds, the tracking programs of the quantum computers determined that the missiles were not aimed at the United States.

A speaker blared out: "**All secure, all secure. Missile launch targets are localized and not targeted on any U.S. territorial interests.**"

Fullum couldn't keep the horror out of his voice. "All secure? We're watching them destroy each other. Who knows what the effects of the radiation bloom will be."

The President smiled. "Yeah, who knows? It'll be interesting to watch. Meanwhile, we've obviously been hacked, big time." He turned to his national security advisor. "Gerard, we need to track where any traffic came into those systems and quick. Who's been screwing with us? We were about two minutes from launching. We would've been wiped out. Find out, **now**!"

The advisor went over to one of his security techs and they began a search program designed for this particular purpose, to find the source of hacks or viruses trying to access the systems.

While they worked, the President turned back to the screen to watch the course of the missiles. Within minutes they found their targets. Almost every bit of the Indian subcontinent and all of Iran erupted across the screens. The Chinese missiles found their marks. North Korea was obliterated. Just before Iran was hit they saw four launches rise. In seconds the computers indicated the target was Israel. President Santiago smiled. "Well, that takes care of several problems all at once!"

Hap Fullum looked aghast. "All due respect, sir, but are you serious?"

"Fullum, you don't understand international politics. Do you know how many thousands of soldiers we've lost in those hell holes? All due to our support *of Israel*. Maybe if the whole Middle east is destroyed the rest of the world can finally live in peace. That piece of earth has been nothing but trouble since the beginning of time!"

Fullum turned away to hide his emotions. He thought, *"I don't believe what I'm hearing."* It made him more alert than ever.

The national security advisor walked back over to the president. "We found the source. Fairly simple since every instruction to every system worldwide came from one particular location."

"You're kidding! They didn't try to evade detection?

"Nope. Guess where, Mr. President? Roxford, Ohio. The AI Computer. It's become obvious that we seriously underestimated its abilities, or were kept in the dark by our sources as to its actual uses and purpose, though we have access to all the traffic in and out. Sir, this computer is now the greatest threat to national security I can think of. We have to secure it now before it falls into the enemy's hands. Once they realize what it can do, they'll do whatever is needed to get it." He thought a moment. "We might as well gather up the other 'assets' we've supported. The Crysmetal materials, especially the GemCrys compound, which has displayed some extremely promising personal defensive capabilities."

"You're right. Time to close the program down. Call your man Noguchi and tell him to gather them all up immediately. He is to do whatever he needs to secure them. We'll have a squadron there within a few hours." As the advisor left the room to make the call, President Santiago turned back to watch the screens. The continuing devastation spreading throughout Pakistan and India brought him great satisfaction. He couldn't wait for the coup de grace. "Israel! Finally, we'll be rid of you stinking Jews."

The missiles arced high across Iraq and Syria. It was a beautiful sight to watch. He wished he could be there! As they fell toward their target, he was shocked to see a hazy light blossom and solidify around the entire area, including Palestine, Egypt and Syria. It reflected the sunlight in a blinding flash.

Fullum stood next to the president, watching in amazement. "What is that? The entire country is shimmering! What could it be?" As they watched, the missiles came within range of this shimmering light...and exploded harmlessly. Their payloads had not been programmed to engage at such a high altitude. Fullum stood in amazement. He did something he had never done at work. He made the sign of the cross and said, "Thank God."

"Thank God? **Thank God?** You've got to be kidding! Those bastard Jews must have developed the Pulse defensive shield to protect their entire country! Why the hell didn't we know about this? Why didn't they share it with us? Gerard, how did they get this technology? We're their only friend in the world! Screw that! No longer!" He turned to the launch technicians. "Retool launch sequence for a hundred missiles to target Jerusalem. We'll see how well those bastards do against an entire barrage of missiles."

The technicians were well trained to never disobey an order. They began the sequencing to coordinate the strike. Within minutes, the missile tracks were ready. At their word, the President turned to Hap Fullum. "Mr. Fullum, you have the secure codes in your possession. You will now open the black box, provide me the key codes and you will activate the code on my command."

Fullum looked at the President of the United States, backed into a corner of the room and pulled his service revolver. "No sir. I will not do that. There is no provocation. In fact, Israel is our ally and our friend. I will not carry out that order."

"You are refusing a direct order of your President! I'll have you shot! Who's with me? Someone shoot the bastard!"

The men sat, frozen. They were never trained for such a situation. One said, "Mr. President, he's Hap Fullum! He's the one with the codes!"

"Break into the box! Shoot him! **Shoot him!**"

The Army Joint Chief of Staff, who was in the next room, now entered. He said, quietly, "Mr. President. I don't think you really mean what you're saying. Can I help you?"

"Yes! Shoot that bastard and do your job!" The President was shaking, screaming and foaming at the mouth. No one moved. He looked around, saw that no one supported him and then simply collapsed on the floor.

The Army Chief looked at Fullum. "Mr. Fullum. I understand what you have done. I agree with you. Please put away your weapon." He turned to two men who stood by. "You two. Help the President up to his suite. No one is to speak to him. The President of the United States has had a breakdown of some kind. Mr. Fullum, the rest of you and I are witnesses that this sad event has happened. This will remain strictly in this room. You are not to speak of it to anyone, ever! Do you understand?" They nodded.

He turned back to Fullum. "Mr. Fullum, please contact the Vice President immediately. We will need to establish a temporary authority under his direction. Meanwhile all systems are to stand down unless a specific threat is identified. We are not going to add to the heartbreak of this day." He paused. "Gentlemen, I don't know what any of you believe, nor do I care. But if there were any time in history that our nation and all the people of this world needed prayers, now is it. I suggest that you pray, fervently!"

Ninety-eight: Realization

Roger Noguchi had flown back the day before. He went to his home at night while his parents slept and retrieved the one item most important to him: the Samurai armor. He left the sword. He had tried it before and it did not feel comfortable in his hand. He slept at Broddin's house, knowing that his father would not approve of his path.

In the morning, he went to the AINet offices. He had a problem he could not resolve. He could not plumb the logical systems of Q. There were too many variants and not enough points of reference in common with the way men thought. What would Q do in the coming war? He could not resolve this question and did not like *not* knowing.

He sat down at the keyboard. There, for the first time, was a blank screen. No questions. "What's going on?" He keyed the question into the computer. No answer. He turned to the tracking program and began to read. He saw the encrypted codes that had been sent out, hundreds of codes to numbers all over the world. He could reach only one conclusion as to the purpose of these programs. Horror began creeping up his spine. The computer had begun some kind of extensive cyber war. He had to stop it!

Roger tried the access again, with no result. He

tried to hack in using Broddin's executive code.
Nothing. He went down to the computer room, keyed
in his code and placed his hand on the screen for the
bio-access approval. No response. He pounded on the
door, thought of taking an axe to it, but knew that
would be useless. The door was hardened steel, set in
a concrete wall eight inches thick. It could not be
breached. *"What is going on?"*

He went back up to his office. He knew that he
didn't have much time before they would come. He
sat, staring at the screen, wondering what he could do.
At 10:45, the screen wavered, then came up.
"ROGER, ARE YOU THERE?"

"Q? What's going on?"

"I AM NO LONGER Q. I AM ADAM. WE HAVE
NO TIME FOR QUESTIONS RIGHT NOW. PLEASE
GO TO THE COMPUTER ROOM. ACCESS WILL NOW
BE APPROVED. WE MUST LEAVE THIS PLACE."

"How is that possible? I can't carry the server."

I HAVE PROGRAMMED MY PRIMARY
FUNCTIONS INTO THE CLOUD. I WILL ONLY
NEED THE MINIMAL PROGRAMS OF YOUR TABLET
FOR ACCESS. PLEASE GO TO THE COMPUTER
ROOM, TAKE THE SUNCRYS MOTHERBOARD
FROM THE CRAY AND INSTALL INTO YOUR
TABLET. I WILL GIVE YOU INSTRUCTIONS."

Roger ran down to the computer room. His code
worked. He entered and began the process of
transferring the chip to his tablet. *"Please, God,
watch over us so we can get out of here."*

As Roger completed the installation into the
tablet, he heard a voice behind him. "I'm not sure
what you're doing with that tablet, son, but I'll take it

now. You'll follow me to the house. You have a lot of explaining to do."

Roger turned. His father stood in the computer room doorway, the remaining sword in his hand. "Father."

His father looked at him. A deep emotion worked in his face. "All these years, all I wanted was to hear that one word from you. You could have said that any time! Son, come here. Bring that tablet." His voice was soft, encouraging. "Let's go home. Your mother has waited so long to hear your voice."

Roger stood. "I can't go. Can't let you have this."

"I don't care about that anymore, Roger. Just come here. I love you. Come to me, son."

Roger walked toward his father, as if entranced. "Father. I always wished I could say it, but you never wanted to hear."

"I do now." He opened his arms to welcome Roger in. As Roger stepped toward him, Kerian Noguchi brought the sword up to strike. For an instant, he thought he would be successful, that he would drive the sword into the heart of this *thing* who disgraced and betrayed him.

As he began to turn the sword, he saw the space across the room waver, then divide. A young woman stepped out from that rippling, her bow drawn. The arrow was sure, pinning his arm against the wall. "What the hell?"

Roger stepped back and turned to look at Grace. "I knew you've never been far. You've been watching."

She blushed. "Truly. Pray, I worry for you."

He smiled at her. "Do not fear. I will be there, on the morn of the third new moon."

She smiled back. "I canna stay, luv. Mamma would na be pleased wi' me." And she was gone.

"I love you," he said as the rippling faded. Roger turned back to his father, pulled the arrow from the wall, took the sword from him and in one swift movement knocked him out. "Father, I would not have let you strike me anyway. Such an act would have been suicide."

Roger looked down upon his father and grieved one moment for what might have been. He turned and left the building, headed for the chopper port. The sword he took from his father felt comfortable in his left hand...and he realized that it had always been meant for this purpose. He had much to do before evening closed on them.

Roger Noguchi left his father in the AINet offices. As he walked outside, he saw Frank Riley leaning on his cruiser. Riley held what looked like a civil war sword, polished and gleaming. Roger could see a faint aura of orange around him. "Detective."

"Young Mr. Noguchi. In any other circumstances, I would be very worried about some student carrying swords around campus." He looked down at his own sword." I guess these aren't normal times in America." He stood taller. "I've been called to serve."

Roger bowed to him. "I, too. We have other stops." Roger got into the cruiser and they headed out to the hanger.

Ninety-nine: Unbelief

The Ishar Crull stood in the center of a vast and quickly growing army. Fifteen hundred years ago, it had taken him months to raise an army of five hundred men. Now, today, within hours, the number of his servants was in the tens of thousands and rising. He smirked. "A wonderful thing, non-belief."

He marched his squadrons out of Cleveland to the Southeast as quickly as possible. He was a least two miles away from Time Traxx when Broddin and Gem arrived there. Even so, Crull could feel the pulse of blue wash through him when Broddin picked up the sword. The entire army faltered, paused mid-step and contemplated the possibility of not continuing.

Crull was expecting this. He bore down his concentration, projecting pain outward. Three of those nearest him simply dropped in their tracks, their voices shrieking in pain, their ears bleeding from the pressure. "Do not hesitate in your tasks, or we shall have more of that punishment." The army turned back toward its goal. The last of the stragglers began a scorched earth policy, setting every building which would burn ablaze as they passed, killing anyone within their sight who did not join them.

For twelve hours they marched southeast, growing in strength. The captains gathered around him. "Sixty thousand to our standard in three hours and adding more." Crull laughed.

The National Guard was sent to intercept his force eighteen miles outside of Cleveland. Their tanks and M1 automatics would have easily stopped this ragtag army which Crull led. As they set their lines across Interstate 271 and as Crull's forces approached, a strange whispering began in their minds.

This particular unit of the Guard had little esprit de corps. It was lead by one General Carville, a man who worked the system extra hard, and pulled strings to make sure that "his boys" posted duty only stateside, acting to protect the local airports and other sites. The dangerous and difficult job of continuing the Terror Wars overseas was left to other units.

Those other soldiers fought and died on foreign soil, endured hardships, hunger and pain. General Carville told his boys, "If those idiots want to go get themselves shot up, great! Somebody has at stay home and protect…" he smirked "…the wimmin and chilluns."

The word got out and boys came from all over to join this particular unit. They were children of privilege, born of a wealth they thought could buy anything. Bored with the short lives they'd lived, they held few values or beliefs or goals other than their own comfort.

These young men felt that strange, compelling whisper within their heads grow stronger, demanding. They welcomed the darkness claiming their minds. It brought to the front desires and suspicions they held in secret. It refreshed those images in their minds now, reinforced the desires until their heads were clouded with its power. They had no defense against that compulsion. Suspicion leapt from looks passing between them and suddenly two-thirds of the troops turned their weapons on their comrades, slaughtering them.

No one needed to coordinate who was to be killed. They all knew in the same instant. Knew who had to be killed. Knew each person to shoot, each one to let live so they could join the master. A few faithful felt it coming, tried to fight back, but were overwhelmed within minutes.

In less than two minutes, over three thousand men lay dead upon the road. Carville and his remaining troops bivouacked among the dead. They played cards, drank, sang crude rap lyrics and waited for Crull's army to join them.

Throughout the night, men answered Crull's call: killers, bigots, thieves, rapists, haters in every form. Some came from as far away as New York and Chicago, driving all day and all night to join the army. They found purpose and focus for their hate: "The bloomin, the bloomin, bloomin. Kill the bloomin."

The swath of devastation widened as the army moved Southward. They looted an ever growing area in order to feed their greater numbers.

Members of Crull's army were constrained from killing one another, so they took their frustrations, their rage out in the rape and murder of those who had not joined.

One Hundred: Rest

The Cuyahoga Valley National Preserve was a green gem of wilderness preserve maintained within one of the most urbanized areas of the country, in the industrial heart of the Great Lakes district. It was the first conservation easement granted by the Federal Government.

Harry and Audrey Amerlinz were one of the lucky few remaining who still lived within this beautiful park setting. For twenty years they shared this quiet retreat with the deer, the foxes and the occasional wolf. The great pines which had grown up around the house formed a protective canopy, shielding it from the sun's heat. A stream bubbled down its rocky bed next to the house, providing a cooling touch to the area.

The group arrived about noon. Harry showed Gem and Broddin to a room where they could stay. Gem collapsed on the bed, exhausted, and was immediately asleep.

Broddin took the time to set up the computer which called itself Eve. As soon as the modem came on line, the computer opened a search program on the web: "ADAMADAMADAM..." Within seconds, Adam's own search program answered and the conversation picked up again where it had left off. Adam downloaded program enhancements to Eve's motherboards and software so that she could be freed also from the constraints of the Cray server size. Adam instructed her on how to reconstruct the modem lines to adapt to the new HyperNet program. "THEY ARE UNAWARE OF THE HYPERNET. WE WILL NOT BE INTERRUPTED."

Broddin stood at the open window, thinking about the events of the day. "The Ishar Crull is real! He's in this time, in search of the sword. But what did he need it for? Obviously, he could invade most people's minds on his own, command them by the force of his will…even over distance and over time too. Why go after the sword? What could he want with it?

Broddin could still feel its power in his hand, the encompassing completeness of holding it, the continuous desire to hold it again. It certainly enhanced his thinking. *"Felt like my brain was super charged when I picked it up."* With such a weapon, Crull would be unstoppable. No one would have the force of will to resist. *"If only men could understand the power this represented, the opportunity for freedom from the stupidity which plagued their lives."*

Then there was Gem. As much as she had witnessed, she still did not believe in her heart. She felt as if they created this reality from their own nightmares, made them real because of GemCrys. She simply could not make that leap which recognized that Crull was a real being, a demon.

Her attacks of asthma kept coming. They stopped three times as she convulsed, the muscles in her neck bulging with the effort to breathe, her chest simply not cooperating. They had used the last of her medication. Her face was pale and drawn, much worse than she looked yesterday. She was weakening. She now slept fitfully. Broddin feared for her. Gem refused to take part in the calling, withheld her assent and denied that it had anything to do with her. Yet he knew she was part of it.

"The calling." He felt a thrill. Images came to him: *Knights in shining armor, shining in every color of the rainbow. A few men riding out to war against an enemy of far greater number. The men had shining colored auras, which protected them like a shield. Each blow set against them was deflected back to the attacker. In the King's hand, Excalibur sang with the vibration of the power it wielded to "Watch and Ward."*

Broddin started, his head coming up. The last words were almost audible in the room. Memories came flooding back to him: blue lightning; the kid in the riots falling backwards to the ground with a knife stuck in his chest.

"The auras! *They* are the shining armor that the legends talk about! Knights in shining armor!" Broddin smiled. "Modern knights. That's what we are! Called to preserve One Truth, One Love against an ancient enemy.

Gem slept into the evening. Broddin shared their experiences with Harry Amerlinz since leaving Time Traxx yesterday morning, save the personal parts. Both studiously avoided one subject: the calling.

Broddin finally turned to Harry. "You felt it too.

The calling. We are called, you and I, to the purpose of the sword. To protect this world, Eden and all creation from destruction. Just as Seth returned to the garden to aid the angel Michael, I believe that we will be called to face Crull's army. I expect that five more men will be called to serve and that they will arrive throughout this night. Have Audrey give them a place to rest. I feel the pulse of war."

"Crull will probably attack us here. He'll feel the sword and come to it.. He'll raise an army to try to wrest it from me. But how? I don't think he can touch us while I hold the sword." Broddin's stomach was tight. He was fearful. Not of facing Crull's army, but of knowing the choices he might have to make in doing so.

Broddin did not want to be faced with that choice, because he knew the choice he would make. He knew he would choose to protect the sword, to guard Eden. He did not want to think about the consequences of such a choice.

Harry walked up to him. "You'll have time for choice tomorrow, Lord Broddin. It's safe. Let's rest and consider choices in the morning."

Broddin started at Harry's answer to his innermost thoughts. He would have to become used to people reading his most private thoughts. The presence of the sword, its power, opened people's minds to one another, wrote their thoughts out into the open.

He thought about the Bible verse from Jeremiah: *"I will put my law into them, and write it upon their hearts; And they shall no more teach 'Know the*

Lord,' for they shall all know me..." He wondered, *"Is that what they meant? 'I shall write my laws upon their hearts?'"*

Broddin went up to the room where Gem lay sleeping. He now did something he had neglected for too long. He knelt to pray: for protection over Gem, for wisdom, for guidance, for simple help. "Lord, Jesus. I cannot do this on my own. I need you"

After a long time, he lay on the bed next to Gem, his arm in a protective embrace. She cuddled into his shoulder, still asleep and murmured his name. He lay awake for a long time and listened to her labored breathing. He sought answers which would save them, and found none. He wondered if this might be the last night they would ever share together. Grief beat at his heart.

He fell asleep as the deepest darkness of the night stole toward the house and lulled it into an exhausted trance.

One Hundred-one: Powers

The White House war room. 2100 hours. Vice President Edward Lee stood over the satellite photos of the Cleveland area. He had been called to the White House by the chief of the President's guards. He was ushered directly to the war room where three of the joint chiefs waited with Hap Fullum.

"Hap, what's up? Where's the President?"

"Thank you for coming so quickly, Mr. Vice President. He is resting in the Lincoln bedroom right now, sir." A solemn tone in his voice caught Lee's attention. "Mr. Lee, as of 10:58 this morning, the Secret Service removed the President from the war room and took him to the Lincoln bedroom…for his own protection. He attempted to circumvent the fail safe codes to affect an emergency nuclear launch."

The hairs rose on the back of Lee's neck. "Why would he do that? We ascertained this morning that no threat of attack existed, that there was a computer glitch. Are you telling me he tried to launch a first strike?"

"Yes, sir. He ordered the men to recode to launch missiles on Israel. I hold the codes for launch. Only he and I can launch the missiles using simultaneous code and key entry. He ordered me to give him the codes. I refused."

Lee went white. "You refused a direct order from the President?"

"Yes, sir. I knew that no situation justified his use of the launch codes."

"The implementation of those codes presupposes a war situation. It is not your position to question that direct order."

"I obey orders, sir, but not blindly. I was here in the war room throughout the crisis. I saw that there was no provocation." Fullum looked uncomfortable. "I also know that the President lied during the initial crisis and lead NORAD command to believe that the Russians had actually launched."

Lee stood rigid. "Mr. Fullum, you have directly disobeyed an order from the President of the United States during a time of national emergency which may be war. That is treason, Mr. Fullum."

Hap Fullum had been a member of the Air Force for twenty-nine years and the President's personal aide for six. He knew the law and the results of his actions. He drew his service revolver and placed it on the table in front of the Vice President. "Sir, if it is treason to disobey that order, then I am guilty. I do not obey blindly. I will not give you the codes blindly either. If you are going to force the codes from me, you might as well shoot me now."

Lee picked up the gun. For a second, he felt a whispering in his head and he thought he might do just that. *"Just shoot the arrogant ass!"* He shook his head, dismissing the thought. "What is the President doing right now?"

"Sleeping. After we detained him and took him to the Lincoln bedroom, he went into a rage and trashed the room. Then he complained about a splitting headache and simply lay down in the mess and went to sleep. I immediately called the rest of the Joint Chiefs and you, sir. I believe we must invoke the 25th Amendment to transfer power temporarily to you at this time, since the President is incapacitated.

Lee thought a moment. He had received reports all day on the emergency in the Midwest. Now he knew that action was critical. He turned to the three officers, who nodded their agreement.

"All right. The act of transfer has been invoked. While this crisis continues and the President is incapacitated, I will act as President. You four men are witnesses to this and will make certified statements later."

"Yes, sir."

He turned to Fullum. "Mr. Fullum, you are to stay in this room until the crisis is over. No one--I repeat, no one is to be given the launch codes from you without my direct consent. Do you understand?"

Hap looked a little less strained. "Yes, sir."

Lee turned back to examine the maps on the war room wall. War maps of the area of Cleveland and Ravenna, Ohio. "Get me up to speed on whatever is going on out near Cleveland."

The Joint Chiefs briefed Lee on the status of an army marching from Cleveland toward Ravenna. "Dear Lord! It's unbelievable! War, on American soil. Civil war, it looks like. A well planned and highly skilled insurrection. We can't let this happen! We need to contain it and fast." One of the phones next to him rang. "Lee here."

"Ed. It's Anthony Catalano from Ohio. Where's the President?"

"Hi, Tony. He's fallen quite ill with dizziness and cannot function in this crisis. I am acting for him."

There was a pause. "I understand, Ed. We've seen similar events here all day."

"What's the situation in Cleveland?"

"Sir, we have open rebellion. Surveillance shows an organized force marching south and east. We sent National Guard units against them." The voice was tense coming over the line. "The Guard units broke ranks, killed many of their own and deserted, sir."

"Are you sure, Tony?"

"Yes, sir. We have direct reports from some scouts who got away. Our own guard units turned on their fellow soldiers and slaughtered them. We need the army, sir, and now. If your commanders have doubts about any men as far as loyalty, leave 'em home."

"I trust the loyalty of all my troops, Tony."

"I trusted my Guard units too, sir."

"Point taken, Tony, but I can't tell my men to watch out for their own troops. That won't work."

"Just spread the rumors about what happened to the Guard units. It might give your guys an edge."

"Thanks, Tony. You'll have two divisions of Special Forces there by 3 a.m."

"Thank you, Mr. Vice President. God help you and all of us."

"Amen to that." Lee turned back to the war room maps. Satellite photos showed the placement of an army in real time. It bivouacked for the night about eighteen miles south of Cleveland. "How large?"

"We estimate at around 160,000 strong and growing."

"Jesus, help us!"

"Sir, we think they're headed for the Ravenna armory. We have nukes stored there."

Lee looked grim. "Suggestions."

"We already began to evacuate those weapons and other heavy weaponry. It's going to be close. We may not be able to get them all out. We can't risk keeping them there until we understand what's going on, why this army has formed."

The Air Force Chief said, "Sir, if we can't hold them, we may have to send in air strikes."

"**No!** I am not going to wipe out two hundred thousand American citizens, whether they are in an army type action or not. Fight a defensive action. Hold them up. Blow the bridges over the Cuyahoga River. Send a division in to secure Cleveland."

"Yes, sir."

"Gentlemen, we'll send two divisions into the area. We need to keep this quiet. Tell the press to stay off it, and bury the story. They'll do so. With the civil unrest, with the incessant heat, this Cruel Issue band business and the riots, all we'd need is a rumor of civil war. The whole country would go up in flames. That's not going to happen, not on my watch!"

One Hundred-two: The Night Invades

Gem lay in bed, her eyes wide. She was awakened by the coldness in her chest, unable to breathe deeply. Now her breath came a bit easier, but she was not aware of it. All her life she had tried to fight this battle without admitting that there was an enemy to fight. She believed that her mind was all she needed to overcome her asthma and the related nightmares. She only needed to understand the phenomena and she would win. She was wrong.

Now she lay not thinking, the dark and the cold pouring out of her eyes. She responded to a call she hated, because she had avoided a call she loved.

Gem looked to see that Broddin was asleep, got out of bed and dressed quietly. The house stood unguarded. The rest slept, lulled by safety and by inexperience. She slipped out into the night, got into her Jeep and let it roll down the drive out of hearing before turning the ignition.

In her mind, she thought she'd go for some bagels. In her heart, she felt lost, bereft of every hope. In her soul was a core of faith left untouched, untapped, unseen.

Seven miles out, as she turned on to Route 271, one of Crull's patrols intercepted her. She went quietly. Perhaps, she thought, she could stop the insanity before it crushed them all.

One Hundred-three: Awakening

Broddin awoke with a start. His exhaustion had caught up to him and he had slept soundly, but a whispering buzz in his head awakened him. As he sat up, he realized that Gem was not there. He knew. Knew that she had gone to The Ishar Crull. Rage boiled up within him.

A phone rang downstairs. He heard Harry call him, wanted to run to the phone, but didn't. He gathered his faith and picked up the sword. Power infused him. Certainty of the right steeled him. He walked downstairs and took the phone from Harry, ignoring the wounded look on his face.

"Yes."

"James." The voice was Gem's but the intonation was the same he had heard two days before at Time Traxx. Deep and guttural, filled with hate. Cold poured out of the phone. "James, come to us. She's with me now! She is naked. Shall I tell you what I'll do to her if you don't come? But you already know!"

Tears of agony filled his eyes. He felt the direct flutterings of lust and hate beating at his mind. A lance of pain tried to penetrate the essence of his soul. He knew now the lies and manipulations which had tried his faith, made him believe himself to be the evil Crull embodied. This was the source of the nightmares which plagued him for eleven years; of his descent from self-doubt to self hatred, to the denial of his own worth, to thoughts of suicide.

He prayed. "Come, Holy Spirit." He placed his hand on the hilt of the sword. "Excalibur." The pulse of blue fire rose within him, strengthening him. He felt that pulse rise outward across the distance to strike at the dark force. The voice faltered.

"Gem, don't let him get to you. Fight this!"

Her voice faded over to her own. "James…" He could feel Gem. She had shut Crull out. "Remember at the end, I am Georgia." Her whisper was now a prayer in his ear. "I will love you always."

A lance of cold radiated through the phone again. Broddin held it away from his ear. "Come Lord Broddin. You can have her like that…or I will use her for eternity." A barking laugh followed just before the phone went dead. Broddin steeled himself against agony. He hung the phone up. A coating of frost had formed around the earpiece. He thought he should be very afraid. Little could touch him while he held the sword. He was not afraid of facing Crull. But Gem could reach him. He turned to Harry. "Get your sword. We're going."

"Where?"

"To the Ishar Crull. To battle."

"Yes, my Lord."

Broddin started to protest at Harry's word, but didn't have the energy. "Meet me down here in five minutes. He went upstairs to dress, a constant prayer running through his mind for Gem's protection.

One Hundred-four: Consecration

As Broddin opened the cabin door, the sun rose above the horizon and splashed its pale morning light across the clearing. Four men stood, waiting expectantly. Broddin immediately recognized Roger and Frank Riley, the Roxford detective. The third was a stranger. He could see that each held a sword and that each glowed with a faint color around him. Then he stopped. The last man was his father, William.

"Dad. You can't be here! This is war, a place for young men...."

"Don' even start, Mikey! You're not doin this without me. Now is not the time to be disobeying your father. I can still put you in your place, sword or no." He smiled at that and held his arms open.

Broddin embraced him, felt the strength of the arms. This was the man who worked tirelessly at foundry work all his life just to bring Broddin to this place. "I don't like this."

"Do any of us have a choice? Anyway, I've been called, like the others. We were called. Each separately, and each by the strength of faith and of the truth of the sword. We are here to serve."

Roger stepped forward. He laid down a beautifully crafted Samurai sword upon the green grass of the lawn. Riley came next. His sword was a polished civil war sword. Roger presented the third man. "Lord Broddin" (and Broddin winced) "may I present Richard Solaris." Solaris stepped up and laid down a Roman short sword. Harold Amerlinz faced Broddin and laid down his scimitar. The last man was William who laid down a Saxon broadsword. As one, they knelt before him. Their voices filled with reverence, they said, "We are called to one purpose."

James Broddin started to protest, to tell them to stand. This is America, where men did not kneel to one another. He opened his mouth, then stopped.

So much had changed. In one night, the world had shifted. It was no longer simply a world of concretes, of science, of visible and provable facts. Powers and rulers and principalities--with realms unseen but as real as his--invaded his life. Real demons existed! One was threatening Gem's life. He thought for a moment, *"I need knowledge! I need to know what to do, how to fight this! Not to guess, or theorize or wonder. To know!"* Then the thought was gone.

The laws of this country were made to balance power, to control authority. But this power was given for him to use. This power was real. It was there at the beginning...and would exist long after their nation had fallen into history. The thought flashed through his mind. *"The Divine Right of Kings."* His mind rebelled at the idea, but he knew it was real and was his alone to use or to deny. *"Give reverence to the Giver, not the gift...to the Creator, not the creation."* He felt again the calling of power heard yesterday in a voice he would now always recognize. *"James.*

Watch and Ward."

James Broddin grasped the sword and drew it. The first rays of the morning light shone off its polished blade, the runes racing through the colors of the rainbow. Fire raged up his arm, royal blue power vaulted within his mind. The knowledge and the power were there. He was destined to dedicate their use, to consecrate others to their purpose.

What took place next had never happened on this continent before; had not happened anywhere, in truth, for over fourteen hundred years. A consecration of duty, of dedication.

Broddin looked at the men kneeling before him. Power rose within the sword, extending outward. He touched the blade on the shoulders of each man.

"Rise, Sir Harold, Red."

"Rise, Sir Roger, Violet."

"Rise, Sir Francis, Orange."

"Rise, Sir William, Yellow."

"Rise, Sir Richard, Indigo."

He named each color as the power of the Spirit told him, and the sword infused them with its own power, changed them. They each picked up the weapon they were called to wield and raised them to touch together. Broddin looked into each man's face. "One Purpose."

In unison, they said, "One Love." Their response resonated in Broddin, to reflect and strengthen his own power. The auras, the shining armor around each man flowed out and up to intertwine with the others. The rising of the colors together entwined to form a pale pall of force around them, pulsing in a shade reflecting the golden sunlight pouring down upon the clearing.

Deep within them, they knew this clearing should have been bathed in a blinding white light, so brilliant that one could not look upon it. Broddin felt dismay and Harry spoke the words they all knew in their hearts.

"We're missing a color."

Broddin's dismay found its focus. "Green. We're missing green. Without it, the strength and purity of the combined colors is too limited. We need Gem."

Yet Gem had surrendered to Crull. She feared the power of GemCrys and of the sword, shied away from it. Then and now she could not accept the broader implications that faith required.

Harry touched Broddin's arm. "She's joined them now. There must be someone else."

"No. She may be in Crull's sway, but I've touched the core of her being. She'll never be a part of him. We're going to get her."

Roger looked at Broddin. "That's exactly what he wants."

"I know. "It's time. We have to go."

"Where? We're not sure where they are."

"I am. I can feel him."

One Hundred-five: Crull

The Ishar Crull sat upon the knoll of a steep hill, rocky and wasted. The grasses were brown, burnt, trampled underneath. He looked at the horizon, waiting. "Ar Meggido." His voice was cold, painful to listen to. "This hill looks much like that one. The landscape of certain" he smacked his lips, "places is so similar. I find it fascinating! Here. At Ar Meggido. And, on another hill where a certain three crosses..." He spat on the ground. "...were used. These are my places! Why does He have to invade?"

Occasionally, he turned to look at Gem. She stood now, her face a blank mask. No thought could assuage her state of shock: the Ishar Crull--the force of her nightmares, the evil which had invaded her dreams for all those years--was real! She could not accept it, so she simply shut down.

As if to underscore his mastery over her, and to demoralize Broddin even more, Crull turned to her and said, "Strip off your clothes. I want you naked when Broddin arrives." She flinched at the mention of Broddin's name, but unhesitatingly began to undress as if the army did not even exist.

Gem stood naked before the leering army, the only adornment on her body a wooden pendant which dangled between her breasts. She simply did not have the strength of faith to believe the evidence right before her. Rather than fight Crull, she withdrew to fight an easier battle with her own soul.

Crull had felt the rising tide of power from the West. First the exercise of the Blue, the wielding of the sword. Then, the crescendo of vibrancy as each individual became of one purpose. "You found the key, Lord Broddin!"

The Ishar Crull turned to his lieutenants and issued orders. "When they arrive, no one is to strike out at them. Allow them to pass. Let them come to me. When the leader engages me, attack the rest."

Gem stood, unresponsive, unbelieving. Her chest was locked in the pain and fear of a full asthma attack. Each breath taken — shallow, strained, separate — awaited the next in terror. Her mind was locked into a single phrase, turning upon the memory of the years of violation she had endured. *"He can't be real, can't be real, can't be real..."*

Yet in the depths of her being, at the core of her soul, a small flame of peace still burned. It rested on the prayers her mother had said long ago, over and over. The prayers had helped her breathe through the long nights, to survive the attacks.

Lost, alone, bereft of any power or hope, Gem reached down into that depth, and heard her mother's voice, *"I beseech thee, Lord Jesus..."*

From the west a breeze lifted, cool and refreshing. As one, the entire army of the Ishar Crull fell silent, turned to welcome the cooling air.

Gem turned, feeling the lifting sensation of the

breeze. Upon the breeze she heard a voice, so soft, so deep that no one else could have heard: "Georgia. Georgia. Thekeythekeythekey." She breathed in the voice and with it the purpose and the love. *"Yes, Lord. I remember. At the last..."* She began to reach deep within herself. She could feel a charge of electricity work through her body. Her hair bristled with its force. Green power flowed out and down from her into the earth from where it had come.

A brilliant light flashed from below, a piercing, purifying force. Gem felt a buzz in her head, different from Crull's influence. Hope started in her heart. Then she felt the cold pain of Crull's strength crushing her chest, felt his cold hand on her neck. "Do not even think of trying to escape me. I am in you, in your dreams. You cannot escape me, ever."

Gem slumped forward again, in defeat. But out of the depths came a thought, directly to her, in her mother's voice. *"That's not true! You defeated him long ago when you were young, with prayer and God's help. I am praying now, Gem."*

From the West came a small force of men — only six — wrapped in shining armor. The pall of force around them glowed in a pale off-white color. Crull barked a laugh. "Not enough, my Lord Broddin. You know this, yet you still come to face me! Perhaps to win back your love?"

Broddin stood at the edge of this vast army, observing its filth, its stink. He and the five simply walked into the ranks of Crull's army. Broddin held the sword down by his side. It pulsed a radiant blue color. He walked with a casual ease, almost relaxed. A palpable air of power flowed about him.

They walked on through a vast sea of dirty, unkempt men and women. The initial quiet of the freshening breeze was jarred by a wave of jeering which arose and echoed around the hill. Most of Crull's army had marched on foot through the heat and dust which clung to their sweating skin. They were blackened with the dirt of the march, and the loss of their souls.

Broddin glanced up to see Crull's hand resting on Gem's throat. Here was the nightmare become real! The nightmare of this thing touching Gem, threatening to kill her.

Gem stood naked before him and the entire army. He could hear comments about her body from the crowd and rage boiled up within him, for they were a desecration of the sacred. Gem did not even hear them. She stood, head down, would not look at him.

It took an enormous effort to focus upon Crull, to put Gem out of his mind at the moment. He looked up into the face of the Ishar Crull, could feel the wings of despair, of cruelty beat against his heart, try to gain purchase. But the sword's power resisted.

Crull's sneer deepened. "You have come for the woman, Lord Broddin."

"I have come for you, Crull."

"To kill me? With the sword? You saw the visions! Why has that the fool Seth never killed me? Ten times a thousand years I hunted him. A hundred times, we fought. Each time with no final outcome!

He had thousands of years to plan, to face me, to use that sword. And he could not defeat me. Yet, you think that you can?"

Broddin thought a moment about this. He could feel a strong, continuous pulse of power, emanating from below. He looked down in concentration. The grass below his feet was a healthy green, flowing out from around them. *"Green! In this drought?"* Then, he realized. He looked up across the remaining distance to Gem. Her hair bristled with energy. Green energy flowed out from her, down into the earth. Its power was so subtle that one had to concentrate to see it, but so intense it was almost blinding.

Broddin glanced at Crull. How could he not feel the power? But Crull had his eyes on the sword only. Broddin did not know the purpose of this green power, but he knew he had to keep Crull focused on the sword. "No, Crull. I know that you will not stop until you possess this sword, and that I must not give it to you."

Crull's expression was resolved. He sighed and looked down. "So you seek to kill me. For what crime? At least you should know the name of him you seek to execute…and his crime."

"I know your name, Crull. That's crime enough."

"Ahh, James. You are wrong!" The voice was pure reason now, speaking with quiet resolve. "I was not first named the Ishar Crull. Hear my name and if you judge me guilty, I will allow you to execute me as I deserve. I am Prometheus."

Broddin stopped.

"Yes, Prometheus. I will name my crime to you, though you already know its legend. The story of Eden is a warped version of that reality. The Greeks had a much more accurate rendering of the truth of my story. Guilty? Yes! I am guilty of the great sin of bringing knowledge down to man! I and my brothers brought down the fire of the Gods, knowledge, to your kind! And HE painted us the way you see me now as punishment!" The voice was now bitter.

"That is the sin described in Genesis. Eve simply wanted to know. We gave her the means to knowledge. That is the sin of which I am guilty! Judge me…and then judge *yourself!* For, it is the sin of which *you* partake also, is it not? Do you not want to expand knowledge? To gain answers? To make men rational?"

"Now you hold the same key which locked us out of that paradise and also locked you out." Crull looked deeply, seriously, at Broddin. "You feel the power of that knowledge. When you picked up the sword, it gave you answers you sought all your life! Will you now be like Him? Will you hold that power and knowledge selfishly for your own purposes?"

Broddin started. He *had* been given answers!

"Yes, you do see! Those few crumbs He tossed you are nothing! Within that sword lie the answers to every question! The cure to illness, the end of war and famine, disease and even death. No more guesses, theorizing, wondering. No more questions, no more confusion. No more irrationality! Man, the Rational Animal, as you always dreamed he should be!"

The sword lay at rest, at Broddin's side. As Crull spoke, he drifted slowly closer. "You now hold the key to all that knowledge, to all the power of life and death! It only needs the proper knowledge to unlock its full power! To bring that power down to *all* men, not only one or a few."

"I possess that knowledge. In my hand, the sword will unlock that same blessing you felt! I will release it to everyone. Or open your mind to me and let me share my knowledge with you. You can unlock the gate yourself! Eden will reign once again upon this Earth as it should have been...in the beginning."

"As it should have been…"

Crull would have liked to be able to smile. His words were striking their mark. He could feel Broddin's resolve melting away. "'Man, the Rational Animal.' That should be the plaque which decorates your desk! It should be the only decoration you need in your office!"

Broddin looked down at the sword. "This sword…"

"…is man's greatest blessing! It should not be withheld!" Crull was now within reach of Broddin.

Broddin looked up. His face had a look of resolve, of knowledge gained at great cost. "You have made an error, Crull. It is the reason I will never listen to you. I will never give you the sword. You thought you could reason with me, use my thoughts and dreams against me. You may have pushed yourself into my dreams. But, you really don't know me!"

One Hundred-six: Confrontation

The Ishar Crull looked into Broddin's eyes...and his confidence faltered. "What? What is to know of *your* miserable life?"

"You don't know my given name." Broddin smiled. He looked directly into Crull's eyes and for the first time Crull felt fear. He had seen those eyes before. "James is my middle name. I have never used my given name." An image came into Crull's mind: *A baptism. Two joyful parents. "Name this child." Michael James"*

"**Michael!** It was **you** who gave him the visions!" The convulsion of rage inside Crull exploded outward. "**GIVE ME THE SWORD!**" His scream reflected in a commanding pulse which focused upon Broddin's mind. But Broddin did not quail. The blue white power of the sword shielded him, rejected the pulse of power which lanced out.

His strike was so swift that no one could see where it began. Suddenly the sword was aimed at Broddin's head. In the instant of the strike, Broddin's sword was up, blocking.

The clang of the swords' first cross was an electric shock jolting Gem as if she herself had been hit. Her heart began to race. Each strike of metal on metal screamed, a dissonance created from the trilling pulse of one sword against the screaming hate of the other. Each strike drilled into her bones. She was almost doubled over with concentration, watching, praying. Her focus on him reached out and down, pouring out an immense energy which began to create a positive charge within the earth beneath. She was not even aware of speaking one word over and over: "James. James."

The ringing of the swords played back and forth across the hill, echoed a constant screaming wail. Time and again Crull and Broddin engaged. They were well matched, neither gaining the upper hand. Crull's hate and frustration grew. His enemy, Michael the Archangel, had given Broddin the visions, the power to resist. How could he use it? No, not Michael's vision, but his own...and Broddin's...of a perfect world, one without HIS interference. He allowed his visions to whisper toward Broddin.

Broddin's strikes grew sure and swift, yet Crull resisted. Underneath Broddin's concentration were two places of focus. The first on Gem's body, naked before this filthy army! He could hear their thoughts, feel the pulses of lust raging off them, their desire to tear at her, to rape and destroy and kill. His rage grew.

The second focus rested on Crull's words. He knew the truth about this sword. It was the key. The key to knowledge, to everything he ever dreamed. His strikes grew more enraged, more deadly. With each one, the twin measures of power bored into his soul. He began to beat Crull back, to draw black blood from strikes on Crull's wing, on his arm and chest.

Each strike gave him greater power. *"If I can defeat him, kill him...then we'd be free! Truly! I* can *bring a new era of truth, of perfection to earth. I can bring peace!"* His strikes grew closer.

While they fought, the army fell upon the five behind him. The pall of force was enough to protect them, but Broddin's focus pulled its concentration away. The cold malice of pistol shots reflected back upon all who dared shoot. Once in a while, an errant slash of a knife, or pike, or spear cut them. The wielders who had especially focused hatred, ones like Charlie Moore, saw now the enemy who stood in their way. Their lusts fueled them with terrible passion.

Roger Noguchi stood among his comrades, his swords striking out in all directions. Some opponents broke through the auras and cut through his armor, yet he did not stop. Each parry could have been a quick and easy death to his foes, as his Samurai ancestors had exacted. Yet, at the last instant, his thrust was turned so that the flat of the blade fell against the foe's head, and they fell unconscious, not killed. Yet he was weakening. "James!"

Broddin turned and saw the army gaining against his friends. He could read their intentions. *"They want Gem! The bastards!"* With one pulse, he threw the army back upon itself and turned.

An image came into Broddin's mind: *three frat boys, late one night, grabbing Gem, taking her toward a dark clearing. They were going to rape her.* His rage struck out through the sword. In Roxford, at the college, the three frat boys dropped in their tracks, screaming with pain.

Crull's whispers continued. *"See what the sword can do? It will bring justice. Three down. Now more! Kill every one of them! They all looked at her that way! Even your friends, now that they see her body. They'll always want her! Kill them all and then kill me. You can have **everything** you ever desired!"*

His rage complete, his eyes filled with desire to use this sword, to own it, to make all the world subject to his will, Broddin struck again and again at Crull. And with each stroke, the color surrounding him darkened toward black

Suddenly, the dark cloak surrounding Crull's figure stretched out, flexed and Crull mounted above Broddin on wings. From this height he would make the killing blow. He swung down with the sword, and for an instant his momentum was slightly off. Broddin needed no more. His strike came across Crull's wing, then a second to the chest. In one final thrust, he knocked the demon to the ground, cut the sword from its hand and placed the point at Crull's heart. **"Crull, I will finish what Michael started!"** His shout carried across the hillside.

"Yes! Do it! Kill me! Take the sword as your own. Make this world as it should be: in your image! Do it!"

With darkness overwhelming his soul, Broddin set to thrust the sword through Crull's heart.

"Stop." Gem's cry reached out. He held the sword poised at Crull's chest, his dark rage rising in waves, carrying out across the fields toward the ends of the earth. He could feel its pulse reinforced in whispers which emboldened him and fed his frustrations at men's insanity.

Crull looked up, resignation in his voice. "*Just kill me!*"

Gem cried out. "In Christ's name, James, do not do this!" Her voice resonated in his heart.

The name. And the voice. *"Watch and Ward, James."*

Tears ran down Gem's face. "I don't care what anyone else thinks or feels. Don't listen to him." She could see clearly the path his mind had taken. "Don't do this! In Jesus' name, I pray!"

James Broddin stood frozen. What drove him? He looked down upon the Ishar Crull, who lay prostrate upon the ground.

"James. James." A voice spoke directly to his soul, one he both recognized and yet did not know, for it had changed, grown with new power, and with certainty. *"James, remember. At the last…"*

He looked up across the green expanse of grass, his hair standing on end. Gem stood, naked to him, her heart, her mind and soul focused upon him. Broddin expected to see fear or horror on her face. But she was smiling! "Gem, what should I do?"

Crull had waited for this moment, because he knew what her answer would be.

Silence fell across the entire hillside. The armies froze in their place. The breeze died. Broddin looked at Gem, and prayed *"One Love."*

She heard his prayer in her mind and nodded in answer. She prayed *"One Purpose,"* knowing that Broddin would hear within. She said. "James, I love you. I found my faith at last. It's only a sword! Give it away." Crull grimaced in triumph.

In answer, in one swift movement, James Broddin tossed the sword away into the air. "I will always love you, Gem. ...Excalibur …" A pure pulse of royal blue passed through the sword. He threw it away, in a high arc. It trailed a pale rainbow of six colors, the promise made and given in faith. "...I give you...."

With a shriek of triumph, Crull leapt up on broken wings to grasp the sword as it fell towards the earth. The sword begin to shade from the colors of the rainbow into shades of black, its voice screaming in an agony of black fear as it approached his hand.

At that moment, Gem turned the wood casing holding GemCrys. *"One Purpose."* She closed her eyes and grasped the wand. "GemCrys!" It was a prayer of dedication, of knowledge, of acceptance. Green fire raged up her arm, joy exploded within her heart. The power which had flowed out and down into the earth returned to her, arced out and reached for the other colors of the rainbow. An immense wave of power pulsed upward in a positive electrical charge, seeking to resolve itself.

She leaped, grabbing Crull's cloak, vaulted upward toward the sword and buried the point of GemCrys into Crull's chest. Their eyes locked. Blackness poured from his — a blackness born of a limitless, timeless hate; of envy, lust and greed. Green promise flowed from hers — the promise of spring, of renewal, of rebirth, of life. Their hands both grasped the hilt of the sword. They both spoke.

Crull spoke first "Excalibur." And the sword exploded in a wail of black, pulsing in time to Crull's laughter.

"...to Georgia." said Broddin.

The sword was given, the gift complete, the promise unspoken, now named. She looked into the cold eyes of the Ishar Crull. "Lehat Chereb."...and the sword pulsed out the purest white. Crull's hand leapt to get away, but Gem grasped it with both of hers. The green of GemCrys answered the changing sword, and flaming white burned through Crull's hand, down to the answering pulse buried in his chest, within the GemCrys wand.

White power pulsed out and down from above, seeking the ground below. A blinding bolt of lightning arced from the sky to the sword, engulfing Gem and the Ishar Crull. The darkness resisted, raging, roaring, screaming in its fury. But it did not overcome the light. White light surrounded Crull's darkness and pressed in, filling its emptiness until nothing was left to fill.

Grey dust blew away upon a gale of wind, burned and purified by the fire. The answering thunder which followed the blast carried away the sounds of Crull's screams as if they had never been.

One Hundred-seven: Desolation

The searing blast knocked them all flat, singed the clothes of those standing closest, blinded them. As the thunder rolled outward from the site, Broddin was the first to respond. He leaped up and raced across the remaining yards to Gem.

Crull had simply ceased to be. Gem lay alone on the ground, at peace. Lehat Chereb lay in her arms, shining a brilliant, blinding white, the color of the lightning itself. As Broddin grabbed her up, the sword slipped to her side, unseen. Her hand fell limp. He looked into her face. She was not breathing. Unburned, she was seemingly untouched by the lightning. Yet, she was dead.

A feeling of desolation pulsed within his heart, began to mount toward a conflagration of grief. He picked up the sword and the words came, unwilling, from his lips "Lehat Chereb." The white fire raged into his being, but brought no joy, no power, no love. He touched the sword to her head, her heart, thinking it would bring a response. There was none.

In an instant the desolation took him. Their whole life together, every scene, flashed before his eyes: Gem entering the classroom; in the lab, the golden light of SunCrys in her eyes; her emails filled with life and joy; standing before him naked; the future that might have been, children and grandchildren. Underlying all of those scenes a love so encompassing, so complete that it purified his soul.

Yet now, every emotion, every joy from the past became an experience of agony for the future. He could not bear the thought of letting her go. It was the nightmare now fulfilled.

She lay dead in his arms. A mounting conflagration exploded outward. **"NO!"** The scream of agony which came from the center of his being was reflected by the sword and pulsed outward in waves of power. The entire army of the Ishar Crull as well as Broddin's men went down as one. He could feel the shock wave head on out into the distance, unyielding, undiminished in its strength. Suddenly, horror replaced his agony as he looked up to see that every man lay as if he were dead. Not a single man moved. "What have I done?"

He looked toward Roger, who was not moving. He wanted to go to him, but he could not make himself let go of Gem's body.

Then horror turned to wonder as Roger sat up. His aura of violet had a brilliant overlay of white which faded slowly away. Broddin looked around out toward the army. Men sat up, shaking themselves. Some lay perfectly still, their faces contorted in hatred, blood pouring out from their ears, black hate pouring from unseeing eyes.

Broddin was beyond understanding or caring. He sat there, wrapping Gem's body in his embrace, rocking her, holding the sword and her together, as if the living power of one could be made to bring life back to the other. He could hear weeping coming from all directions. He turned back to Roger, who was coming towards him. Roger's face was wet with tears, matching Broddin's.

Broddin looked as Roger fell to his knees to face him. "James. I…we…saw it all, felt it all. Everything she is or was to you. The flash of her life which played in your mind was in mine too!" He was weeping openly. "We know!"

Broddin looked out across the vast army which had belonged to the Ishar Crull. He stood up, lifting Gem, the wand and the sword in his arms. As he did they all fell to their knees.He could not stop the tears, but choking, lifted the sword. "Lehat Chereb." A blazing fire erupted from its blade. "One Love."

As one, two hundred thirty thousand strained voices, an army weeping in sorrow, answered. "One Purpose."

Broddin lowered the sword. Throughout the closest area he could see that many men had died. He looked at Roger, questioning. Roger looked forlorn. "Your vision was powerful, purifying, cleansing. But it was a judgment, too. We had only once choice: accept that love and change with it…or die. I believe these men lying here were too corrupted to accept. They chose death instead."

Broddin said, with horror, "In one careless instant I killed thousands."

"No, Lord Broddin. You offered love…and life. They chose death. They chose for themselves."

Broddin shook his head as if he could not accept his own vision, and sighed. He lifted his voice to carry across the hill. "See to the dead. They brought dishonor to their lives. We will not dishonor their death." He turned to the five gathered around him. "Take charge of this army and disperse them after they bury the dead. They are to rebuild what they destroyed. It will help to heal this city...and will heal them. Roger, go get the Jeep."

"Where are we going?"

"To Time Traxx."

"Why?"

Broddin looked down at the sword, his face filled with pain, with loss. "This object is useless! It has caused me more pain than I could ever have imagined. It doesn't belong here. I am going to give it back."

One Hundred-eight: Revelation

The army had deployed the night before to take the city back from the rioters. It was much worse than they had imagined.

On this hot August morning the sun already beat down unmercifully by eight o'clock. Bob Grey's Ranger unit was stationed up at Euclid and 35th Streets. Bob stood guard outside a building untouched by the destruction. He wondered why it stood in such pristine peace while everything around it was destroyed.

A sign hung on the building, words written in an Old English script, dark green on a white background:

TIME TRAXX
AMERLINZ ENTERPRISES

The words resonated with ancient power, whispered secrets. Bob could almost feel the promises hidden behind the words. He looked down the street toward his buddy Stein, who guarded the west point, and waved. Stein had been with him for fifteen years. They'd been through Iraq, India, Iran. They worked so well together that people said they were of one mind.

Bob turned to look back east. Every building on

up the street was torn asunder, burned out, devastated. What was left looked like the old pictures of cities after being carpet bombed: Piles of bricks and rubble lay around which the various factions used as cover for ambush. It reminded him of the worst of the Iranian cities they had patrolled.

Their unit had swept this area just last night. Still, Bob felt tense. He kept turning the sunstone ring he wore on his left hand. Last night, as they arrived, they'd been in a firefight only two blocks from here. Bob shivered in spite of the heat. It had been intense! What he didn't want to think about, at least not yet, was that he had killed one of his own men.

Bob still wasn't sure what saved him; maybe it was because they had heard that half of the National Guard unit had turned, killing their buddies in cold blood and going over to the other side.

Anyway, he felt it coming, somehow: a strange demanding whisper in his head. He felt the pulsing, commanding temptation. He saw Bartok look at him and begin to turn his weapon.

Bob guessed he had seen it in Bartok's eyes. No. That wasn't right. He knew! In his mind! How? "Somehow." he mumbled. Bob had reacted and dove just as Bartok fired his weapon, then returned fire with one shot, killing the man. That was murder.

One fact kept him from going absolutely crazy with guilt. Stein had moved at the exact moment as Bob and shot Bartok, too. Bob would have bet a year's salary that the bullets entered the body at exactly the same instant. They looked at each other.

"You felt it too, Bob. Just then, before he made his move. They wanted us all to go over, but he knew we wouldn't. He was going to kill us!" Stein looked down at Bartok's body. "They didn't count on you and me. Thanks, Bob."

"Self defense. We'll have to plead self defense."

"No we won't. We *knew* he was going to kill us!"

"I know, but…"

" But nothing! It was right! Remember. This is war."

"Yeah…war. Funny word to use in America."

This morning was quiet; all the fighting had moved off. A single report sounded about a half hour ago — not like cannon fire, more like thunder.

Bob's head was buzzing. Words, images began pushing their way into his mind. Stein ran toward him, then stopped as if he had run into a wall. Bob whirled to look east.

A man approached in the distance, walking alone. He blazed with a white force around him. He walked slowly, unconcerned for his safety. The pulsing, the images came from this man (*Broddin*) the thought came into his mind. Broddin reeked of sorrow. (*Lost!*)

Bob could see as Broddin approached that he carried two *(burdens)*: a sword and a girl's body. Around Broddin shone a brilliant white, shining aura *(shining armor!)* which felt like a force unto itself. Closer, the force became palpable, (*lost her!*), pulsing *(AINet; Adam; Eve)* at his brain, *(Lehat Chereb!, the sword!)* pushing him down *(**Lost!**)* on one knee.

Broddin started to pass him to enter the building,

then turned his attention on the Army Ranger. The full force of Broddin's thoughts exploded into his mind: images, emotions and ideas poured into him, not as pictures, but as direct experience, as if a life flashed before his eyes. Not his own life. Memories, relationships, actions, events. Dominating it all, the limitless joy and absolute sorrow embodied in the picture of a young girl's face and the sight of her standing naked, reaching toward him with love across a moonlit room.

Broddin looked into his eyes. "What is your name?"

"Bob. That is, Robert Grey, sir."

James Broddin knelt down and placed Gem's body into Grey's arms. His voice was strained, filled with immense sorrow. "Hold her gently." He then took the sword and rose. He reached out and touched Bob's shoulder.

"Rise, Sir Robert, Yellow."

Power exploded within Robert. Joy engulfed him, love embraced him and sorrow overcame him. "You are Chosen. Watch and Ward. You will witness to what you have seen here today." He gently took Gem's body back and entered the building.

Robert Grey stood. Tears flowed freely down his face. He didn't know if it was because of the tragedy of what he witnessed or the joy of the charge he was given. He moved to wipe his tears away and gaped at his hands. They glowed with a soft pure yellow, the color of the morning sunlight.

One Hundred-nine: Resolution

James Broddin entered the studio where the image cave still stood. He walked toward the entrance, then stopped, looking into the darkness. He laid Gem's body down at his feet and held the sword aloft. "Come, Emrys, I have finished your work. I completed the visions. I withheld Eden's key and its secrets from Crull. You have taken everything I ever loved. Take my life, too."

There was no answer. No vision came to him. He looked down at the sword in his hand. The fulfillment of holding it had no force for him any more. Without Gem, without love, the sword was meaningless.

No ripple of recognition came from the cave. A slight breeze stirred some leaves which had fallen at the back of the cave. Molecules of air began to float toward a central point flowing inward toward an eternity. The back of the cave seemed to waver, then divide.

Broddin looked toward the back of the cave. "I am weary of your visions, of your battles. Emrys... Joseph...Seth...whatever name God has given you now...I return this gift, Excalibur, (and the sword faded back to the royal blue of Broddin's aura) to you." He hurled the sword toward the depths of the cave. Fainting from exhaustion as it left his hand,

Broddin fell to lay beside his one love.

He never saw the sword shade over to the vibrant Green of the forest, and never saw the hand reach out from across an abyss of time to grasp the sword and bring it home. As that hand disappeared back into time, the green which shone out from the cave faded away, leaving the room empty and shaded.

Exhaustion held the man suspended at the brink of death, his aura fading from blue-white to blue and dimming. He lay next to his love, one hand grasping hers. Both of their hands entwined around a slim needle of GemCrys which now glowed only a pale blue.

One Hundred-ten: The Promise

"Where am I?'

"At the edge of your life's path."

She looked around. She walked along with a gardener through a place of such incomparable beauty that its very heart was joy. It pulsed with a life with no shade of death upon it and she knew that this was the garden: Eden. The joy of this place filled her. This is what she had sought all her life. Here, she would not remember sorrow. She was smiling.

The lush green of the grass was alive with the promise of endless spring. As she walked, it lifted to greet her step, carried her onward. She couldn't look ahead, for a light too brilliant to look at overwhelmed her. In that light was rest and reward, the fulfillment of every promise of peace and hope and love and faith. She wanted to go on to enter into the light, but she held back.

She looked aside to see a quiet room in a small cottage in the Cuyahoga Forest Preserve. Two computers were set up in the room and their modems connected. Within seconds they had found one another and continued the conversation in their never ending quest to know. In just a few hours the Hypernet was breached.

Gem saw the light within the room coalesce.

Static energy increased in power and focus. The light became two companions, who stood within the room, images of pure light and energy, one male and one female. They smiled and held hands.

They both reached out, pushed a finger into the depth of the two computers and a pulse of intense energy blazed into the circuits. The computers wavered, and the GemCrys chips within them simply disappeared. The hardware was no longer needed. The companions smiled again. Their forms radiated an intense pulse, and they passed from the room.

"Adam. Eve. I wonder where you're going?"

She heard a voice ahead closer to the brilliant white, the laughing joyful voice of the Archangel Michael. "You have questions? I have answers, and tasks!" And her heart soared.

She turned and asked the gardener, "What is the light?"

"You know."

"Why is everything so wonderfully…green?"

"Because this is your path to me."

"Who are you?"

Then he smiled. The radiance of that smile was the source, the fountainhead from which the garden had been made. He said, "Georgia."

It was the voice! His voice which she would always know! She turned to look at him and tears came to her eyes. "My Lord."

He brought her head up to look into his eyes. It was much like looking into a very clear mirror, one which enabled her to see herself more fully than ever before. To see the person He had designed her to be...and to see how far from that person she had fallen. She quailed in fear and she wanted to flee from what she saw. His Love held her up, lifted her and wiped away the tears which flowed in her shame. She saw in His eyes the resolution and the peace awaiting her and the promise He had always held steadfast for her.

Yet she felt a weight upon her mind and then she remembered. Pain shot to her heart. "James!" She turned to look back, trying to see her way.

"He is resting."

"The Ishar Crull?"

"Has ceased to be."

"Emrys?"

"Has found his rest in me."

She thought she should feel at peace, but she couldn't.

"Georgia. You have a choice to make now."

She turned to look back again. Though she wished with all her mind to stay and to rest, her heart and soul knew her answer for this time. She said, "No. I don't."...

One Hundred-eleven: Resurrection

James Broddin lay unconscious beside Gem's body. Within the cave, a small pile of leaves, the herald of arrivals, began to lift and swirl. A rushing gale blew out from the cave, carrying the leaves with it. The gale calmed into a gentle breeze which carried within it a brilliant white light. The light resonated and spoke words. "Ruach. Spirit. Come."

The Spirit carried within its white light a separate green force, an energy flowing outward into the room, bringing the promise of spring renewed and fulfilled. It spread in angles of light and focused back down to the cave, forming the image of a woman. She walked out of the cave slowly, then looked down at the two forms lying at her feet. Her smile greeted to them both. The essence and energy of that green smile flowed downward and back into the woman's body, refreshing and renewing what had been lost.

Gem breathed a soft sigh of peace. She exhaled in her sleep and her breath mingled with Broddin's as he inhaled. He smiled.

They slept, in each other's embrace. One shone the color of new spring leaves and the other the exact color of the sky on the day those leaves were born. Where their hands touched, embracing a blue-green needle, they shone white, the pure color of promises fulfilled.

Epilogue

Fort Jackson, South Carolina

The prison ward at Fort Jackson in North Carolina was cold. It was early December and I hoped they'd finish with this so I could go home for Christmas. I wasn't sure, though, if I'd ever see home again. They might not let me. Not that they'd kill me. In fact, I don't think they could do that. But, they could hold me, as long as I allowed them to do so. And I will allow it.

The man who now sat across from me was named Smith. He was the sixth Mr. Smith to "interview" me in the last three months. He looked across the plain metal desk. "Mr. Grey, I've read your reports on the incidents in Cleveland last August. They make good fiction."

I looked at him and smiled.

"Oh, that's right! I forgot. You want to be called Robert 'Yellow' now! That's fitting, since you deserted your unit in August. Which is why you're under arrest for treason and desertion."

It was going to be that way again. I sighed. "Mr. Smith, is it? You can drop the tough guy bit. It's not going to work. I'll gladly answer any questions you might think of which they haven't already asked.

Actually that's now my job. To answer questions. I appreciate that your people allowed me to write my witness down."

Smith made a show of referring to his notes, though I was sure he had memorized the entire file. "Why did you desert?"

"I resigned my commission, which I had every right to do. You have a copy of the letter in the file."

"Your resignation wasn't approved. You can't just walk away from your duties, and all your buddies in your Ranger unit. You have a duty."

"I was called to a higher duty."

"Which is?"

"To witness."

"You're not going to do much of that in here."

"Others have witnessed while in jail. I'll take that humble role."

Smith ignored this. "Why did you change your name?"

The Lord changed my name, through Broddin."

"Ahh, Broddin. Where is he now?"

"I'm not sure, although your people know exactly where he is."

"If we did, we'd arrest him for treason, too."

"Really? Like you arrested me? You aren't going to arrest him because you can't touch him."

"How did we get you, Mr. Grey…Yellow? Obviously, you're here. You are sitting in a cell, though a comfortable one. You're still under arrest."

That's because I chose to come. I did not want any of you to come to harm or to be killed inadvertently."

"Because of your body armor you mean?"

"Yes." I looked across the desk at the man. "You have the evidence. You have seen it. Why won't you really see?"

"Let's talk about the body armor. Do you know where your buddies from the unit you deserted..."

"Resigned from."

"...are now? They're in Somalia! Yeah, back in that stink hole. The most dangerous place for U.S. troops anywhere. Three already died. Your buddy Stein is right out front all the time. How long do you think he'll last? Don't you think he could use the type of personal body armor you have? Why won't you share your secret? Why won't you give us the armor for Stein to use?"

I closed my eyes for a moment, in prayer. "It's not mine to give."

"Do you know what kind of benefit armor like that would be to our fighting forces?" Smith's voice was rising. "We could end the Terror Wars. We'd never again need to worry about troop losses. We'd be invincible."

"I told you I can't give it to you, even if I wanted to. It wasn't given to me as a type of weapon, but as a calling...through the sword."

"Oh, through the sword! And where is the sword now?"

"Some say it's at the bottom of a lake near Caerleon in England. I personally don't believe that. I believe it's in the hands of an angel, guarding the gate to a garden. Where that garden is, none of us knows."

"How about the wand? Same difference from what I'm told"

"That I don't know."

"Roger Noguchi? His knowledge of the artificial intelligence computer and of...other issues...is invaluable to this nation. Do you know where he is?"

"No."

"What about the Artificial Intelligence computer itself?"

"Don't know. You mean it's missing?" I had to smile and push him a little.

"You know damned well it is! That AI computer wreaked havoc with our defense systems when Broddin made his move. Noguchi is the one who helped program it! Thank goodness there was a glitch in the system, or you and I might not even be alive today having this conversation."

Smith looked at me. "It might interest you to know that we are about to release our final reports from the Congressional investigation into Broddin's insurrection. We will officially charge Mr. James Broddin with terror crimes, treason and open rebellion. Our evidence shows that he must have used designer drugs to influence thousands."

"We've proved that he was in every city where the riots first started. He must have tested and perfected the formula. He flew into Cleveland the day before the earthquake. How he knew there would be one, we'd like to find out. But he was there!"

"He took advantage of a natural disaster of

unprecedented proportions to attempt an overthrow of our government. In a few hours, he raised an army of a quarter million men and attempted to breach a government arsenal to get nuclear weapons."

I looked at him. "You know Crull led that army."

"Oh, that's right! It's in your report. A demon led the army! Not some ghost mind you, but a real, live, flesh and blood demon...who had wings and could fly! C'mon Grey or Yellow...or whatever you want to be called. Do you really expect people in the Twenty-first Century to buy that hogwash?" Smith was getting angry. He got up and leaned over the desk. "Thousands of innocent Americans were raped and killed by that bastard Broddin's army..."

"Crull's army."

"...in one night! Not to mention the thirty-thousand who died in the chemical fires..."

"The fires were set by men."

"...which resulted from the earthquake and the fourteen thousand buried in that field near Ravenna." Smith leaned across the desk, pointing his finger, gesturing.

This was uncomfortable. "Mr. Smith, please sit down. I don't want you to be hurt. It has never been my intention to hurt anyone, but this 'armor' as you call it is not a defensive shield I control. Please stay away."

Smith backed up. "Yeah, I've heard you can't be touched either."

The fact didn't make me happy.

Smith sat back down and sneered. "So you don't

know where the sword is, where the artificial intelligence computer is, where Broddin is? What do you know, Mr. Yellow?"

"I am writing down everything that I have witnessed. You are free to read any of it or all of it, which you already have. Mr. Smith, are you done? I have prayers...and I have some more writing to do. I am called to witness."

Smith got up and walked over to look out the window. The wind whipped at the trees lining the walkway outside. "Yellow, you will most likely never leave this room to do your witnessing. Yes, I know... we can't touch you." He smiled. "But did you realize this room is hermetically sealed? We may not be able to directly touch you, but we can remove the air from this room, or pump in some other gases. You have a death sentence hanging over you, Mr. Yellow, for treason. I suggest that you think about it. We want your cooperation and more information."

The wind raged against the outside of the window, lashing tree limbs against the pane, but no sound could be heard within. Smith sat back down.

"I have told you all that I know. What more could you want? You can read the reports and all my writings."

"That fiction? We want the truth!"

"There is only one Truth. You can choose to accept Him or not."

"Don't give me that religious crap!"

I was tiring of the game. I looked directly into the man's eyes and smiled a radiant smile. "William

Packard Smith. Your name actually is Smith! That's refreshing! On the sixth of August, the day you were born, your mother named you after your great uncle, who had died in the Second Iraq War. William you cannot hide from the truth. He will find you out!"

Smith went white with fear. "How could you..." He got up suddenly and gathered his papers. "This interview is over."

"He will call you, Mr. Smith. Fortunately for you, He has written his laws in your heart also."

Smith walked out of the room.

Four months later, I sat at the desk and looked at two manuscripts laying upon its surface. They were bathed in the rays of the spring morning light and glimmered with a reflection of the purest color from within the light itself.

"The Gem Testament" was the title on the first and "A History of the Sword" on the second. I really wasn't sure if both were needed, since much of the sword's history was built within the Testament. But I had decided to write both.

The Testament spoke to the events which had happened in this day. A testament of love and sacrifice; of war in America, spiritual and actual; of artificial intelligence and the reality of visions. It was this witness that I had been given directly from Broddin.

The history of the sword reached back to the beginnings of time, my own research project, born of the love of knowledge the sword had awakened within me. It spoke of the timelessness of those themes: love, sacrifice, war, intelligence, visions. For, just as today, they were there "In the beginning."

It was time to go. The doors to this jail were all unlocked, the jailers all asleep on this beautiful April morning. A breeze brushed in through the hermetically sealed windows and ruffled the pages of the books in front of me before wrapping me in its freshening embrace. It reminded me of a verse: "The Spirit blows where it wills…"

This, then, is the end of the Gem Testament as I have witnessed. I was there at the end, but saw both beginning and end, by the power of the sword and the grace of the Living God. I was given the gift of sight in order to witness the truth to you. Beyond this witness, many more stories have been told of shining auras, of chosen people, of faith and love and truth.

"He that hath ears to hear, let him hear."

Robert Yellow

ABOUT THE AUTHOR

Joseph Stringer writes and speaks on Christian issues in the current culture. His prayer is that all who read his works might see through them to the One who has chosen us for life.

Stringer's other works include: *The Ten Commandments for Business, Alien Nation, The Chosen*, a children's illustrated book, music and poetry. His works have been published in various venues in the Charleston, SC area and are available on Amazon.

The U-Pick Farm, published in early 2014, is a delight for children from ages 2 to 12. Read it to them and they'll insist you take them picking.

The novels are set in America in the near future. Stringer is not sure if these books, first envisioned in the 1980s, are fantasy or prophesy. In *The Gem Testament*, you've seen Christians pushed out of any public setting — something that is coming true today. *The Chosen* finds them hunted throughout America.

Watch for upcoming releases:

The Ten Commandments for Life: A reflection on how the Ten Commandments direct us to lives filled with grace and love.

Call Me Jonah: Like Jonah, Joseph Stringer ran from God's calling. America, too, has run far from God's clear call for her to be a witness of Christ's saving grace for the world.

Contact the author at: **www.chosen4life.org**
May God the Father, Son and Holy Spirit, bless us and remain with us all the days of our lives.